TOGA

Arca Book 5

KAREN DIEM

Copyright

Copyright © 2020 by Karen Diem

Cover art by Deranged Doctor Design.

***

eBook version 1.0.1.

First Paperback Printing: July 2, 2020.

ISBN: 978-0-9975740-8-1

To contact Karen Diem or subscribe to her newsletter, go to http://www.karendiem.com.

Dedication

Dedicated to everyone who spent too long reading Greek myths and/or who felt the world needed another superhero portal fantasy.
Also dedicated to my dog, who hasn't chewed up my computer... yet.

Table of Contents

Chapter One

She had no idea what she was doing wrong, but making the mistake was awesome.

Snow flew beneath shapeshifter Zita Garcia's snowboard as she sped down the gentle mountain slope, leaning eagerly into the chill wind. She focused, letting her body find its balance naturally, despite the delightful speed and unfamiliar sensation of having both feet bound to the board. *This was worth the money for the secondhand gear. I needed to get out of my home gym and away from my weight set.*

Fiercely, she shoved aside the memories of the endless search of the mudslide for the missing, especially the last few days where she found only the dead. She fixed her gaze on a small snowbank between two trees. Her mood lightened as she contemplated it. *That could work as a tiny ramp. I'm certain I've got going straight correct; it's turning that I have to master. Since my Arca form's identical to my natural body, other than the hair, face, pointy ears, and fingerprints, it should be a fair test whether I've got it without being too risky. Unless the long hair throws me off. Por supuesto, if I could figure out how to use that like a rudder or a cheetah's tail to turn, I'd be ahead of the game.*

Zita shook her head to make the long black braid down her back settle into a more comfortable position. She chuckled at her own silliness. The noise temporarily silenced the jeering birds, which had been the only sound on the isolated mountain other than erratic wind gusts shaking the trees and the crisp slide of snow under the snowboard.

Her sole companion didn't speak. He rarely did.

She craned her neck to see where the taciturn mercenary was and glimpsed him weaving in and out of the trees on a course paralleling her own. Although his speed matched hers, his movements still held an economical strength and control she envied. *He gets the fun run while I'm on the baby course? He might be the teacher, but I'll catch up. Of course, if I fall behind a little, he does provide eye candy. I bet you could bounce quarters off… I need to focus on what I'm doing and stop ogling the poor man.*

Warmth spread through her as the familiar presences of her two best friends filled her mind.

Trying to keep irritation from her mental voice—they might need her for something important—Zita sent, *Hey guys! What's up? I'm in the middle of something.*

Can you come to the air park right now? Wyn sent.

Zita glanced at Freelance. By the additional tension in his stance and the way his head had lifted, he knew she was up to something. She forced herself to move her lips as if whispering, since she'd told him that her friends communicated with her using a magic subaural device previously. In truth, Wyn's telepathy tied the three of them together in a link they called "party line," but she wouldn't be the one to give away her friend's secret ability. She tapped her ear at him and made the phone signal.

He nodded.

That done, she answered Wyn's question. *I'm in Colorado, snowboarding with a buddy. I can be there after I get rid of him and* get far enough away that he won't catch me teleporting, but it'll take a few minutes. *¿Qué onda? You guys okay?*

A wave of curiosity came from Wyn. *I thought we agreed we'd all take more time for resting after the mudslide rescue we did in March. You worked yourself into exhaustion, emotionally and physically, and haven't said a peep to anyone about it since then. You know I'm here if you want to talk about it, right?*

Learning a new sport is relaxing, and thanks, but I don't need to talk. As her mind filled in the acrid reek of the mud and buried... things... that she'd been trying to forget, Zita suppressed the memories before they could leak to her friends. She didn't bother to mention the extra working out she'd been doing since then either.

We'll come to you. It's bad, Andy sent.

What's going on? Is it Dragon? She prayed it wasn't. When Dragon was angry, the death toll was always ugly. Not only had Zita had more than enough of corpses, but she also couldn't do much directly to stop the colossal shapeshifter.

Wyn responded immediately. *No, she's still keeping a low profile somewhere in Egypt or Libya. The African metahuman team is monitoring her. We're almost to Colorado. Can I use my tracker spell to pinpoint your location? Are you there as Arca or Zita?*

Thank you for asking first. Go ahead, and I'm here as Arca, mask, costume, and all under my coat. Zita glanced back at her path and noted she was closing on the snowbank and a stubby tree that had been hidden behind it. She tried to bleed off speed and turn, remembering too late to align her leading shoulder. *Carajo, I'm too close.*

The edge of her board caught.

Zita catapulted forward. A lifetime of martial arts and gymnastics had her instinctively rolling and twisting to avoid the tree, even with the cumbersome attachment to her crimson boots.

She stopped at the very base, the bottom of her board thudding into it.

The branches above dumped snow on her. Icy crystals cascaded over her head and slid down the back of the too-large thrift shop coat she wore.

Too close to what? Are you okay? Wyn sent.

Coughing and sputtering, Zita yanked her orange goggles off and threw them aside. She wiped the snow out of her face, half-snickering at herself. After lifting her feet in the air, she jiggled her feet until the vibrant colors on the board shone through. That done, she stood. *Fine, just... fine.*

Her friend's mental reply was brief. *Good. We're in the air.*

After pulling her jacket away from her back, Zita wiggled her shoulders and hips, trying to dislodge the tree's frigid gift. "¡Frío! ¡Frío! ¡Frío!"

A stolid black snowboard came to a halt beside her. Freelance stared at her, his head angled to the side. Despite the dark layers of clothing he wore, the fabric couldn't hide the outline of a taut, strong form. A grappling hook gun hung on one side of his lean hips, a handgun on the other, with a row of little pouches sandwiched between them. A balaclava hid his face as usual, and his goggles whirred as he considered her.

"I'm good," she said, licking her chapped lips and tamping down the hormones that roared at his proximity. By habit, she slipped into a fake Mexican accent, a comfort and camouflage she always used speaking aloud in her Arca form, even among friends. The tips of her ears burned. She didn't mind failing, even in front of the seemingly always-efficient man, but she preferred not to seem an idiot doing so. To help herself focus, she brushed snow off the purple coat she'd livened up with random splashes of glittery gold paint.

"Distracted before call. Too late to commit. Control speed, flat and straight one second, then turn. Shoulder alignment," he said, the mechanical rasp of his voice changer having grown familiar. He picked up her goggles and tapped them against his hip to dust them off, offering them back to her.

"Thanks. That must be it. I'll get it next time." Zita flashed him a smile and hung her goggles on one wrist, relieved she wouldn't have to struggle anymore to get them to stay over the mask hiding the upper half of her face.

Freelance returned a brusque nod.

At least he doesn't want me to go back to stationary practice on turns, she consoled herself. She shrugged at him and removed a large, folded plastic bag from her pockets. After stripping off her gloves, she unzipped her coat. "Trouble. My friends and I need to handle something, so I guess the lesson's over. Thanks for texting me to join, and I'll hit you back when I have something fun in mind. I owe you some tightrope lessons, too."

"What?"

Guessing at his question, Zita shrugged. "They didn't say. I'm certain they'll fill me in when they get here, any minute now."

Freelance nodded. As he tilted his head skyward, his goggles focused on something with a soft whir. He took a few steps back so he stood in the shadows of a tree, almost invisible despite his dark clothing in the bright landscape.

She followed the direction of his gaze, absently stuffing her coat, gloves, and goggles in the bag. Hopefully, the mercenary wouldn't notice that she'd left the top button of her neon orange snow pants undone. *I was lucky to find winter gear in May at all, let alone in cool neon colors. It'd be nice if the pants were one size larger, though. Ah, well. I better get it all off since my costume is the only clothing that'll let me shift wearing it.*

With Wyn in his arms, Andy descended from the clouds until he hovered a foot or two above the snow. He wore the male version of the costume beneath Zita's winter clothes: a deep purple sleeveless tank top instead of a sports bra, matching bicycle shorts, and a mask that covered the top half of his head. His straight black hair was also bound back in a braid, but his was tidy, uniform, and missing the snow that no doubt decorated hers. Unlike her, he wore a fluttery cape that matched his shirt. Andy's eyes widened, and he gave a visible start when he caught sight of Freelance. *Next time mention that he's the buddy. He's way too easy to miss.*

"Arca. Freelance." The second word dripped with figurative ice. Preferring magic to a mask, Wyn wore the illusion of a ghostly blond woman, one whose physical beauty Zita privately considered too sharp-edged and perfect to be real. Her deep purple eyes narrowed as she glowered at the mercenary. Golden magic twined around her slender arms, and a small, floating arrowhead pointed at Zita. After a curt gesture, the glow disappeared and the arrowhead dropped into her hand. *Why is he here?*

"Guys. What's the emergency?" Zita brushed a layer of snow off her pants, trying not to shiver. *We were snowboarding. He's cool, relax.*

Freelance said nothing, but his gaze was on her friends.

Andy rubbed the sides of his pants. "It was quicker to come to you than the alternative. Zeus, Jennifer Stone, and their gang have resurfaced at a new tourist site in Greece. They've barricaded themselves inside a cave with hostages. According to the news, none of the closer teams are available. The Africans are keeping an eye on Dragon, and the Europeans are handling a French riot in progress."

Zita took a second to swear in four or five languages. "Right, we've got to go."

Wyn eyed Freelance, her expression frosty. She shook out her long white-blond hair. "Sorry to interrupt your... date?" For some reason, she'd chosen the short, glittery club dress and high heels version of her favorite disguise, rather than the one in impractical but flattering winter gear.

With a wave, Zita hurried to correct the misconception. *Let's not give Freelance a reason to avoid joining me. It's hard to find a good extreme sports partner, especially one who doesn't ask questions that require me to lie much.* She buried the thought that attractive, relaxing ones were even harder for a woman in a mask to find. "Oh, it's not a date. We're just hanging out, practicing sweet moves."

Her expression screaming doubt, Wyn shrugged. "My mistake. We need to leave now though. Who knows how many they killed before the kid posted the videos on the Internet and they went viral? Jennifer Stone seemed quite unwell."

Sympathy welled in Zita at the memory of the schizophrenic metahuman, whose introduction to her powers had been triggered by a villain's torture. She turned to Freelance. "Did you want to come with? You've been after Jen for a while, and she could be with them." *Zeus threw away a small army in Brazil, but we don't know how many they started with. If he brought a lot of guys with him, Freelance could really help us.*

Her posture stiffening, Wyn shot her an accusing glare. *We don't need his aid unless you want people to die.*

Depending on how big of a force we're facing and what the local authorities have managed, we might need him. He's effective, and the last time he helped, he didn't kill anyone. Seriously, you shouldn't let the man spook you just because you can't read his mind. Move your lips if you're going to talk like this. He thinks we have magic subaural transmitters. Zita rolled her eyes.

His mental voice apologetic, Andy sent, *In all fairness, he has a tendency to sneak up on people.* He did make the effort to move his lips.

And shoot them. Not knowing when he's there or his intentions would be considerably less discomforting if one could be certain he was not about to murder one, Wyn added.

The mercenary broke his stillness with a small shoulder twitch. "No. Jennifer Stone requires medical expertise and medication to ensure a safe extraction. No time."

Wyn relaxed. *Praise the Goddess!*

I didn't know he could use full sentences, but maybe the extra words fell out after being exposed to the fluorescent overdose of Zita's outfit. We have to save those people. Andy straightened, and after another glance at them, he jerked his chin at the clear slopes above. "The mountain has a big open area up higher. We'll go there, and I'll shift to Wingspan so we can go straight to Greece from here. Muse, will you get the GPS out?"

"Right, we don't have the time then. I'll be right there, guys, once I get enough stuff off." Zita worked to free the bindings on her feet, some part of her mind calculating if it would be faster to run through the snow to Wingspan or to remove her remaining gear to fly. *Flying would work best given the board. Once I unfasten it, I can shift to a cat to get out of my snow pants, and then carry it all as a large bird to my friends.*

With one last cryptic look at Zita, Wyn let herself be led away.

She glanced up and smiled at Freelance, her hands busy. "I'll text when we're done and let you know if Jen ends up in jail so you can work with whoever it is. Hasta." Zita collected her snowboard and planted her feet, preparing to shift.

He called her name. Her vigilante name, anyway. "Arca."

Surprise and curiosity stopped her. *Usually he disappears without a goodbye or waiting for me to finish a sentence.* One hand automatically sought the pocket she kept snacks in, but then she remembered she'd already eaten them all. She checked her other pocket. The backup food was gone too, and her water was mostly empty. "Did I forget something?"

Freelance closed the distance between them. His goggles hummed as they focused on her, and he held his body in a strange, tense position she could not identify. "We're not dating? I thought... My apologies."

Her mouth fell open, and she dropped her snowboard. "Wait, what?" she said, blinking. "You—why?"

"Why else spend so much time together with obvious mutual interest?" His head tilted.

"Because we both enjoy awesomely fun things, and we're using secret identities so we can't include friends and family?" Zita frowned. "Wait, obvious? I was obvious? I was trying so hard to be all respectful and subtle. Caramba."

Whether it was tactfulness or his customary reticence, he did not reply.

Her jumbled thoughts caught up to the rest of his question. "Momentito, you thought *you* were obvious? In a full-face mask and body armor? You never made a move or said anything. I mean, you don't usually say much, but you never said... I don't even know if you're single. Did you enjoy all the climbing and other sports or were you just humoring me?" She frowned.

One of his shoulders twitched. "I am. I did. My apologies. Cordial still?"

Words poured out before she could think about them, perhaps because of all the other thoughts jostling each other. "Órale, I'm not opposed, just surprised. If you're—we're—interested, maybe we could see where it could go?"

The mechanical sound of his voice held no clues to his emotions. "You're a hero. I'm a mercenary. Reputation protects you; dating might damage."

She nodded absently and picked up her board again. With a frown, she traced the edge, flicking off snow. "True."

A chorus of male voices sent a single word in unison, letting her know that Andy already wore his Wingspan shape, a jet-sized golden eagle, without needing to check. *Ready.*

For once, Wyn's tone was harsh. *Are you coming? Those people need our help.*

Usually I'm the impatient one. I'm coming. I need to finish something first. Zita tilted her head. "Just a few seconds more," she said, speaking aloud in her distraction.

"You must go."

"Sí, I do, but—" Zita turned back and saw he was gone. "Wait, are we dating or did we break up or what?" Swearing, she ran toward where her friends waited.

***

"Are we there yet?" Zita peered over the edge of Andy's enormous wing, eyeing the area below.

The vivid cobalts and emeralds of the ocean stopped abruptly at sharp, sheer cliffs of khaki rock and olive grasses on an arthritic finger of land gnarled with rolling mountains. Tiny clusters of ruins and rugged villages, isolated from each other, were either joined by a single narrow, winding road or not at all. Terraces, both natural and not, drew jagged horizontal lines on the stone like giant claw marks. As if to underscore the isolation and austerity of the area, the few beaches bristled with rock instead of smooth sand. Even the brilliant swirls of colorful blooming wildflowers in the mellow afternoon sun could not soften the hard edges of the land.

Zita made a mental note to check out the rock climbing in the area later. Her stomach growled, and she appended visiting a local eatery as well.

Still wearing her Muse disguise, Wyn made no attempt to get up from where she rested in the center of Andy's back, studying a map on her tablet. "If it looks like a remote Greek peninsula with an ancient lighthouse at the very tip, yes. The cave is on the coast, directly west of a set of ruins and set into steep hillside. It's only accessible by foot or small off-road vehicles and was discovered following a large earthquake several years ago. Up until then, the major attractions were a demolished church, the lighthouse, and a different, flooded cave. The Goddess only knows how the boy got enough of an Internet connection to upload the video, but perhaps the recent increase in tourism explains that."

Despite the weariness that was just making itself known now that she wasn't focused on snowboarding, Zita jiggled her leg restlessly. *Cramming my usual chores into a few hours to go snowboarding with Freelance might not have been the best idea, especially since we agreed to meet at dawn. It did stop that annoying meta who was nagging me in my dreams, though. Again. No time to dwell on her or her warnings about crossing lines and lizards. Wyn healed my bruises, and my gear will be safe in her purse, so I should focus on the problem at hand.* "I don't see none of that, but I'm guessing the gunfire and flames might be a clue to our destination."

Wyn sighed. "So much for hoping the local authorities have it all contained by the time we arrive. Did you wish to review the video again?" Without waiting for an answer, she raised her hand and used an illusion to display the scenes from the shaky video again.

A woman and a child exclaimed as boulders thrust out of the ground. Other voices in the background were an unintelligible, nervous murmur of sound. Three large men in bulletproof vests steered a barefoot, brown-haired woman, whose gaze was distant and cloudy, in a wide circle around the cave. A vest hung open and unfastened on the woman's tall frame. Huge rocks speared up from the ground to either side of the small group, as if called to mark her path.

Of the four, Zita could identify only one. *Jen Stone, and definitely still off the medication.*

The view changed to show a group of men, armed with a variety of assault rifles, advancing on the camera's position.

"Run, boys!" the woman's voice commanded, and the mutters changed to panting and screams. The camera jostled and bounced wildly, finally coming to a standstill in the grass. The long, uncut strands blocked sight of anything more than changing shadows, but the microphone picked up a small zapping sound, followed by a man's cruel laugh and a cold command in English.

"I've got this one. You get the tourists. Kill the locals."

Zeus.

Through the grass, Jen stared at something near the camera, her gaze clouded, and lifted her hand. "Children aren't dangerous. Leave the little one alone."

A kid's voice whispered in English and the view shuddered, settling on a view of rock, "They've got my mom and big brother. Help us! Send, send, send."

Someone off-camera wailed, a young, high-pitched sound of anger or fear, and then the images disappeared.

Zita licked her lips, hoping the kid or kids in question still lived as she peered below. To aid in picking out details, she did a partial shift to a harpy eagle. Feathers whispered instead of hair when she turned her head, but her vision sharpened as she'd hoped.

The already mountainous area had been transformed into the kind of ground she would've expected to see in one of the Andy's beloved video games. A narrow path wound between natural terraces with one ridge showing signs of significant modification. Forbidding spires of stone thrust out of the ground, filling the gaps between walls she guessed were natural and ones that had the bare look of newly unearthed rock. Separate from all the others, one spike impaled an off-road motorcycle with an official-seeming symbol on the side. Fire bloomed from the remains of other multiple off-road motorbikes and the nose of a boat stuck out of the water by some huge rocks. A few limp forms lay unmoving here and there.

Hidden behind the barrier spikes blocking off the warped terrace, a deep crevasse split the ground in a gap wide enough to swallow even a large vehicle. Past that, several small, rocky enclosures squatted with the long, deadly noses of guns pointed out from all but one of them. A burning rope dangled above an eerie cave mouth, where the entry had been closed with stone bars.

Zita frowned. The Grecian police or military... or both... had set up a wide perimeter around the rock. Armored vehicles blocked off the narrow two-lane road that seemed to be the only access to the general area from the closest town. Several boats floated offshore, two with guns large enough to see from a distance. With one exception, they stayed just barely within what she guessed was eyesight of the shore. Clusters of men, most in uniform but a few with the practical, worn clothing of locals, hid in a ragged semicircle around the cave, under terraces and behind rocks. In the air, multiple sets of spindly metal machines flew.

"Something's not quite right," she murmured. "Neither side is making any sense. Most must be sitting inside, because I don't see Zeus or his buds, just a bunch of thugs with guns. If they're in the cave, why aren't they using it as cover?"

Wyn lifted her head from her tablet, sighed as she tucked it away, and got to her feet. She drifted over just enough to peek below. "That is odd. The cave is renowned because deadly gases make exploration impossible without special breathing apparatus, so I can't imagine why Zeus would herd his people inside. He seemed far too narcissistic to kill himself the last few times we've heard from him."

With a nod, Zita pointed at the clusters of military people. "Verdad. Plus, the Greek authority-types are here, but they're not doing anything. Why do they have their men positioned so Zeus' men have one—no, three—escape paths, if you count a possible sea route? Why haven't they closed the circle? Why are the boats all so far off? They have enough men and firepower to shoot the guys outside the cave to pieces, assuming Zeus' men aren't all bulletproof. Why has the military deployed drones over the sea? In case they have attack tuna or something?"

Craning her neck, Wyn tried to peer more closely and then backpedaled rapidly to where she'd been. She assumed a cross-legged, seated position and held out her hands. "I'm going to see what I can discover. Don't leave before I can tell you the results."

Zita nodded. "Por supuesto, I'll wait unless someone is in immediate risk of death."

"That's the best I can expect, I suppose." Party line cut off as Wyn's face took on a distant expression.

Movement by a spike drew Zita's attention, and she focused on it, grateful for raptor vision. When she resolved what she was seeing, she could not refrain from wincing and swearing. *That poor kid! Did Jen think she was doing him a favor?*

Wyn was too engrossed in whatever she was doing with her telepathy, but Wingspan shrieked and flapped his wings, sending thunder booming.

By the time party line returned and Wyn finally spoke again, a few minutes later, Zita was pacing in a tight, impatient circle as she ran through possible rescue plans.

Wyn spoke aloud; they knew from experience that Andy could hear everything said on his back. "It's all any of the Greek commanders are thinking about, so I found the problem. Someone's commandeered the drones and computers in the area and is blocking voice communication. They've also intercepted text commands and inserted false information, so that can't be trusted. Additionally, they're under surveillance from their own hijacked equipment. The teams on the ground were attempting to coordinate using hand signals, but the couple tries they made to move ended with Zeus' men concentrating fire..."

Zita winced. "They're pinned with no way to request backup."

Wyn nodded. "They believe the drones are broadcasting their moves, but no one is willing to destroy the expensive equipment without a high-ranking officer's permission."

"Which they can't get because comms are down," Zita said.

"Correct. Utilizing their own computerized systems against them, the hacker has already run one boat aground. The hacker has partial control of another ship, the one separate from the others. Navy reinforcements are remaining outside what they believe to be the radius of the hacker's reach."

After considering the boats, Zita nodded. "No drones close to the boundary either, so they're probably right. That'll help. In case you missed it while you were rummaging through brains, one of the rock spikes is hollow and has a kid stuck inside. If anyone tries to ram it, they'll kill him, so he's got to be top priority. The top half of the spike is missing so we can see his face and his hands—I think he's trying to get out, but he lacks the upper body strength. I don't see anyone else in the others, but we'll need to tread with care."

Only one child is trapped above ground. All other hostages are below ground, Wingspan added in one of his rare comments while in bird form. His voice echoed like that of multiple men speaking in unison, and anger vibrated through the statement.

Knowing Andy's bird form had a homing instinct for people in trouble, Zita nodded, even though logically she knew he couldn't see her. "Thanks, that makes things easier. How's this for a plan? Mano, drop off Wyn either by the ruins or behind that outcropping near where the river joins the sea. Then, you get the kid out of the rock and drop him off with her. If he's stuck in the rock or something, you're strong enough to bring the whole chingado thing with us so he can be extracted later. Once he's safe, you can draw fire from Zeus' guys so the official Greek-types can get into better positions. I'll see if I can find the hacker and shut down his controls. If I can do that, the military can use all their nifty toys again. Wyn, can you help me find him quicker by scanning the area and narrowing down where the hacker's at? Once you've got the boy, keep him safe and see if you can put any of Zeus' thugs to sleep."

Wyn frowned, chewing her lower lip, then nodded. "I'll see what I can do. Set me down in the ruins above the cave. The Greeks had a team that attempted to come in from above, and they've got serious injuries that need treating as well. Between the walls and the team up there, I should be safe enough, and I can see better from there." She sighed and wrapped her arms around herself.

Zita padded over and patted her friend's arm. "Look on the bright side," she tried, "we've got an advantage because Zeus' thugs have a major weakness."

"What's that?"

"Freelance was with me, so they didn't hire him or his team to fight us. So, even if the numbers seem overwhelming, bad leadership is likely to sink them. Jen is too sick to be coherent for long, Pretorius is in some Brazilian jail, and Zeus is obsessed with being on camera. Tiffany and Garm might be a threat since they're not brainless, but they're all wrapped up in being dramatically evil, which handicaps them." Zita ticked off names on her fingers as she spoke, concluding with a smile.

Her friend's eyes narrowed as her attention moved to Zita. "We'll need to revisit the Freelance thing later."

"Oye, got to go find me a computer geek. Where am I checking at?" Smile gone, Zita leapt from Andy's wing and shifted to a golden eagle.

Chapter Two

Taking down the hacker—a middle-aged woman with amazing manual dexterity but poor reflexes—took next to no time once Zita had a rough area to search. Sporadic gunfire echoed on the mountainside as she flew to rejoin Wyn. Below her, the Greek forces scurried into new positions, abandoning vulnerable spots and cutting off Zeus' escape routes, as the drones stopped moving. The boats remained a distance away.

She circled high over the ruins where Wyn hid. *I'm incoming. Tell people not to shoot me.*

Near the edge of the cliff above the cave, a tight rock grouping sheltered a crumbling building. Based on the floor plan, revealed by the lack of a roof, it had once been a chapel. Now it held Wyn in her Muse guise, a boy that appeared to be about ten years old, and a cluster of people armed for war. Half were military, recognizable by their faded uniforms, bulletproof vests, and muscular bodies held with rigid correctness. The other half were weathered, lean-muscled men in serviceable civilian clothing that she assumed were locals. A young man with an enormous bloody blotch on his uniform seemed to be issuing orders, and was the only one with any rank insignia visible. Ropes, backpacks, and gear surrounded them and filled their hands as they spoke. Standing out among the other standard equipment was a handful of breathing apparatus, similar to scuba tanks, but far too few to accommodate the number gathered.

Wyn glanced up and waved.

Zita took that as her cue and dove, slowing at the last minute to land on a half-destroyed wall. She shifted to Arca.

The men greeted her return to human form by pointing a variety of firearms at her, both military and not.

Wyn held out an arm and spoke in rapid Greek. "Wait, this is one of my friends. Don't shoot."

Wiggling her fingers at them, Zita sat down, keeping her arms loose and away from her body. "Relax," she said in the same language. "I'm unarmed and on your side. Not dangerous at all." With a smile, she swung her legs, wishing they reached the ground, so she'd feel less like a five-year-old on a too-big chair.

The military leader harrumphed, but his gun returned to its holster at the waist of his bloodied uniform. "Down," he commanded in Greek as he approached. The soldiers complied, but the locals kept their weapons trained upon her.

She held as still as possible in case someone had a twitchy trigger finger.

Stopping beside her, the military leader set a heavy hand on Zita's shoulder. Angling his head so he glared down his long nose at her, he barked, "What happened to the hacker?"

Given that most adults and many teens are taller than me, the purposeful looming is more annoying than intimidating. Zita's chin jutted upward, and she slid out from under his grasp. "The computer chick's tied up on top of a rock. Someone will need to do a little climbing, but she can't get down by herself, based on her swearing. Her electronics stuff is all in the cave. Other than turning it all off, I left it where it was so I wouldn't mess up whatever evidence you can get from it. Now, what's the next move?"

The military guy started to speak, but a grizzled local, who was probably younger than his weathered countenance suggested, tugged on his arm. They had a whispered conversation.

"Enough, Nikos. This is my decision, not yours." The soldier turned back to Wyn and Zita. "You and your friends can stand down. Please recall your flying man. We thank you for the help, but we can handle this now. Leadership has requested additional breathing apparatus, and we'll be mounting an expeditionary force once we've gotten things together. You can wait here with the child until our reinforcements arrive as it would be unsafe for you to leave until then."

Nikos' face creased in deep, unhappy lines as the local man lifted a shaggy eyebrow. "Milo..."

The young military leader cut him off. Milo said, "Three people is not enough to defeat that group anyway. We wait for reinforcements, and that's final."

The words slipped out before Zita could stop them. "But they're morons, and we've won against them before! If you haven't noticed, we're trying to be all polite about it and—"

Wyn cut her off, offering a smile. "What my esteemed friend is struggling to communicate is that we're here to help, and we'd love to know how we could best assist you."

"I was going to say please. Rescuing goes a lot faster if you don't have to dance around stupid political shit. Seriously, Wingspan can crush the bars with no problems and I'm familiar with using breathers," Zita grumbled in English.

Nikos snorted, his mouth twisting upward. He waved a hand at the others.

The last of the guns lowered.

Zita's shoulders relaxed, losing some of the tension.

Jaw clenched, the military man gritted out, "You are still civilians. We appreciate the assistance, but this is our job." One of his hands drifted toward the bloodied section of his shirt, and then he let it drop. The other men watched avidly, and the boy whimpered.

Wyn's smile grew forced, and she walked over to tap Zita's arm. She switched back to Greek. "We're more than happy to do our part and work with you. It'd be lovely if you'd wait over there while I talk to the nice men, Arca. I'll call our friend to come here." She reinforced it mentally even as she waved at another section of the crumbling structure. *Let me handle this. Andy, can you meet us at the ruins?*

His reply came quickly. *Sure, I'm getting shot at by both sides anyway. It tickles.*

With a sharp nod, Zita jumped off her perch, landing lightly on her feet. She strode in the opposite direction, toward the edge where she could assess the situation. *You know if they don't let us help, we're going to have to step in anyway since the European super team isn't here.*

Wyn soothed her. *We'll do it our way, but let us at least attempt diplomacy. We have to wait for Andy in any case.*

Mollified, Zita crouched behind a large pillar of rock and peeked below. A scurrying sound won a glance behind her.

The boy came to her side. His English was pure American. "You saw my video! You can't just go! You have to get my family back! The other lady promised you would."

We shouldn't make promises we may not be able to keep, Wyn, Zita sent.

He sniffled, biting his lip and hugging a tablet in a battered case like a stuffed toy. Liquid welled in the kid's eyes.

Oh, no, no crying, especially close to a cliff. Traitorous words slipped from her mouth. "If we can, we will. You did real good with the video. Now, why don't you go sit in the ruin and ensure the military know how many hostages they have."

Wiping his eyes on the back of a grimy arm, the boy nodded. "They took seven people, including my mom and my big brother.

You can tell him from the others because he looks like a big, stupid dork. You'll really try?"

She nodded.

"Good." He scurried back to stand by Wyn, who stroked his hair and murmured something.

Pebbles crunching alerted her to additional visitors. She glanced over.

Locals separated from the military, and Nikos came up beside her. The rest hung back and spread out, their bodies blocking her view of the military men, Wyn, and the boy.

As her body tensed, Zita turned sideways and slipped into a defensive posture. "What?" She stuck to Greek.

Nikos watched, his dark eyes spearing her.

The wind brought the murmur of Wyn's voice and the deeper tones of the men, as well as the rapid clattering booms of bursts of gunfire from below.

"Your friend is unhurt by guns?" He nodded upward as Andy flew by overhead.

She nodded as hope flared. *Bulletproof is its own diplomacy and a handy one at that.*

He nodded and snapped his fingers. A pair of his men separated and hurried off.

"My grandmother would hate it if Milo weren't around to marry my niece next week." He lapsed into silence.

Zita barely dared to breathe and instead studied the landscape. With the hacker out of commission, the military had gotten their most vulnerable units under cover. Their ships still lingered in the same spot, but she could see a flurry of activity on the deck.

Two locals returned, carrying the breathing gear. They set it down in front of her and then joined the others obstructing the ruins from sight.

"Show me your expertise," Nikos said.

Zita picked up the closest of the units and examined it for weakness, even detaching a few pieces and reattaching them. "Above this, good. Below that, bad." She pointed to the appropriate values on the gauges. Finally, she adjusted the straps of the backpack to fit her petite frame and slid it on. *And my brother Miguel told me scuba diving would never be needed on my resumé. Too bad I can't tell him about it.*

He grunted and shot her a disapproving glance. "Military's ten minutes out."

Negotiations just ended. He wouldn't listen, Wyn complained.

Zita lifted her hands in surrender. *Lucky you brought me, then. I totally just talked this guy into lending us his kit so we can go into the cave whenever we're ready. Come over here so we can move in before the military-types.*

Nikos nodded and wandered back to his friends.

Coming. Do you actually have the expertise to use such equipment? Curiosity ran through Wyn's reply.

Andy kept it simpler. *Just landed. On my way.*

Zita smothered a smile and checked the other two packs she'd been given. *No hay bronca. Scuba gear is similar. I've taught in a dive shop before and even had sex a few times while wearing it. I don't recommend the second, by the way.*

Way TMI, Andy sent.

The crowd of locals split to allow Andy and Wyn through.

Keeping it real. We got about ten minutes before they can follow us in, so we got to hurry. Other than having fewer dials, these don't seem too different from what I'm used to. She slapped a backpack into Andy's hands and assisted Wyn with hers, making certain that Andy could copy what she'd done. As she went, she provided low-pitched instruction in English.

Andy shouldered his pack without complaint, but gave the full-face mask an unhappy look.

Zita batted Wyn's hands away from the straps and tightened them for her. She grinned and double-checked the valves. "You're good, Muse. Wingspan, you going to carry us down fast so we don't end up with bullet holes? We can't let the oxygen tanks get shot or set on fire unless you want them to explode." She double-checked Andy's pack and stripped off her own.

Wyn grumbled. "The pack's heavy and ugly."

"It's not that bad. I've carried worse. Can I get a piece of my chalk from your bag, Muse? The air will be limited, so move fast in there," Zita replied.

After a second, Wyn handed over the chalk.

"How limited?" Andy frowned, but he lifted Wyn with one arm and held out the other to Zita.

She shrugged, tucked the chalk in a pocket, and piled her own gear on Wyn. "After we've had them on a while, I'll check the gauges, but we should have at least an hour, assuming they don't have any major differences from diving gear. I'll go small, so Wingspan has less to protect, and put it back on at the cave mouth." *Let's go before Nikos' ferocious abuela descends on us or they realize that fighting Zeus and his crew might damage their equipment.*

***

Moments later, Wyn and Andy crouched low at the top of the cliff above the cave. Zita hid in the long, scratchy wild grass near their feet as a coyote, blending into the foliage. In the ruins nearby, she could hear the locals still distracting the military.

Wyn settled into Andy's arms, her lap full of breathing equipment. "Arca, could you sit on his shoulder so we're all together, please?"

If you say so, but I'd be safer if I flew separate. Zita shifted to a hyacinth macaw and fluttered to his shoulder. Fastidiously, she kneaded the smooth, slippery fabric, trying to anchor herself.

"Try not to rip my clothes with those claws," Andy grumbled.

As his near-invulnerability meant she couldn't hurt him, Zita dug in more, though she did attempt to keep from piercing the fabric. She cawed out a laugh. When her friends winced at the noise, she switched to party line instead of speaking. *Sorry about the squawking. Should I sit on your head instead? Trust me, mano, if I were going to rip off anyone's clothes, I wouldn't pick yours. Let's go.*

"Shoulder's fine, but I've got a blind spot where you're sitting now. I'll have to go fast to avoid being shot by the one or two baddies that the Greeks haven't dug out of their holes yet. Or the Greeks themselves." Despite his grousing, Andy rose a few feet off the ground and flew over the edge, descending rapidly.

Wyn freed her hands enough to make a few gestures, and a bubble appeared around them.

Well, at least we'll be safe from magic, assuming they brought Tiffany or someone like her. Zita cocked her head sideways, blue feathers fluffing around her.

Toying with a long lock of hair, Wyn answered aloud in English. "This is a new version of the spell. It protects against bullets and other physical attacks, though I'd prefer not to test it too much. We end up at or around gun battles far too often to not develop a way to keep myself and those I'm with safe. The biggest drawbacks are that I can't cast anything else while it's up, and it doesn't protect against magic as my attempts to combine the two shield spells have thus far been unsuccessful."

Zita clicked her beak in approval and felt her body relax. *That's awesome. You the witch!*

With a tight, relieved smile, Andy said, "Great! I can be more careful then." Their descent slowed.

Gunfire boomed. Tiny specks of light flared on the shield, but the protection held.

"Maybe not that slow." Andy sped up again and landed by the cave. He set Wyn down beside the entrance, which had thin bars like tiny stalactites barring entry.

Zita was already off his shoulder, though she was careful to stay in the gleaming shield. Shifting to a fluffy black cat, she peered through a gap between the bars. While she saw no one, her sensitive nose alerted her to another problem. Her stomach lurched.

With an inner sigh, she withdrew and returned to her Arca form. "Looks clear inside, but I smell dead people, so brace yourselves." She reclaimed her gear from Wyn and hastily put it on, double-checking the gauges as she went.

Andy stepped in front of the cavern. With no visible struggle, he closed his fingers around a stone bar.

It cracked, splintered, and crumbled to dust.

Methodically, he began to clear the opening.

"Right, you get that. I'll double-check our gear in case something shifted on the way down." Finished donning her own, Zita checked her friend's equipment once more.

Accompanied by the rapid rattle of assault weapon fire, tiny sparks flew along the magical shield around them. Nothing made it through the protection.

"I really like that spell," Zita said.

A wash of pride came from Wyn.

"Done." His expression sickly, Andy closed his face mask and clambered awkwardly past Wyn and inside. *Underground is not my favorite.*

Zita shifted partially to a cat, just long enough to gain the improved vision for the dark and hearing, and stopped the shift while still humanoid. She tightened up her mask and gear for the subtle differences in her form and followed him in, with Wyn close behind her.

The trio stood inside a small limestone cave with just enough room for them to crowd close together in what little light snuck in from the entrance. Damp and dripping, stalactites and stalagmites formed the walls, leading to a narrow Stygian passage that leaked a gauzy mist near the ground. The ceiling loomed overhead, only inches from the tops of Wyn and Andy's heads. Rock was clammy and unyielding beneath Zita's feet. While the cavern magnified the mechanical breathing sounds of their masks and the shuffle of their feet, the gunfire outside was muffled, and the soft susurration of the ocean was almost absent.

Andy fidgeted with his gas mask strap. *I don't like these things. Or caves.*

Noticing the tiny green LED gleaming on the back of his pack, Zita grumbled to herself. *We need to keep them on or we'll die. Don't turn your backs on the bad guys in these things; they've got little lights that will give your position away that I didn't notice in the sunlight. On the bright side, it's just enough light to let me see where I'm going... and that. Caramba.*

In what would've been a great ambush position beside the cave entrance, a muscular woman in jungle fatigues was crumpled in a bloody puddle. A rifle on a sling rode her back and a very modern breathing apparatus lay beside her.

After setting the weapon out of the woman's reach, Zita leaned in, intending to see if the stranger still lived. However, when she had to lift her to remove the firearm, the face—or more accurately, the gory lack of—became visible. Gagging, she let the corpse return to its original position.

Wyn waved her hand, and a glowing orb appeared. "What? What's wrong?" she whispered.

Zita shook her head, and her ears, longer and furrier than usual, flicked with irritation as the brilliant light stung her newly dark-sensitive eyes. The stale, metal-tainted air from her gas mask drowned out any other scents, thankfully. Keeping her voice as low as possible, she said, "Put out the lights. Using those paints a target on us and makes it even harder to see through the fog. That's probably the bad air, by the way. Since it's all close to the ground, that'll give us more time to get out if our gear malfunctions since we won't immediately get poison up our noses."

"I can't see once we get farther in! How can we do anything if we're blind?" Wyn peered deeper into the cave and shuddered.

Biting her tongue, Zita calmed her breathing. "Can you tone the light down? I doubt you want to look too close at the dead chick right inside the entrance. Since she doesn't dress like a tourist, tour guide, or Greek military, she's probably one of Zeus' people who got hit on the way in. Hard to tell with her face mostly gone. She's got a gun... and a mask she didn't get a chance to wear... I guess I should take the breathing gear for the hostages." Steeling herself, she tugged it free, grateful the unknown person had died before putting them on.

"Goddess, the poor woman." Wyn turned her head away, and her light brightened.

Zita winced. "Seriously, can you bring that down a notch?"

Andy set a hand on Wyn's shoulder. "I'll stay with Muse. She'll use a small light so we can see, and you sneak ahead and let us know what's going on. It's what you'll do anyway, and the tunnel won't allow more than one of us to walk at a time."

"Bent over, at that," Wyn grumbled, eyeing the ceiling and ducking.

Zita managed a weak grin, not that they could see it. "True for you, anyway. I'll do that. I won't be too far ahead in case you need me. Let me know right away if you get headache-y or dizzy because that means you might have a problem with your breather. Can we bring down the brightness?" She pressed the spare breathing apparatus into Andy's hands, and he reflexively took them.

The light decreased.

Thanks. These tight confines will make fighting tough, so I'd rather avoid it if I can, especially since I can't shift without losing the air tank. Zita ghosted around a corner, swinging her head back and forth as she stretched her senses to detect hidden traps or guards. While the gas mask filtered out the smells, the stone and air cooled more as she descended a primitive set of steps. From the uneven but rectangular surface beneath her bare feet, she assumed the steps were not new to the passageway. An orange-painted stalactite divided the corridor. The mist grew dense and clutched at her legs as it seemed to pour out of the left corridor. The ground and anything more than a few feet away was hidden.

Her toes brushed fabric, wrapped around something too pliant to be rock.

Swallowing hard, Zita bent to find out what it was.

At her feet, a beefy man lay unmoving. He wore green combat fatigues, similar to the woman at the entrance.

She knelt beside him, noting his fixed stare. Swallowing, she checked for a pulse.

He was warm, but no pulse met her questing fingers. *Found another of the bad guys, dead. This guy's got to be six feet tall and close to three hundred pounds, so I can't move him out of your way without risking mangling his corpse. Sorry.*

Zita closed his eyes gently and crossed herself as she stood. The dead man was once again lost in the fog. *No living enemies so far. I'll keep going to ensure it's safe.*

Unhappiness came through the line from Andy. *Fine, we'll watch for him. If we get a chance later, I'll move him so his family can know what happened to him.*

"Dios keep you, even if you followed an idiot in life," Zita whispered as she stepped over the dead man and continued through the passage.

She glanced down both tunnels and picked one, making a small arrow with her chalk on the painted stalactite so she could backtrack. *Since it'd be far too easy if the way we want is the one without the poisonous gas everywhere, I'm going left at the fork in the tunnel. The intersection has a neon orange stalactite that should be hard to miss with an arrow pointing the way.*

Sounds about right, Andy said.

Indistinct voices came from somewhere ahead.

Tension and excitement chased down Zita's spine as she inched along her chosen corridor. *I must be close.*

Chapter Three

Her assumption was confirmed as she peered around the next corner.

Three more uneven steps led down to an enormous cavern. Near where Zita crouched, statues of a headless sheep and a bull stood guard by stone tablets too degraded to read. A man lay crumpled on the ground by the statues.

In the center of the cave, a swirling wall of wind raised a thin sepia-tinted screen of dust and mist around a half-destroyed temple. Despite the steaming stream of water that ran along one side of the temple, the ever-present fog was curiously absent around it. Stalagmites and stalactites that had joined comprised the remaining standing columns; any manmade ones had long ago fallen and left only irregular, jagged stumps. Tall tripod lamps flooded the walled area with harsh white LED light, but only deepened the shadows outside of their limited radius. Portable generators growled at the bases of the lamps. The voices she'd heard came from the three groups of people gathered near the crumbled edifice.

Using the stone bull for cover, Zita inched closer to the immobile man, avoiding the blood. Even though the charred, gory mess of his back and the odor made life unlikely, she had to see if he still lived. Steeling herself, she reached out to his neck, some corner of her mind noting his khaki shorts, hiking shoes, and unblinking stare. No life thrummed under her fingers. She crossed herself and sent a message to her friends. *Body at the entrance to a big cave. Local or tourist. Make sure you turn off your light when you hear the voices—you don't want them to spot you.*

Hope in her voice, Wyn said, *Could they still be alive?*

Zita's tone was flat. *No, he fried. He real dead. I'm guessing he tried to run, and Zeus zapped him. The poisonous gas probably didn't help either.*

Had she not been partially shifted, she would've found it too dark to see well outside of the temple zone. As it was, it allowed her to notice that what she'd taken for a bit of rubble outside the whirling wind was actually a motionless stack of men in bloodstained fatigues. *In addition, a few of Zeus' thugs must've dragged themselves in here before they died. They're too close to him and his surviving people to check, but they're stacked in a pile and not moving or complaining. And they all smell dead.* She felt her friends flinch via their connection. As she waited for them to join her, she scanned the assembly.

To the right, four adults and two teenagers huddled together. Their shared miserable expressions identified them as the hostages. A strange brown mark marred all of their foreheads. While a teenage girl clung to a man with similar features, a younger boy, maybe fourteen, held a camera shakily pointed at the people who stood directly opposite. No one guarded them, but painted ground surrounded them with a circle. Of the large symbols adorning it that Zita could make out, some were Greek words, and the rest seemed to be sloppy, unfinished shapes.

Her head throbbed as she contemplated the nonsense writing. She waited, recognizing the source of the hurt as one of her powers. Once the new language had added itself painfully to her linguistic repertoire, she understood more.

She sent an update to her friends. *Found the other hostages. One of those magic circle things is around them, Greek and some kind of*

Germanic writing along with meaningless scribbles. I'm no expert in magic, but this is screaming bad juju and an obvious sacrifice.

Proto-Germanic runes, perhaps proto-Norse futharks, given Tiffany's choice of Halja as a name? That would be the obvious linguistic option, though it's hard to tell with someone as incompetent—Ow! A sharp pain radiated down the link.

Everything okay? Zita studied the largest group in the cave.

Crankiness emanated from Wyn's reply. *Yes.*

Across from the hostages and beside a carved arch, a big blond man postured, his rich red cape hiding the people behind him. He lifted his chin and smirked, his attention glued to the camera held by the frightened boy hostage. A car battery sat at his feet, and a faint smudge marred his forehead.

Zita wrinkled her nose and bent to lower her profile, placing each foot with care as she crept nearer, hiding behind rocks whenever possible. *Zeus must be thrilled. Not only does he have a camera to play to, but the battery plus the generators will let him throw around lightning when we have to fight him.*

Concern swirled in Andy's voice. *I hate that you're probably right that this is going to end up as a fight. That said, Wyn hit her head hard enough to start bleeding. We need a minute so we don't start at a disadvantage.*

It's not a serious injury, but I prefer not to suffer needlessly or provide blood for our enemies to use against us. While the presence of Zeus, Tiffany, and Garm is inauspicious in and of itself, the circle is an ominous portent of their intentions. I prefer to have a clear head to deal with whatever mangled magic Tiffany is attempting this time.

A tangle of grim acceptance and unhappiness radiated from Andy. *We'll be there as soon as we can, so don't do anything yet.*

After a moment, Zita nodded. *They outnumber me, and I'm not an idiot. I'll try to wait, but I'm moving closer so I can intervene if they go to kill someone.*

When Zeus struck a pose, the people behind him shuffled a step back, becoming more visible. In a cheap folding chair, Jennifer Stone sprawled, apparently insensible to the world, her head lolling on her neck and body drooping. Her eyes were closed. At the edge of the circle, facing away from everyone else, another woman hovered a foot off the ground, arms raised and eyes blank. Her hair waved in a breeze that existed nowhere else in the cavern. Fifteen men, most carrying a variety of weaponry and massive backpacks, stood behind the women. Blood colored the makeshift bandages on three of them, one of whom seemed liable to collapse at any minute. Another set of nonsense scribbles glinted in the circle surrounding this group. Their foreheads bore a different symbol than the hostages, except for the floating girl, who had no mark. As Zita watched, Zeus smoothed his hair and blurred the mark there until it was barely more than a grayish smear.

Fewer mentions of sacrifice around the second group, Zita thought as she translated a few of the symbols, and then switched her attention to the remaining group of people.

In the center of the temple, the marble statues of a robed man and a three-headed dog loomed. At their feet, a blindfolded tourist knelt in a pile of ashes mixed with yellowed shards. Her bowed head suggested submission, but her body was tensed and alert rather than defeated. Beside the oversized dish, a skeletally thin woman in an out-of-place white business suit used a long paintbrush to deface the statue's robes with more scribbles. In an eerie mirror of the statue above them, a wolf with midnight fur crouched at her feet, his adoring gaze on the standing woman. Yet another circle ringed them with the same mix of characters and squiggly marks.

Tiffany and her favorite furball, Garm. Awesome. I'll have to be extra careful sneaking by or he'll sniff me out. Maybe the scribbles are gang signs they're trying out or something? Zita tried to plan the most logical approach to get as close as possible without risking the hostage.

As if she heard Zita's internal grumbling, Tiffany lifted her head to reveal a fabric mask hiding the left half of her face and a pair of mismatched eyes—one solid blue, one all black, and neither with any pupils or sclera. She glanced down and smiled smugly at the three-hundred-pound canine.

He licked her ankle, and his tail thumped once.

The sorceress began a soft chant, the volume too low to make out the words.

Sí, sí, still winning the creepiest couple of the year award. With a shudder, Zita updated her friends, telling them what she'd seen.

Andy groaned mentally. *Have I mentioned how much I hate fighting Jennifer Stone? It feels wrong to hit someone who's that sick, but if I don't do something, she buries me beneath the ground or tries to impale us on spikes.*

Pues, Jen looks like she's passed out in a chair, so we might get to skip fighting her, Zita replied. She crept closer, keeping out of the light as much as possible.

Tiffany raised one arm high, holding a dagger and a small compass. She checked the compass, rotating until something lined up, then continued speaking almost inaudibly.

The giant wolf watched.

Zita groaned internally. *They have the Key of Hades again. How inefficient is DMS if they can't keep one cursed knife out of the hands of lunatics? Hurry, guys. I don't know what Tiffany's doing, but she's waving that weapon near a tied-up lady. If she's gearing up to stab the hostage, I don't want to be too late to save her, especially if that's the kid's mom that Wyn promised to save.*

Andy focused on the question. *The Department of Metahuman Services will probably be more efficient now that they no longer have a traitor trying to establish his own drug operation in their midst. We're coming to you as fast as we can.*

I revised the spell on the dagger so they can't use it to gather power anymore. Wyn seemed affronted.

Zita did a controlled breath. *Do you think Tiffany remembers that? If nothing else, they seem to want to get all stabby with it. Besides, we know you're awesome, but they're idiots and might not have figured that out. Next time you should turn the knife into a pretzel stick or something.*

Homicidal idiots. Andy's mental voice was grim.

I can't make a knife into a spoon or something innocuous—well, I don't know how to off the top of my head, though I suppose I could devise something with adequate time and materials... Academic interest leaked through Wyn's communication.

As Zita returned to sneaking toward the temple, something nagged at her about the people gathered there.

I sense magic building. The spell is nascent, not fully activated yet. She'd need a power source to trigger the spell. Her runes previously have been abysmal, so she might need to correct the smudged sections too. Once I get closer, I'll better be able to determine how to dismantle it. Wyn's mental voice tried for lightness, but worry ran through it.

Zita stifled an exclamation when she realized what had bothered her. *None of them are wearing gas masks! So, either the air is clear there, or the weird whirlwind is making it possible for them to breathe. That would explain why they're stupid enough to use generators in an enclosed area... Maybe the floating girl is holding back the poison gas? She's the only one obviously using powers.*

Andy groaned. *Right then, no punching her unless we want everyone to die.*

Concern ran through Wyn's mental voice. *I'll see if I can put everyone but this air elementalist to sleep when I get there. I can't risk having her stop providing breathable air, though, so much will depend on her proximity to the others.*

Shuffling sounded from the mouth of the cave.

Behind the hostages, Zita froze, but no one reacted to the noise, probably missing it under Zeus' endless droning about himself. She glanced back, grateful he had apparently neglected to bring anyone who could see well in the deep twilight by the entryway.

Wyn and Andy hid behind the bull statue, or tried to.

I can get all the bad guys but Tiffany, Garm, Zeus, and the flying elementalist. The bigger problem is the magic. It's Tiffany's usual substandard sloppiness, but on top of a much more intricate and skilled spell, like a beginning pianist trying to play a complicated symphony by themselves and making up bits of the melody at random. Wyn's tone seemed torn between academic interest and disgust.

Andy sighed mentally. *I'll run toward Zeus' group and attract their attention since they won't hurt me if they shoot. Wait until I get farther from you, Wyn, so ricocheting bullets are less likely to hit you.*

One of the guys in Zeus' group seemed to freeze, squinting at the direction of Zita's friends, but then he cast his attention away with a studied casualness.

Did Zeus accidentally recruit someone with a conscience? Zita had an idea. *Wait. If Tiffany's still building the spell, let's get out at least a batch of the other hostages while they're busy. Wyn, you can do an illusion that the hostages are still there, right?*

Over the connection, Wyn hmmed. *I could do that, but I'll need to stand among them for the effect you want.*

If you're hanging out with them, Wyn, you shouldn't need your breather thanks to air girl. We've got a spare I took off the lady at the entrance. Andy, do you need to breathe? You fly us into space all the time.

Enthusiasm warmed his mental voice. *I see where you're going. Good idea. Given that I've gone really high as myself without the lack of atmosphere being a problem, I don't think so. You could use my mask too.*

Wyn caught on as well. *Yes, absolutely. Their safety is our priority. Use mine.*

Zita could've rubbed her hands together with glee. *Great! So, I can sneak out three hostages at a time using your gear and the spare. Once we've got most of them out, Wyn can do her sleep spell on the bad guys and pass the kid the spare to get out. I'll free the altar hostage and, if I have to, fight Garm. Andy, you've got Zeus—*

Wyn interrupted before Zita could finish. *When we enlighten the miscreants of our presence, I would be delighted to educate Tiffany on the responsible use of magic. Whatever she's casting is worrisome. Prior to that, I'll alert whoever we're moving out first so they do not inadvertently ruin our deception.*

Andy ventured, *Won't that give away your telepathy?*

Party line transmitted Wyn's amusement. *No, I'll tell them it's a spell that lets me to augment whispers, not telepathy. The captive at the altar and the boy will need to be the last two we rescue. With Zeus' narcissistic obsession with being on camera, he'll be the hardest to get out. Tiffany and Garm are almost on top of the woman, which will make her hard to sneak out.*

Plus, your illusions don't smell the same to a canine nose, Zita sent absently.

By the bull statue, Wyn straightened for a moment, and then ducked back down. *They don't?*

Didn't I tell you that? Zita winced, recognizing the warning tone in her friend's voice.

Ice was warmer than Wyn's tone. *No, you neglected to mention that fact.*

Andy broke in. *I'll wait near Wyn, so I'll be closer to Zeus and able to jump forward to save the woman at the altar if Tiffany tries to sacrifice her while Zita's gone.*

Whatever her annoyance at Zita's omission, Wyn focused on the rescue. *If you're in the front with me, that makes the illusion easier to maintain since I can anchor it to you and me. It won't extend far enough to hide them by the statues or the bodies given the amount of detail required, though.*

Forgetting her friends couldn't see her, Zita nodded. Belatedly, she repeated herself on party line. *That works. Worst comes to worst and we need to speed things up, I can hold my breath for several minutes—had practice while diving—so I'll give my mask to someone too if we're heading directly out. Freeing the captives might break Tiffany's circle and help wreck the spell too. It won't do anything bad to the people inside if the lines get scuffed, will it?*

Wyn's mental voice softened. *You were listening when I was talking about magic circle theory at yoga last Saturday? I thought you were focused on lifting weights in weird positions. I don't think breaking these circles, no matter how inept they are, would hurt anyone.*

Yeah, I totally listen. I'm a listener. Umm. Sometimes. We got a plan then?

Assent hummed along the line from both her friends.

Wyn sent, *I'll contact the gentleman with the teenager and one of the others so you can lead them out. When party line comes back, that's your cue to move.*

Party line dropped.

Zita settled into a crouch to wait.

***

At first, the plan went well. Once her friends arrived, Zita led out the first three hostages—the man, his daughter, and an elderly woman—and had just returned with her arms full of breathing equipment. Thanks to Wyn's illusion, it seemed as if nothing had changed from their original foray into the cavern. The majority of Zeus' thugs stood inside one circle, listening to their leader pontificate. Tiffany chanted something at the altar, with her lover in wolfen form at her feet. The hostage at the altar had pushed her blindfold up slightly, based on the strange angle of her head and the subtle attempts to back away on her knees. In the last circle, a young teen held a camera, with other hostages standing behind him. Even knowing it was an illusion, she still did an involuntary double-take at seeing the people she'd just freed back in their old positions.

Zita began creeping toward the hostages' backs. Once she'd gotten behind them, she could see Wyn's and Andy's backs, as well as that of a sturdy gray-haired woman and the kid. Andy had the tense posture of someone expecting to pounce, while Wyn kept sneaking glimpses at the runes around them and frowning.

She sent her friends a summary. *I'm coming up behind you now. The first three are out, and the Greek officials have them. How do you want to handle the last three? I don't think your trick will fool Garm in close quarters, but we could get the kid and the woman next to you out. The military will be joining us soon.*

Wyn sighed mentally. *The youth with the camera is the son of the blindfolded lady. He won't leave without her. The older lady behind him is a vacationing law-enforcement officer who feels she has to assist them in escaping before doing so herself.*

Zita concentrated on moving stealthily and not allowing the equipment she carried to clank.

Wyn continued, *The spell's still building, but Tiffany will have to trigger it soon or risk it dying or exploding. While I don't think she has the power or skill to make it succeed, I'll have to drop the illusion to counter the spell, as I can't do both at once. Whatever source spell she's using is unexpectedly complex, so combined with her bumbling, the magic will require all of my attention soon.*

Got it. I'll set down the air tanks behind you for the hostages, and then head over so I can grab the mom whenever you make your move or they figure out we're here. Sound like a plan?

Similar to a plan is not actually a plan, you know. Andy grumbled but his assent sang over the link.

Wyn just sent wordless agreement.

Before her friends could say more, Zeus smoothed his hair. "Give us more of a breeze. It'll play better onscreen, and I'm tired of the smell of dust." He extended one hand toward the car battery and the other toward the flying woman. A tiny spark leapt from the generator to his hand and then to the girl.

The wall of wind around the temple area faltered as the flying girl flinched and squealed. She blinked, turning toward Zeus. "Don't do that! I almost lost track of what I'm doing! I hope you're almost done, because I'm getting tired. I can't maintain this much longer."

Tiffany sneezed and pointed the dagger at the pile of wood where the blindfolded hostage stood. "Stop with the breeze before you destroy the altar beneath the pyre. We need the ancient sacrifices here, not scattered around the room. Now, don't break your circles or interrupt me." She wiped her eyes with a tissue, then began to chant, her words either mispronounced beyond recognition or mumbled too quietly to make them comprehensible.

With horror, Zita realized that the mass of ash was the cremated remains of previous sacrifices. *No mames, you're not adding that lady to the pile.* She sped up. As she crossed the swirling wind barrier, it strengthened and shoved her more roughly than it had before, but she reached her friends without dropping anything.

At the altar, the giant wolf lifted his nose, sniffed, and stiffened. "Intruders! Wingspan, Muse, and Arca, somewhere." He got to his feet, his beady eyes squinting in the bright light.

Swearing internally, Zita set down the air tanks by Andy.

The breeze died, though the outer barrier keeping out the poisonous air remained in place.

Zeus' smile faltered and turned into a smirk. "When we find them, we'll handle them. Perhaps we'll allow one or two to worship us once we become gods."

Tiffany glanced around, and her chanting grew faster. "Don't break the circles," she barked.

Her motions gentle to keep them quiet, Zita removed her own breathing equipment, placing it by Andy, but separate from the others. *I can't risk ruining this if I shift. It's probably the one closest to the boy's size anyway. He's taller than me, but he doesn't have the shoulders of a man yet. I'm going ahead with our sort-of plan. If the hostages run for it, worst comes to worst, we can hold our breath and sprint for the cave entrance, or at least get far enough into the dark that I can teleport us all home.*

Understood. I will maintain the illusion as long as possible, but I've been analyzing the tangled mess that Tiffany's made of her spell. I can't tell if she's summoning, or endeavoring to create a portal via sacrifice, or attempting to directly gain power from elsewhere. I'll actually work on unraveling it as soon as I can drop the illusion. The young man's agreed to don a mask so he can be prepared to escape once his mom is free, and the policewoman would enjoy leading the others out. I suspect she would love to arrest Zeus even more, but that objective is outside reasonable expectations. Tension rang through Wyn's mental voice.

As Zita exited and slunk through the darkness by the swirling wall of dust and deadly air, she was careful not to dip into the well-lit area. She had to smile at her friend's assessment of the remaining hostages, however. *Dream big, cop lady. Prep the other two to run for it. I'm going to grab Mom there. If I can get her far enough away from Tiffany and her wolf-toy, you can get the hostages out while I keep Garm busy.*

Since they're going on their own, I'm giving the officer one of your backup flashlights from my bag, Wyn sent.

Andy cracked his knuckles. *I'll handle whoever I need to.*

Garm's head snapped in their direction. "I found them," he breathed, and his tongue fell out of the side of his mouth in an evil, canine grin.

Zita froze.

Oops, Andy sent.

While Zeus and most of his men stared all around, their guns ready, the wolf's head turned toward the noise from the circle of hostages, and then swung toward Zita. He padded to the edge of the markings surrounding him and sniffed. Garm snarled. "Muse and Wingspan are hiding among the offerings! Arca's closer, somewhere."

Tiffany doesn't have the power for whatever she wants to do, but don't let her make her sacrifice! Whatever she's been building will trigger then, and I haven't had a chance to unravel the spell yet! Wyn sent urgently. The illusion dropped. Pink clouds rose around the feet of Zeus' people.

Guess the time for tricks is over. Zita shifted to a gorilla and clambered up the small hill as fast as possible.

Garm charged at her.

Scooping a double handful of the ancient sacrifices and praying it was only animal remains, she threw the powdery ash and bone fragments into his face.

He sneezed and pawed at his nose.

Zita grabbed the hostage and leapt off the pile, kicking up a small cloud as she did. She landed hard, unaccustomed to jumping in the much heavier gorilla form, almost dropping her burden. Her knees shrieked in protest. Clumsy, she stumbled across the lines of the circle and lurched toward her friends.

I had to help the cop with her breather. She's going to help the kid with his gear, Andy sent.

Garm lunged, but Tiffany seized his scruff.

He tilted his head at Tiffany. "What? I can get them! Should I leave the little witch for you to kill?"

"Don't break the circle. I need you here. We're out of time." Tiffany slashed the air in the direction of the arches in a pattern and muttered something about death. Lime green dripped weakly from the weapon.

Stubby legs moving fast, Zita sent, *I've got Mom, bringing her to you.*

In Zita's arms, Mom Hostage squirmed and fought. She froze when she felt fur.

Zeus held out a hand to his car battery, and electricity rose and coiled around his fist. He made a gesture as if to throw it at Wyn.

Andy leapt into the way of the bolt, and it dissipated around him.

Zeus swore. His men opened up a hail of gunfire.

Wyn's shield appeared. *I can't work on undoing Tiffany's spell if I'm shielding against bullets!*

Mom Hostage clawed at Zita's eyes.

"Calm down! I'm rescuing you," Zita tried to say, her upper lip curling as she tilted her head away. Given her current form, it came out as a series of quiet hoots and grunts.

The woman she carried screamed. Small arcs of light shot from her hands and ran through Zita.

As her muscles locked and the world turned into blinding pain, Zita tumbled to the ground, an impact she barely felt through the other agony, though she could hear Zeus laugh. *I hate it being tased.*

Wyn and Andy cried out in protest.

Zeus laughed. "I hope you got that on tape. Do a close-up of her stupid monkey face."

Dimly, Zita heard the hostage say "Oops" and the patter of running feet. Multiple voices murmured. Since she couldn't turn her head, she stared at the altar.

Wyn sent, *The boy said his mom's shocks only last about a minute or so. Andy has to finish disarming Zeus' men so I can lower my shield and get back to unraveling the tangled mess of magic in this room.*

The wolf made as if to leap at Zita, but Tiffany grabbed him. "No!"

His great muzzle tilted toward the sorceress. "I need only a second to finish her!"

From her position by the statues, Tiffany stroked the midnight fur on Garm's head, and her voice was oddly gentle as she painted a rune between his ears. "Stay with me. We're out of time and the spell has to be triggered now or never. It'll only work with someone who was in this circle during the casting. Garm, my love, I need you." She drew him closer to her as she backed away from the combat, onto the pile of ash.

"I am here," he said, following her and pressing his body against her legs. "They will not get you."

Tiffany turned her head away and her voice barely carried. "No, my love. I do not require the beast. I require your heart." Her voice still held an odd note that made the fur on Zita's spine raise.

Garm had no hesitation. "You have it always, my queen."

Her face studying his, Tiffany nodded. "Thank you, my faithful Garm." She rested her forehead on his and closed her eyes for a second. Below his chest, her blade gleamed silver under the harsh white LEDs.

Zita tried to shout a warning, but her tongue was thick and unwieldy in her mouth, though her body quivered as she fought the effects of the shock. She hauled herself to her knuckles painfully and promptly fell again.

Tiffany leaned back and buried the blade in Garm's chest.

The hostages shrieked behind Zita, and she heard multiple thuds.

The great beast stared at Tiffany, his dark eyes wide. "L-love?" he said. Blood poured from the wound in his chest, and he staggered.

Zeus laughed, a low, nasty sound. "So much for Romeo."

As the pain abated, Zita managed to turn her head to see what was happening.

Behind Zeus, his people clutched at their chests and fell, with the exception of the oblivious girl floating in the air. Even Jennifer Stone convulsed in her slumber, falling out of her chair and collapsing. Andy stood among the fallen, a rifle in his hands and confusion on his face. He snapped the gun in half and hurried to disable the rest of the weapons.

Wyn moaned. Her shield disappeared. "Oh, Goddess. What an unstable mess. She's killing all of them to power the spell and unbalancing it even further. The spell she's ripping off wasn't intended to be a death spell. You have to stop, Tiffany!"

Snarling, Tiffany paused just long enough to glare at Wyn. "You know nothing! It's a death spell by a death god, and I will be a goddess, no matter the cost!" She returned her attention to the wolf, stabbing him again.

Zita flopped forward and pushed herself up on her hands. *You can't get a heart out without cracking the ribs open or coming from underneath, so she's just hacking... Gracias a Dios that Mom Hostage doesn't have Zeus' voltage and a gorilla can take more than a human.*

Her eyes gleaming with tears, Tiffany brought a coppery bowl under Garm's chest and made a sawing motion. The blade must have been stuck on bone or... something... as she grimaced, pulled out the knife, and struck again. The lime green of the magic glowed brighter. She whispered, "I will always remember you, my beloved."

The lights flickered.

Garm cried out and fell.

Nausea overwhelmed Zita as she forced her sore muscles to move, but she staggered back to the altar. She headbutted Tiffany aside and grabbed Garm, throwing him awkwardly out of the circle.

Zeus finally noticed what had happened to his people. He touched his own forehead. "It was ruining my appearance," he muttered.

"No! You smeared my mystic runes, you vain fool!" Tiffany wailed and slashed wildly.

Agony shot through Zita's shoulder as one of the sorceress' berserk blows landed. She ran to half-carry, half-drag the dying werewolf to her friend to heal. *I hate that knife.*

"Arca!" Andy cried out, and something clattered on stone.

Wyn cried out. *The magic just increased in strength exponentially!*

Zeus snapped out a hand to his car battery and roared. "Traitorous bitch! You were going to sacrifice me too!" He threw lightning in the direction of the altar.

Andy jumped into the bolt's path.

It coruscated around him and died down.

As soon as the light faded, Andy shoved Tiffany down and yanked the knife from her. He hurled it against the farthest cave wall.

The Key of Hades shattered into pieces that glowed like tiny malevolent eclipses, sickly lime green and red outlines around each lightless shard-shaped hole.

Tiffany's face was feral and angry. "No! I will be a goddess! Let them all die!"

From the entrance, a man swore in Greek. Two heads, faces hidden by breathing equipment, peered into the cave.

Zeus grabbed another handful of lightning. "Oh, you want your precious dog dead? I'll finish him and then you!"

Zita dropped the wolf shapeshifter at Wyn's feet and returned to her Arca form. "Heal Garm or we'll lose him, all the hostages, and Zeus' flunkies!"

"I don't know how much time I can spare! The spell is devolving!" Wyn argued, but her hands were already in motion.

"Then just stabilize them! Fix the magic after!" Zita shouted to be heard over the increasing noise.

Tiffany shrieked.

Andy interposed himself in front of Wyn and her furry patient. "Back off, Zeus," he snarled. "Don't we have enough going on?"

The lights flickered and an unearthly wail of wind began whipping around the cave. Outside the whirling air, the three hostages lay on the ground, gas masks in place. A flashlight rolled on the ground by them.

"I can help him and the others by extension, but the magic here has become completely unstable!" Wyn shouted as her hands flew in patterns and the gentle light of her healing spell poured out over Garm's injury.

"Just the magic?" Zita shouted back. "I'll check the hostages."

I'm sorry, I thought I was helping when I destroyed the Key, Andy sent. Another bolt of lightning dissipated over him.

Pressing a hand against her wound to slow the bleeding, Zita sprinted toward the wall of wind. On the other side, the cops from the doorway ran over and began carrying the limp hostages away.

The floating girl chose now to pay attention. "What have you done? You're not leaving!" She gestured.

Dust swirled as the wind formed a giant club and swung at Zita.

She rolled out of the way in time to avoid being hit, but pain from her shoulder stole her breath.

The generators threw out a handful of sparks. Above everyone's heads, light bulbs broke—one, two, three—showering the ground and Zeus' crew with plastic shards.

The cave went dark, an utter, unbroken blackness.

Verdant green incandescence sprang forth from Wyn's hand, illuminating her and part of a motionless Garm. A moment later, vibrant cycling colors bathed the circle that had held the hostages, fading from blue to green to white. Andy stood protectively at her side while the wolf stayed still under her ministrations. The light flared, rising upward in a column that hid Zita's friends.

Tiffany exclaimed as gangrenous shades of gray and green ignited her circle. It rose around her, hiding her from view.

Finally, Zeus' circle ignited, white with a gray center that seemed to pulse with black shadows. Inside the circle, Zeus and the air woman shouted a variety of curses as they too were hidden from sight.

Wyn's panicked voice came over their mental link. *The spells are exploding! I can't shield everyone, so I'm dropping the counterspell to shield the hostages and military! Go join them.*

A shimmering, transparent bubble appeared over the hostages and the men trying to help them to the doorway.

Not leaving you here. Zita reversed direction and ran to the circle with her friends. She hit it and bounced off. While she caught herself before falling, it jarred her injury and her vision darkened at the edges for a precious few seconds. Fingers wide, she touched the circle. It stung, and she drew back her hand. This close, her friends were blurry images.

A multitude of colors flashed and spun around all three rings.

Andy curled over Wyn protectively. *Go home, Zita. I tried to carry Wyn out. It won't let us cross the circle.* His mental voice shook.

Go. Wyn huddled under him.

Lights flashed around them, and the keening wail of the wind drowned out all other sound.

"Fuck that melodrama! I got your backs!" Zita teleported to her friends. For a second, she seemed to hang in nothing... but then she burst through, like breaking the surface of water, and was beside her friends. *The hostages have gas masks.* She grabbed their arms, stuck one foot into Garm's oddly silky fur, and prepared to teleport to the abandoned air field. Her head and shoulder throbbed.

Lightning-bright colors seared her eyes before everything went black.

Chapter Four

Darkness. Warmth. Pressure from above.

Zita lifted one eyelid and turned her head to the side. Someone else's hair that tasted like herbs and chemicals filled her mouth, and she grimaced, spitting it out. Daylight leaked in around the edges of whatever was atop her. Disoriented and pained by the light, she shut her lids again. Her head felt as if it had been ripped in half and then the raw edges had grown fuzzy mold. The rest of her was painfully pinned, as if she were slowly being squashed in a press. A heated, breathing press that smelled of books and flowers, windy sidewalks and desert. Some corner of her mind recognized and was comforted by those scents, lowering her alarm but not eradicating her resistance to being held down. A snuffling sound was echoed by a delicate snore, then a louder droning growl.

She blinked, coming fully awake as she leapt to her feet... or attempted to. Something lumpy and heavy lay on top of her, and she rolled sideways to win herself more space, squirming out from under it. Agony ran through Zita as her injured shoulder took her full weight during her escape maneuvers, wringing an involuntary cry from her.

The weight atop her fell away.

Despite the continuing mental fogginess, she sat up. Vertigo assailed her, but she closed her eyes and knuckle-crawled a few feet away, grunting as she forced sore muscles to move. While she tried to avoid aggravating the searing misery of the stab wound any more than necessary, it still protested with the movement. *The Greek cave. The magic. That chingado knife. Well, my adrenaline wore off or I wouldn't hurt so much. So, it's been at least a few minutes.*

Once her whole body was bathed in warm, dry air, Zita stopped for a second to rest. Sunlight painted the edges of her eyelids in red, and she held still long enough for the dizziness and pain to pass or at least recede to ignorable levels. Once it had, she opened her eyes. *This... is not a cave. Did I bring us here? I don't remember teleporting, and this isn't a spot I've memorized.*

She was in a grassy meadow on the side of a hill or mountain, based on the slope and the view of a verdant valley. Beech trees gathered around the edges of the clear area, their brilliant green leaves rustling like a cluster of whispering gossipers, with the occasional pine or oak pretending not to listen in. In the shadier spots, moss draped small rocks that broke through the rich chocolate brown of the forest floor. Beneath the tang of blood, the air held the flavor of undeveloped land, with nothing to override the scent of the greenery and the earth. Her spine prickled with the nagging sensation of being watched.

When a breeze, a couple degrees cooler than the ambient air, brought a whiff of the familiar from behind her, Zita spun to check.

Close by, with a line of disturbed ground where she'd wiggled out to her current location, Andy and Wyn slept. A line of drool trailed from Andy's mouth, and he smacked his lips. A long piece of grass tickled the bridge of his nose. When he snorted and swiped at the grass, he flopped onto his back. He didn't awaken. The thick purple cape covering most of him pulled away, showing how he had been curled protectively over Wyn and why it had been so dark beneath them. The witch was face down on a mess of low-growing green plants, but a dainty snore revealed that her friend still lived. As she watched, a chestnut ringlet slipped free of a fancy hairnet to rest upon the curves of a cheek.

Zita relaxed, seeing both friends alive and well, if sleeping. *It figures. They fell on me. Tall people never look down before they faint. That explains why I couldn't see anything between the two of them and that cape on top of me. Wait. Brown hair? Dios, where's Wyn's illusion?*

On the other side of her friends, a mass of midnight fur sprawled. An enormous, snarly snore ripped from Garm's wolfish mouth, and his tongue hung out the side of his mouth. His hind legs shivered in his sleep. Dried blood and a line of white fur clumped the otherwise flawless black in lumpy swirls and lines, centered around his heart.

Apparently, enough time has passed for his healing power to mend his injuries, or Wyn's magic did the job. Too bad I'm still sore, though it's not as bad as it was.

Realization hit. *He can't be allowed to see Wyn's true form. I need to teleport us all somewhere I can get back to. Once I drop Wyn off home, I can wrangle Garm to a police station when he wakes.*

Pacing, Zita tried to figure out the best place to go. She set a hand on each of her friends and stretched out a bare foot to touch the wolf. *For such a pendejo, he has really soft, fluffy fur.*

She teleported to the abandoned air strip she and her friends used regularly to meet in their disguises.

Or tried to, anyway. Nothing happened.

Carajo. She tried teleporting a few inches to the left.

That worked.

Right. No teleporting home. It must be a magic thing. Still, Garm can't see Wyn's real face. Zita dashed to her friends. With a cautious glance at the sleeping wolf, she shifted to a gorilla. After grabbing Wyn, she carried her behind one of the bigger trees, an oak, and then repeated the process with Andy. She leaned them together against the stout trunk, and then noticed their clothing.

Wyn wore a long, draped affair that extended to her wrists and ankles. A belt gleamed under her chest. Elaborate pentacle pins held the fabric in place at her shoulders and arms, and a dainty leather bag tangled about one wrist. The cloth was a fine lavender linen, and the hem held a repeating pattern of tiny pentacles and eyes, embroidered in glinting silver and white thread. Whatever shoes she wore underneath sparkled from beneath her skirt. A few ringlets framed her face, having escaped the complicated hairstyle visible under a metallic hairnet embedded with tiny moons and gemstones.

In comparison, Andy's darker purple dress—or toga, Zita guessed—left his arms bare and stopped at his knees. Leather boots with the slight imperfection of handmade stitching ran from the soles of his feet to the bottom of his outfit. His hair was bound in a high bun and tied in place with a white woolen string. A Native American thunderbird in one of two alternating styles, followed by a swirling symbol and then a rain cloud, decorated the hems. Pins holding his outfit at the shoulders copied the same motif, as did the larger one keeping the thick, plum-colored cloak in place. The only unchanged item was the mask hiding the upper half of his face.

It's possible she was wearing the dress under the illusion, but I know he wasn't. Weird. Magic is a fashion critic, now? Interesting how the thunderbirds match the ones on that blanket Andy's mom made him for Christmas. I need to focus on hiding Wyn's identity, though, before Garm wakes or Zeus' thugs find us. They could be around here anywhere. Zita surveyed the meadow, but saw no one else. The only sounds were the distant calls of birds and the rustle of the trees.

With a shrug, she removed Andy's cape and tore off the bottom half of it. *That should leave him enough to cover his butt... maybe. It's not like I have a lot of options.*

After ripping the remnant into strips as a gorilla, she switched to her Arca form for the dexterity granted by human fingers. She went to Wyn and began wrapping. The need to hide her friend's hair meant that the final result was a lopsided turban-mask, and Zita spent far more time than she intended stuffing errant curls under the cloth. *Wyn's all about the fashion, so I should make it fancy.* She changed the last knot to a bedraggled bow.

Close enough. Zita stepped back to admire her handiwork and wiped her hands on her skirt. Fabric hid all but her friend's eyes, nose, and mouth.

Wait. Skirt?

Blinking, she looked down and verified that her usual sportswear had also been replaced. Her toga was a violet one that left her arms bare and featured a hem with numerous animals cavorting and leaping, matching the shapes on the pins at her shoulders. Her waist had a belt of rolled fabric in the same shade. After a second, she realized it wasn't a belt. It was the skirt of her toga rolled up to allow the bottom of the garment to stop a few inches short of her knees. Since anything as long as Wyn's would hamper kicking or movement, she left it as it was. An ugly brown blotch covered her sore shoulder, and dirt and dust smudges decorated the entire garment. An actual leather strap wrapped under and around her breasts like a harness and her feet remained bare. Now that she thought about it, she felt layers of cloth binding her generous chest almost painfully tight beneath the outer garment. *Well, at least I'll have support when I move, though I hope magic underwear doesn't come with drawbacks. This is way too weird for me.*

She slid the toga off her shoulder to assess her injury. Although jagged and swollen, the wound had stopped bleeding and seemed relatively clean. Her gesture cautious, she moved her arm in a circle to assess the puncture's depth. It twinged, but she could make the motion. Impatiently, she pulled the toga back into place. "That'll do until I can get it healed."

Tapping her foot, she stared at her friends as she attacked the next problem: waking them. She idly gathered up the last, leftover strip of cloth and toyed with it. "Come on, guys, time to get up."

If they won't get up, we'll need water and shelter. This spot is pretty, but I've got no supplies or weapons except our clothing, the pins on it, and my ability to shapeshift, not that I can go far with them— her, anyway—so vulnerable. If she were conscious, we could raid her bottomless purse for all the food, blankets, and other things I've stored in there.

Rapid hoofbeats—oddly off balance, like a running animal— approached. Zita positioned herself in front of her friends, hands spread and weight balanced. She let the strip of cloth drop. *Hopefully it's something harmless, like a deer—or a donkey?*

Carrying a fat man and two big ceramic jugs on her back, a jenny burst through the trees, heading toward the grassy meadow with a determined lope. From the beast, Zita's presence rated no more than an ear flick. The man on her back, however, shrieked, and threw an ornate cup high in the air when he saw her. He cried out as he reached for his cup. "No! My goblet!"

His words were Greek and yet not; she guessed it to be an archaic form with an odd intonation. A stitch of pain rippled through her head, though not as much as when her abilities granted her another language. She darted forward, bounced off a nearby oak to gain a little height, and caught the flying vessel. Landing on her feet, she straightened with the cup, the nagging pain of her shoulder abating as she stopped moving.

Coming to a sudden stop, the donkey began to graze, apparently unimpressed.

The man threw aside the cloth that had been draped over his waist and wrapped under him, revealing that he wore nothing underneath. He slid unsteadily from the donkey's back to land in a heap on the ground. While he was bald on top, his remaining white hair was long, falling down his back to mingle with copious back hair like a mane. Green oak leaves stood out in a crown upon his head. Ears similar to a horse's wobbled as he struggled to stand. His overlarge eyes stared at her from a long, chubby face that had a snub nose reminiscent of a pug, abundant laugh lines, and a beard that would've required a chain saw to bring it under control.

No real muscle tone and smells like he's been rolling in sour wine. How did a nudist wino with strange ears get into the middle of the woods? We must be nearer to a town than I thought. She offered him his cup with a sheepish smile and spoke in Greek as well. "Sorry to startle you. Here you go."

After tottering to his feet again, the strange man accepted the cup back and cuddled it. His face held a strange mix of emotion that she couldn't quite read. "Thank you. I am indebted to you. I would greatly mourn the loss when we still have hours to journey before us, provided this ungrateful beast will carry me onward."

As she automatically translated the words to a more modern version, Zita grinned. "You owe me nothing. Food and drink are serious business."

After a pause, a smile escaped the snarled mess of a beard, and laughter boomed out. "So it is, so it is! It is delightful to find wisdom in one so young. I am Silenus of the silenoi, late again from a meeting. Not to worry, however. Like any democracy, real work will not be done until sudden exigency demands it or everyone grows weary of arguing." The man executed a sloppy bow that almost landed him on the ground again and revealed a long horse's tail growing out of his backside.

"They call me Arca," Zita said, trying not to stare. "Where are we?"

He glanced around. "I did doze while riding, for I've been long in conference with the most boring assembly of... never mind you that. It is likely Mount Belus, but it could be Olympos. The sun is not so high that the lazy beast would have gotten much farther, not with me upon her back!" Silenus laughed again.

Zita grinned, unable to help herself. "Is there a town near here? Do you need help getting there?"

"Why, you are a sweet little thing, aren't you, to have such concern for your elders?" Silenus commented, despite the fact that he stood only an inch or two taller than her.

She twitched and prayed he wouldn't pat her on the head. "Uh, whatever?"

"Nay, I should leave you to your journey, goddess. Once your friends arise, you will wish to go. They perhaps partook too much of the sweet fruit of the grape for their constitutions?" His tone was approving, and the old drunk winked at her. Alcoholic fumes wafted from him.

Aloud, Zita said in Greek, "Goddess? Not. What journey?"

Silenus frowned. "To Olympos. The gods always go there. It would be best if your claim settled quickly before those that would oppose you can woo the undecided."

"Is there a trail?" Zita waited with only minimal fidgeting for answers. *Hopefully, Wyn will wake soon, fix whatever the magic broke, and I can teleport us all home without needing to go anywhere. If not, my friends need shelter if they're going to remain comatose.*

His eyelids lowered, and he considered her. "No. Those who need to be there find their way or they must seek a guide."

It's never simple. Pues, at least I can make sure the old dude gets somewhere safe to sleep it off. He's tall enough that he could help me move my friends without dragging them on the ground. On second thought, with that muscle tone he won't be lifting anyone. Still, maybe I can make him feel useful. Zita summoned a halfhearted smile. "How about you?"

"No, I am simply a foolish old drunk who is returning home to ensure my son is not led into too much wisdom. Bright boy. Takes after his mother, and thus he desperately needs my guidance to keep from prudence. Also, my satyrs will have dinner roasting, and

I should hate to miss a meal." Belching thoughtfully, he scratched his stomach and stared at her.

Not about to ask. Zita sighed. "Well, then, thanks."

Staggering over to the donkey, Silenus set his cup on the blanket. After he pulled a jug from her back, he uncorked it and drank until liquid overflowed from it and stained his beard. He wiped his arm across his mouth. The wind stank of wine even from where she stood. "Verily, I am ready, though perhaps not drunk enough. Am I ever drunk enough to forecast to the gods again? This once shall I do so, as to repay my debt and your kindness in saving my cup."

Zita blinked. "What?"

He lifted his face windward and jammed the cork back into the jug. "Your foretelling must be now, for when the fang burns, your fate will be as the old gods always were, changeable as the wind or your garments."

Uneasy, Zita lifted her hands. "No, we cool, man. I don't need nothing. You don't need to do whatever you're doing."

His eyes distant, Silenus intoned, "You walk a path of trouble and stone. Others seek to shape you to their will, and you resist. Bound or free, it shall be as you will. Fight against the many-headed creature without change, and you will win only a lifetime of cold unfeeling rock."

She gaped at him. "What?"

After a prolonged belch, Silenus tilted his head, horse ears twitching. "And now I am done. My debt is expunged. Good day to you—and to you!" He lifted his jug to her and toward the oak sheltering her unconscious friends, then packed it back onto his mount.

Something rustled nearby, and her skin prickled for reasons that had nothing to do with the balmy wind.

The donkey brayed, and whirled around as her ears flattened to her skull. Her tail flapped, and she turned to stare at something beyond Zita.

Following her instincts, Zita somersaulted away, landing in a balanced guard position between the old guy and whatever it was.

A heavy, black shape pounced on the ground where she'd been. Garm whirled to face her, growling. Evil red eyes glared at her as his ruff spiked around his head and back.

I'm not sure why, given my track record, but I'll take a stab at being diplomatic. I hope he didn't see Wyn before I finished her mask. Her feet began a slow, cautious ginga, the basic dance of capoeira, even as words escaped her in accented English. "Wake up on the wrong side of the… uh, forest floor? Good to see you feeling better. I'm, um, sorry your girlfriend stabbed you."

If anything, her attempt to communicate seemed to enrage him further. He lunged again. "Die!"

Silenus picked up his cup, swirled the liquid in it, and drank.

Zita let Garm build momentum, and then stepped to the side, seizing him and redirecting his charge into a sapling. Her shoulder complained, but she ignored it. *And Wyn said having Andy come at me on all fours during sparring was silly.*

An unfamiliar female voice shrieked. "Be gentle with the tree!"

She spared a glance around, but the only other woman was the unconscious Wyn. She returned her attention to the bigger shapeshifter.

The donkey trumpeted and snapped at the wolf.

Silenus winced and chugged his drink. "I'll just be gone, then. Before my sweet jenny forgets she is no warrior." He staggered to the jenny and collapsed over her back, squirming into an almost upright position. Lifting his mug, he slapped her neck and shouted, "Homeward!"

Garm barely spared the naked alcoholic or his mount a glance, and simply howled. In the outpouring of sound, Zita made out a single sentence. "Why couldn't you let me die?"

"Because it was the right thing to do. You're welcome. Besides, are you going to let Tiffany win by giving up like that?"

He snorted and padded a few feet forward. His voice wavered. "Spoken like someone who has never truly loved. It is not about winning or losing. I am better for having had her as my queen, though it was never meant to be. Your emotions must be as shallow and weak as the rest of you."

"Wow, talk about judgy. You don't know me or how I roll. Did you get tired of talking smack just because I'm not a self-healing giant werewolf?" Zita put her hands on her hips.

He snarled. "You had no right to drag me here. Why did you?"

"It wasn't me. Your ex's spell exploded or something. I woke only a little before you." *Gracias a Dios that I got up first, or he likely would've killed me and Wyn. I don't think he could do much to Andy.* She suppressed a laugh at the mental image of Garm gnawing uselessly on Andy's leg and her friend trying to shake him off.

The donkey jolted into motion, after sidling under her burden and letting loose a long, loud string of complaints.

The massive wolf snorted, shook himself, and eyed the animal sidelong. "Meat should avoid calling attention to itself."

With a last snort and a threatening stomp with her front hooves, the donkey plodded off into the trees. Congested snores rose from her back.

"Leave them alone." Zita snatched a pine cone from the ground and winged it at the other shapeshifter.

Garm's malevolent gaze returned to Zita and her sleeping friends. As his lips lifted in a canine sneer, his ears went flat. His words echoed her earlier thoughts. "So concerned about meat and an ancient drunkard? You should be grateful that you woke first. I would've murdered you and at least the lesser witch if I'd been first. Would you kill me for that or try to?"

"No, but I won't let you hurt anyone," Zita said, narrowing her eyes and stepping between him and her friends. The discarded scrap of cloth caught her eye. She returned to gorilla form and snatched it up, twisting it between her hands. *I'm injured already, and he heals. If I put his bite out of action for a bit, that buys me time to figure out how to take him down, plus Silenus can get farther away. Poor old guy might be too drunk to feel anything, but he wouldn't stand a chance if Garm goes after him.*

Garm shifted position to keep his gaze on the slumbering Wyn, and his hindquarters wiggled. He leapt toward her.

Twisting the cloth in her hands, Zita rolled in front of him, snapping the cloth taut between them just in time.

His mouth closed on the twisted material.

She quickly circled his jaws with it, pulling it tight with her gorilla strength.

He whimpered and slashed at her with a paw.

Zita jumped out of the way of his attack, rapidly crossing the cloth over and under his mouth. Her fingers were clumsy, but she knotted his muzzle shut. Once she was done, she released him and backed away.

He backpedaled, clawing at the makeshift gag. Rage filled his eyes, and he shook his head as if that would free him. A long string of undecipherable complaints came from him as he worked on gnawing through the impromptu restraint.

Andy yawned and rolled over, falling facedown into the detritus of the forest floor. "Turn down the TV, girls."

After returning to her Arca shape, Zita danced in place. "Órale, stand down, Garm. We don't need to fight when our time might be better spent figuring out how to get home. Just standing here beating the crap out of you is a waste of time."

While the fabric muzzle rendered his vocalizations unintelligible, the hate radiating from Garm's tense form implied he'd enjoy hurting her.

Get in line, hombre. You're not interested in my friends now, are you? As she backed up, Zita glanced at her sleeping companions and moved away from them, stopping under an old, knotted pine.

Garm stalked her, finally managing to paw enough of the gag off that he could snap the remaining cloth. He snarled, crouching low, and lunged at her again.

Zita jumped and grabbed a low-hanging tree branch, pulling herself up and flipping onto it. Nimbly, she climbed higher. "Hombre, seriously." *Don't make me shift to a dinosaur and maim you.*

The wolf whirled and clawed at the tree. "Get down here!"

A woman moaned nearby.

"Oh, come on, can't I get just five more minutes?" Andy groused, spitting out dirt. He opened his eyes and stared around with a puzzled expression. "What the?"

At the base of the pine, Garm snarled at Zita. "Fortune saves you. Your friend awakened before I killed you."

She snorted and made a rude gesture at the canine. "Lucky nothing. I beat you last time we fought, and I could do it again."

Andy frowned at her, his eyelids drooping. "Where are we? W—Muse? What's wrong with Muse? Why are we wearing bedsheets? It's comfortable, but not really my style. Aw, man. Garm again? Give it a rest, man." He interposed himself between the wolf shapeshifter and Wyn.

Before Zita could answer, a young woman peeked out from behind an oak tree. Absently, Zita noted she had the streamlined, lightly muscled form of a casual runner and a sour expression that seemed carved into her face. Clumps of green curls cascaded around her slim, entirely nude body. She murmured, but whatever she said was lost in the distance between them.

When the green-haired woman spoke again, the words were loud enough to be understandable, if old-fashioned. "I prithee, instruct your handmaiden and dog to cease damaging the trees!"

Garm groaned. "Just what I needed. More humans."

Andy blinked and then whipped his gaze away from the girl. The tips of his ears burned red. "Pardon? What did she say? Is she cold? Here, give her this!" He whipped off his cape and held it out toward the stranger, giving it a little shake when no one moved to take it.

The stranger seemed to catch on that the men didn't understand her. "What did they say?"

Zita grumbled internally. Without leaving her branch, she provided a quick interpretation of all that had been said.

"I am no human! No mortals walk these lands, only animals, immortals, and you gods, unless someone keeps forbidden secrets. My sisters would not do that. What one of us knows, all of us do in short order. And no, I need no so-called favors from any male. He may put away his garment," the green-haired woman said, emerging a little more from behind the tree. She tossed her hair over her shoulder.

Zita frowned and replied in Greek. "We are so not gods."

Andy and Garm looked at Zita.

"What'd she say?" Andy asked.

No need to feed Garm's ego. Zita ran a hand over her hair, back and forth, and said, "She announced she's not human and there aren't any humans except for us here. Also, she doesn't want Wingspan's cape."

Garm snorted. "Good. I am done with humanity." For all his words, he was no longer tensed to fight.

She couldn't let that pass without pointing out the obvious. "You're still human, just a meta who really likes wearing a fur coat."

That brought his hackles back up for a moment before they smoothed out again. "Not anymore. Now I am just wolf. I had only one reason to ever wear two legs, and that is gone."

Zita let herself drop lightly to the ground and strolled over to stand next to Andy, forcing her muscles to untense as much as possible. If that put an additional body between Garm and Wyn, it was for the best. "Drama, much? You know, instead of swearing off humanity because of Tiffany—"

"You're not worthy to speak her name!" Garm bared his teeth.

Andy coughed, keeping his eyes fixed on the wolf shifter and averted from the nude woman. "Can you ask the girl where we are? And if she's not human, what is she?"

Even though she'd wanted to be nicer, a few opinions slipped out. "Can't you just get wasted and pee on a few public buildings? Then you can sober up, pay the fines, and get over Tiffers like a normal guy? After that, you could devote yourself to good deeds to atone for your past. You've been a very bad dog, you know. If I had a newspaper..."

His hand over his forehead, Andy muttered, "Stop helping, Arca. I don't think he's ready for your tough love approach."

Garm ignored both Andy and the strange woman, his focus on Zita. "Be warned, little shapeshifter, I will not lie down to die for anyone. Not anymore."

While people weren't her thing, Zita could practically smell the lie. Pity curled in her heart. "And I'm not real interested in proving you wrong. Chill."

A growl rumbled out of his chest. "You're just afraid that I'll kill you."

Andy tensed, his body shifting subtly into a defensive position.

"You could try, hairball. How's that worked out for you so far? Dude, relax." Zita loosened her shoulders, ignoring the stab of pain from her injury.

Garm snarled, fur lifting on his back again.

The green-haired stranger squeaked, dropped her pose, and hid behind the tree.

Andy shouted, "Guys! Can we concentrate on where we are? I'm not... I should just know, but I don't." He rubbed his hands on his thighs, his forehead furrowed.

"We're on Mount Belus, wherever that is. I was told we should go to Olympos, so I was going to take us that way," Zita said. *As soon as I figure out where that is.*

Her comment was almost drowned out by Garm increasing the volume of his growl.

"Enough!" Wyn moaned. She squinched one eye open and glared at them, then threw out a hand.

A shimmering bubble appeared around Garm.

Wyn's hand dropped limply back down, and she massaged her forehead as she dragged herself into a sitting position. "I feel as if the foul allure of tequila ensnared me again and you three are my punishment. Fight more quietly."

"Gracias a Dios, you're awake!" Zita bounded over and hugged her friend.

Wyn squeezed her back. She released Zita, eyes widening as she noticed their surroundings. "The enthusiasm is appreciated, but could we bring it down a notch?"

"Let me out!" Garm roared.

"Then hush your mouth and let me have a moment. Would you agree to not attack us?" Wyn said. Despite her words, she made a curt gesture, and the glimmering bubble disappeared.

"I do as I wish." Garm prowled to the edge of the trees, moving away from all the humanoids.

Andy and Wyn both relaxed when he stepped away.

Wyn's head tilted when she saw the green-haired woman peeking out from behind the tree. "Now, who is this? Are you well, miss? Do you have injuries that require tending?"

Zita shrugged and threw the wolf to the witch. Figuratively. "I don't know. We were going to talk to the girl, but Garm kept distracting me."

"Me?" Garm's fur rose in spikey tufts along his back, but he came no closer.

The green-haired chick only speaks weird-ass Greek, Zita sent. Knowing her friend would pick up the right language once she used it, she interpreted Wyn's questions for the nude woman.

Emerging from behind the tree, the strange woman tossed her hair. "Ah, I needed to wait for the higher-ranking goddess to awaken, then? Greetings, my lady."

Muse inclined her head and replied in Greek. "The pleasure is all mine. We don't do rank, really, and goddess is a bit much, don't you think?"

"It shall be as you ordain, lady," the green-haired woman replied.

"Apparently even nudist colonies have suck-ups," Zita muttered in English. *It's got to be the only explanation for all these people wandering around in the woods without any clothes. How do they expect to survive without pockets? How do they carry their snacks?*

Although her expression was serene, the thickening of her natural Southern accent and her tense posture revealed her nerves as Wyn switched back to English. "Arca, Wingspan, where are we? What's with our new friend here? And where are Tiffany, Zeus, and the others?"

The stranger had the steady blank expression of non-comprehension until Wyn's last question. She inhaled sharply and dropped into a very low curtsy. Her eyes darted from side to side. "Zeus Hypatus? Did you meet him? Are you one of his company?"

Garm snarled. "They're likely in Hell."

Twitching, her body language screaming fear, the green-haired woman stared at them. "What did he say?"

Zita replied in Greek. "Don't know Zeus' last name. He's a creep that we were fighting before we wound up unconscious in the woods. I'm sorry for ignoring you, but the wolf is a jerk. It's not you, it's him."

"As if I could believe anything said by a trickster. You could not convince me your friend is aught but a goddess even before she used her power. One has only to regard her, even when you've hidden her perfection in needless bandages." She gestured to Wyn.

Wyn took a handful of her dress and studied the trim on the fabric. She touched her face, and then her long, elegant fingers explored the fabric on her head, lingering on the bow. When she finished her quick exploration, she offered the stranger another nod. In Greek, she said, "Thank you for the lovely compliment. Who are you?"

Tossing her hair over her shoulder again, the green-haired woman replied, "Of course, my lady. I merely said what was obvious to all. I am a dryad of the oaks."

"I am known as Muse. These are my friends Arca and Wingspan. The wolf is Garm. Don't trust him. What is your name?"

The nymph jerked backward as if stung. Her whole body tensed and poised to flee. "I am no mother nor a god's lover and do not seek to be. Why would I need a name?"

Warmth flooded Zita's mind as the mental link with Wyn and Andy slid into place.

Apparently, the poor thing has been so crushed under the patriarchy that she doesn't feel she has an identity without a man. Despite the dry tone of her mental words, Wyn's gaze softened. She held out her hand to the dryad. "You need not fear oppression with us. We will protect you if we can."

The nymph pursed her lips.

Zita shrugged. "Muse was only asking because names make is easier to talk to someone." *If she doesn't give us a name, let's just call her Greenie.*

"Exactly," Greenie replied.

After exchanging a puzzled glance with Zita and summarizing for the men, Wyn asked, "What is this place?"

"A random naked drunk told me this was probably Mount Belus or Olympos before he rode off on his donkey. He was pretty wasted though, so his directions might be a bit sketchy." Zita volunteered what little information she had.

Wyn pinched the skin between her eyebrows. "Somehow, that seems normal given how today has gone. What happened to our clothing?" She gestured to her dress, frowning at a smear of dirt and rubbing at it with a finger.

"Fashion magic? You'd know better than me." Zita switched to party line. *For some reason, I can't teleport home. I tried earlier. Now you're both awake, Andy can fly us back and Wyn can fix my power so it works again.*

I don't think I can, Andy sent. *I'm not certain where back is.*

Zita blinked at him. *You're never lost. Even when we blindfolded and teleported you somewhere that one time, you knew where we were.*

You're right. Up until now, that is. I don't know where we are, though now that I think about it, I had the same problem when we visited the place with the dinosaurs.

"Any mud is from when your trickster threw you upon the ground. The local greenery is blameless in the stains." Greenie gestured at Zita.

Wyn raised an eyebrow at Zita. "You dumped me in the dirt?" *Do I want to know why my head is wrapped like a purple mummy?*

Your illusion was missing, so I covered your head to keep your identity secret. Garm woke up not long after, so it's a good thing I got that done. Zita lifted her hands in the air and exclaimed in English. "In all fairness, you and Wingspan were on top of me when I awakened. We're all wearing dresses too. Except Garm. And he might have one on under his fur if he ever takes human form again."

"For the record, I prefer to think of mine as a toga rather than a dress," Andy said.

"Technically, they're chitons, I believe, possibly with a peplum over it. Togas will do for now, though, I suppose," Wyn mused.

"I won't walk as a man again." Garm's lips curled back over his teeth. "Do not think me one. Now my queen is gone, there is only the wolf. As I am free, I will rampage across this world bringing death and Ragnarök."

"Pues, you want to let up on the drama, Garm? That was a hypothetical, not a question," Zita said, though her tone was softer than usual given the anguish in his voice. She tried to quash sympathy for him.

Apropos of nothing, Wyn noted, "This appears to be the wrong mythos for it, but Garm howling and breaking loose of his chains could be considered a sign of Ragnarök, the Norse apocalypse."

His attention on her, the wolf grew angrier and snapped at Zita. "I'm surprised your vocabulary extends to polysyllabic words. Did you eat a few books?"

Zita rolled her eyes, losing sympathy for him. "At least I'm a better judge of people."

Pain crossed the wolf shifter's face.

She amended, "And I'm more fun. You won't catch me hanging with Zeus or sniffing butt all day."

Garm snarled, but anger pushed out the sorrow in his expression, making him easier to watch.

Wyn fingered the symbols on the hem of her outfit thoughtfully as she considered them. She frowned at Zita. "Is that blood on your clothing? Come here and let me heal you." *Where did you find purple bandages? Your efforts are appreciated. It's very... well, it matches.*

Obedient, Zita strode over to her friend and submitted to the spell. She couldn't help a pleased moan as the soreness dissipated. *Andy's cape.*

He scowled. *Wait, what? Why did you have to pick on my cape?*

Her hands glowed with the gentle green healing magic, and Wyn smiled serenely.

Still poised as if to run at any second, the nymph said, "Is there aught else you need, my lady?"

Zita shrugged at Andy. *You had the most fabric to spare, and I was in a hurry. I did leave you enough to cover your butt in case a rogue videographer popped out of the bushes and started filming us. We still don't know where Zeus and his thugs are. He's vain enough to have brought one.*

Not funny, Z. Andy examined what was left of his cape.

As she finished the spell, Wyn pursed her lips. *I'll check for Zeus and his companions. Keep the dryad here.* She closed her eyes and party line evaporated.

Zita cast around for a conversation topic. "Don't suppose you want to show us how to get to Olympus? It seemed important to that Silenus guy that we go there."

If possible, the nymph's expression grew more disdainful. "Of course not. Do I seem as a guide? How can you be so unlearned? What animal suckled you? It is clear you were not blessed with a higher nursemaid."

"Hey now, no reason to be insulting. My mother is a saint!" Zita scowled.

From where he skulked, Garm lifted his head and taunted her. "Does the new girl recognize your inferiority, little one? Do interpret that last interchange."

Greenie said, "You and your friends should all flee to the north as soon as you can, and cross over into the barbarian lands. Olympos is not for you, especially not your gentle lady."

Zita kept her reply short. "She wants us to skip Olympus and go north to the so-called barbarian lands."

The warmth of party line reappeared as Wyn opened her eyes. *I don't sense anyone familiar except Garm. If I scan for nonhuman life and eliminate animals, I can find a few small clusters of sentients, including a group heading down the mountains. There are very few human-like minds at all in the area compared to home. It's... a refreshing change. Restful.* Aloud, she said only, "We are not in our world. This is... someplace else."

"If she can't guide us, we would love to have any aid she can give us with directions," Andy said, glancing at Zita. *I don't know what you're saying, but you should probably stop antagonizing the only local around to help us.*

With a sigh, she interpreted for the nymph.

Greenie would have none of it. She backed away, resting her hand against the oak at edge of the meadow. "Oh, not me. I'm merely a harmless dryad among many. I do not show the way nor challenge the natural order."

One hand lifted as if to forestall Greenie's departure, Wyn asked, "We understand. Is there a path to follow?"

"No, those who are meant to find it, do. Those who are not, die. It would safer for you to forget the words of the old drunkard and leave this land. Do not continue upward. Find the north where your kind may be safer. No more aid will I give you." Between one blink of an eye and the next, the nymph melted into the tree and was gone.

This time, Wyn interpreted for the men.

Garm sauntered a few steps away, the hackles on his back still raised. "I'm done listening to you all babble about petty human concerns. If she says you must go up or north, I am going down and south. Do not follow. I have no interest in returning to our old world, not if the dryad told the truth of this one being nearly free of the scourge of humanity." He sprinted away. True to his statements, his path led away from theirs.

Andy rubbed the back of his neck. "Well, that could've gone better."

"We could say that about so many things," Wyn murmured. "Should we go after him?"

Zita pursed her lips. "No. Not yet. Let's figure out a way home and collect him when we leave. Even if he's an asshole, the furball deserves some privacy to sob into his kibble before we drag him back home and to jail. Tiffany did a real number on the poor guy. Talk about heartless!"

Andy blinked at her. "Were you trying to make a joke? That's pretty dark humor for you."

She frowned at him. "What?"

"Because she stabbed him in the... never mind. Now what do we do?"

Chapter Five

No one had an answer to his question.

Zita strode from the shade of the many trees surrounding the alpine meadow into the sunlight. Her upturned face soaked in the sun's warmth, and she heard nothing but her companions and wildlife in the distance. The breeze carried the familiar scents of her friends and their surroundings, and nothing more. "So, the green-haired chick was no help at all. Now that you're awake, I don't think we got to go to Olympus anymore. How do we get home?"

"That will be a trick. Based on the magic here and the dryad, this isn't our world." Wyn drifted closer to Zita, Andy following behind.

That required a few seconds to sink in. Zita dug her toes into the dirt, still scanning the area for the wolf shapeshifter or any other enemies. "Is this like the dinosaur place? Once we find the door, we can go home provided we don't take any magic rocks with us?"

Wyn sighed and plucked a flower, her gaze thoughtful. "I don't think so. If it is, we are far enough from the boundaries of it that I cannot see any spell weavings or track the magic to a single source, as I did there. This place is both more and less solid, just as magic but built of many different types of power. My guess would be this is a spirit realm rather than a spell supporting a prehistoric area.

Based on the nymph, it's one oriented to Greco-Roman mythology."

With a tilt of his head, Andy said, "So, the reason I'm unsure where I am as Wingspan is because my internal compass is set to Nihalgai, not this world? That would explain a few things. Home, I always know where I am, at least in relation to the Southwest and Pacific."

Wyn's eyes went distant for a moment. "Yes, that would make sense."

"Ni-what?" Zita asked. One leg jittered with energy she tried to repress.

Andy waved his hand. "Nihalgai is what the Diné call our world."

Running a hand back and forth over her long hair, Zita said, "Okay. Navajo myth then. What does that mean in practical terms? Preferably ones I can do something about."

"It means that the most likely route home is to comply with the local mythic cycle, perhaps by finding a traditional mentor figure. Those are usually aged wisewomen or wisemen, or a mythological creature," Wyn said. She eyed Zita and shredded her flower.

Andy pursed his lips. "If it's like the ones in myth, we'd either need a guide to lead us on a quest to the exit, or we'd have to prove our worth to a council of wise elder spirits. If it's more like in gaming, it'll be an old guy with a map in a tavern."

Wyn nodded. "Indeed. Courtesy and consideration toward the mentor would be paramount."

"So, we need an old drunk know-it-all who hates people? Easy. Where's the closest Metro?" Zita grinned.

Wyn and Andy exchanged worried looks.

Zita gestured in the direction that Silenus had gone. "More seriously, the geezer on his donkey told me we should go to Olympos before you got up, but he took off. Well, his donkey did. He was passed out on it though, so that probably counts. We could chase him down, I guess, but we'd need to sober him up to get any help. His name was Siren... no, Silent... Silenus, that's it! I asked if he'd be a guide, but he said no."

Wyn pressed her hands against her temples. "If that was who I suspect, I'm not certain it would be possible for him to be anything but inebriated. He would've worked as a guide, however. Olympos—I'm guessing that would be Olympus—seems the most likely course."

Andy spoke, his phrasing slow and careful. "If it's at all like the stories my mother told me, we can't risk a wrong word or deed that goes against the precepts of the world, Arca."

"Greco-Roman myth is full of quests given both as punishment or to prove worthiness," Wyn added.

"Whatever," Zita said. "So, we have to do a mission to find the way home? How do we figure out what we need to do?"

"Traditionally, a god would send a messenger, a counselor would advise us of it, or we'd understand the mystic symbols hinting at the right path." Wyn pinched the skin at the bridge of her nose.

Andy smiled a little. "We're going to need a guide."

Zita nodded. "So how do we find one of those then since Silenus and Greenie both took off?"

"We should proceed in the most likely direction to find someone else. We'll need to be courteous to all we meet, in case they're the one who can show us the way." Wyn narrowed her eyes at Zita.

Andy nodded, his dark eyes grave.

Zita crossed her arms over her chest. "Do I have food caught between my teeth? Fine, I get your passive-aggressive point. I'll try to be extra nice, though I'd like to say I tried that with Garm, and it didn't work out well. We're going to Olympus then, since it's the only place we've heard of?"

With a pat on her shoulder, Andy said, "Cheer up, Arca, you can be our secret weapon. Silent but deadly." He snickered.

She rolled her eyes. "¿Neta, fart jokes? What are you, ten? Since the dryad said we have to go higher, how about I fly and see if I can find the town? That should make you both happy since there's nobody to talk to up there. First though, why don't you pull one of my meals from your endless purse so we can refuel? I think I put some chicken barbacoa tacos in there last weekend before yoga. Those would be a good choice."

"How did eating slip in there?" Andy grinned. "All jokes aside, I am hungry."

Smiling, Wyn reached into her bag. When she pulled out her hand, she had a cloth-wrapped parcel. Her face fell.

"What's that?" Zita asked. "The tacos were in a butter container."

"I did retrieve the tacos. Up until I pulled it out of my purse, it felt like one of your containers, not this." Her brow furrowed, Wyn picked open the knot keeping the cloth closed, revealing a rough clay bowl. She tilted it toward Zita and Andy.

Tacos nestled in the bowl, though the tortillas had the uneven, irregular quality of homemade rather than the mass-produced ones she'd purchased. The cheese had changed from cheap grated parmesan to what appeared to be goat cheese. Everything else was the same: chicken, radishes, cilantro, and tomatoes.

Andy blinked. "What happened?"

The witch pursed her lips. "My supposition is that inanimate objects transform to fit within the mythic framework of the realm once they're here. That's likely what happened with our clothing as well. Anything I take out of my bag will change."

"So, we have no supplies?" Andy said, his frown deepening.

Wyn sighed. "We do, but no technology greater than that available in this time period to preserve it. Given that, we will need to be judicious in what we remove or we will have to replace a great many items."

"That sucks." After surveying the food for a moment, Zita plucked two of the tacos out of the bowl. "Well, these won't keep in that. We might as well eat them all."

After a moment, her friends ate as well.

When she'd finished her share of the food, Zita considered the panorama visible from the meadow. "Going to scout now." She shifted to an eagle and flew up to assess the area.

When she landed again, she returned to her Arca form. "I didn't see anything even remotely like a town, but it's a big mountain. Lots of peaks and gullies and stuff. It would've taken me much longer to check out everything. We should probably split up so we'll cover more ground. By split up, I mean you two travel together, and I'll take another direction."

In her absence, Andy had switched to floating a foot above the ground, one leg curled as if he were poised to run in midair. His eyes glowed bright white as he grunted. "Never split the party. Never works out, especially in games or horror movies."

Raising her eyebrows at him, Zita frowned. "What? It's a solid idea. We all want to get home soon. My way is faster." Since she didn't trust Garm not to double back, and the nymph had seemed shifty, she sent her reasons over party line. *Jerome's off on a consulting gig, and I'm supposed to help with his koi—they got to be monitored more in real hot weather and the fish lady who regularly does it only comes once a week. I told Quentin I'd go do some crafty stuff tonight to be a supportive sister and cheer on his recovery process. Plus Mamá is coming to visit. Miguel wants to meet for coffee or something so he can tell me what to say, and I can ignore him. I got to clean my place before then and prep some food. If I don't, she'll assume I'm starving and spend all her time cooking and telling me what I'm doing wrong. Not to mention, life won't be worth living if I ditch the big dinner where she meets Miguel's girl on Monday.*

He's serious about someone? Is it that vet, Linnea? Wyn asked.

Zita nodded and squashed down the urge to think about Freelance's admission earlier. She focused on her family instead. *Miguel's serious enough that he wants her to meet Mamá.*

That's wonderful! I wish them all the best. Give your mother my love. I've got work, and my aunt will require a renewal of the spell that holds her Alzheimer's in abeyance next weekend. Additionally, I'm supposed to touch base with my lawyer about some motion my parents filed and be in court next week. If I miss a hearing, my parents will use it as proof that I'm not dedicated to my aunt's care. My lawyer can bat it down, but it's extra cost and delay. Wyn wrung her hands.

Andy huffed, but made his own confession over the telepathic connection. *Yeah, Z, hug your mom for me too. I'm scheduled to work for Dad this week. Detroit and St. Louis both went with someone else for their open professorships. However, whoever took that position in southern Maryland already quit, so the job reopened. My phone interview went well, so I have an in-person interview Monday afternoon. And I have a—thing—scheduled with a friend.*

Good luck on the interview! Should I review your resume again? Wyn sent.

He shook his head. *They have that already. This is the in-person interview where I find out what the catch is. They were cagey about what exactly I'd be doing other than it would be an assistant professorship with the possibility of tenure and a housing allowance. It'd be great to be able to stay near Dad and you guys, relatively speaking, and it's at the same university as Farnswaggle! I'd actually get to meet him!*

Sounds good! ¡Buena suerte! They're nuts if they don't hire you. Zita nodded. "So, back to the plan for the search. If you guys need me, I'll get there as soon as I can. I'll cheat if I have to, and neither of you like to travel with me when I do that," she said, obliquely referencing her ability to teleport.

Wyn turned a delicate shade of green. "Yes, let's not travel like that again. In fact, I'd only slow Wingspan. Leave me here. I'll be fine in my bubble, as we know Garm can't cross it. Greco-Roman mythology is fairly well documented and I've studied aspects of it, so it'll take me some time to review my memories. I can accomplish that better on the solid ground, as opposed to when I'm dangling high over it."

After a moment, Zita nodded. "If that'd help you think, I guess so. Call on party line if you need us. Wingspan can zip here in a flash, and I'll get back pretty fast too."

Andy shook his head. "I'd like to register that I'm doing this under protest. As much as I'd like to get home faster, all of the mythology I'm familiar with says that something bad will happen if we split up."

"Are you referring to actual religious lore or to video game and movie conventions?" Wyn inquired, her tone dry. She raised an eyebrow.

The tips of Andy's ears burned pink, but he admitted the truth. "Bit of both."

Zita tucked a long strand of hair behind her ear. "Right, then, it's settled. You take the side to the west with the higher peaks. I'll take the east—it's got water near it, so I can skim the shoreline. A town should stick out pretty well in a deserted area like this. Let's get this done so we can be home in time for dinner. Or breakfast. Or maybe one of those afternoon teas Muse likes with the tiny, weird sandwiches and cakes."

"Go, before Arca disrespects the sacred ritual of teatime further." A smile softened Wyn's words as she settled onto a large rock in the center of the sunny clearing. She waved a hand, and a transparent bubble rose around her.

"Fine, but I still think it's a mistake." Andy rose higher. Once he reached the clouds, he switched to his giant avian form.

Thunder grumbled as he flapped his wings and rose higher, spiraling west toward the snowy peak.

Zita patted her flat stomach. "Now I want cake."

Wyn giggled. "When do you not?"

"True that." She shifted back to an eagle and took off.

***

Under other circumstances, Zita would've enjoyed the search.

The mountain was an intriguing mix of different areas, most of which seemed unspoiled and ripe for exploration. Different forest types decorated it in zones, beech giving way to pines, with more variety at lower elevations. Grassy plains turned into swamp by the numerous small rivers and babbling streams. Sheer cliffs begging to be climbed towered over picturesque, rock-strewn meadows splashed with color and drenched in floral scents by hundreds of alpine blooms. A warm breeze lifted her higher as she admired what would've been a challenging scramble up a slope covered with sharp, loose rock. A dizzying array of animals grazed or stalked each other unmolested by mankind. Her eagle instincts urged her to stoop and have one little beech marten for lunch, but she dragged her attention back to her search.

Although the hunting was doubtless wonderful, she had yet to see any signs of settlement, let alone a town or even a fancy house that would qualify as Olympus. She sighed. *At this point, I'd settle for tents. We need to get back. My brothers have a hard enough time thinking of me as a full-grown woman instead of as their baby sister, so if I miss meeting up with Miguel or Quentin's thing, they'll both assume I'm ditching them to go be irresponsible.* Zita flicked her wings, and felt her body prickle with wariness.

Obeying her instincts, she threw herself to the side abruptly.

A strange bird, with taloned feet stretched as far out as they would go, dove through the air where Zita had been.

Zita blinked. For a second, she'd thought she'd seen a snarling woman's face and heard a screeching Greek curse from the creature. She climbed higher to improve her maneuverability as she scanned the sky beneath her for the attacker.

Below, the round form of the creature pulled out of the dive and began flapping her way back upward. At the slower speed, she could make out a haggard old woman's face, neck, and chest with an impressive and gloriously silver mane of hair attached to the heavy body of a black-feathered bird. For some reason, vultures sprang to mind. Instinct warned her, and she checked above herself.

Two additional shapes lurked there, squawking with what sounded like laughter. While they shared the elongated oval face of the first one and the beaky nose that almost reached their chins, one had wiry spirals of steely curls, and the other had a cropped-close buzz cut of pure white.

Zita shifted to a pterosaur and flared her wings, hoping her increased size would warn off the oncoming bird-women. From her peripheral vision she tried to track the original one. *Guys, I'm being attacked by fat-ass birds with abuela heads and boobs? Seriously? This place is loca.*

The two above her—she dubbed them Curls and Buzz—rose higher and began a downward arc that would translate into a dual run at Zita. Their claws were large, the hooked and wicked weapons of a raptor, but crusted with an uneven layer of white and brown material that flaked off as the bird-ladies dove at her.

Alarm filled Wyn's mental voice. *Harpies! Don't let their claws touch you. They're famous for their filth.*

Oh, hell no, I'm not playing aerial chicken, especially when there's three of them. Zita snapped her long, toothy beak in their direction. She prepared mentally for her next move.

When they reached her, she shifted to a hummingbird and darted out of the way.

The pair of harpies tried to halt their descent but crashed into each other in a cloud of feathers and imprecations. They fell, locked together.

Claws nothing, you should hear their mouths! People say I have a potty mouth, but I'm a kindergarten teacher compared to these old hens.

Curls separated from the other harpy, with slow, labored flaps, but her companion continued to fall. Buzz let out a piteous cry, one wing bent wrong.

Zita prepared to dive to catch the falling harpy, but Curls rescued Buzz first. "Trickster! You will know our vengeance!" one cried out.

Andy's giant bird form hovered at the edge of the mountain. *You should have killed them.*

Uh, mano, seriously? Zita was so shocked by his comment that she almost missed seeing the bird-woman with the long hair streak toward her from below.

He made no movement to approach closer. *You can hunt.*

I'm not killing an old lady-bird-thing! Not going to let them hurt me, either. Zita shifted to an ankylosaurus and bellowed as she fell toward the approaching harpy.

Panic filled the long-haired harpy's face when she noticed the change, and she veered away, toward her slower-departing sisters. The wind brought the rank odor of spoiled meat and another chain of foul language as she assisted Curls with Buzz.

Zita stared after the departing bird-women, lazily shifting back to a golden eagle and pulling out of her descent.

Wyn's mental voice interrupted, stress and fear running through it. *Help! Apparently, I spoke too soon when I said I'd be fine alone.*

***

Wingspan flew faster, but Zita could cheat.

And did.

She changed the color of her feathers to a brilliant azure similar to the sky as camouflage, and then teleported to a spot well above Andy's massive form. His size made him easy to find, even in the distance.

As Andy shifted to his man form and descended to the clearing where they'd left Wyn, Zita dove. Once she reached the edge of the meadow, she shifted to a northern sparrow hawk and circled, debating her options as she stared below.

At the edge of the woods, Wyn was inside her bubble. The nymph from earlier, or her identical twin, stood beside her with a dull brown knife to Wyn's pale throat. After Zita drew closer, it became obvious that one of the dryad's fingers had changed from being a regular digit to the weapon, rather than it being a separate object.

How do I disarm someone when their blade is their finger? Zita's mind whirled, half-forged plans spinning as she surveyed the others standing nearby.

Andy was motionless, floating a few feet above the ground near Wyn's bubble.

A semicircle of half-men surrounded the bubble. Most had a well-muscled man's torso sprouting from the body of a horse where the neck should have been. Half held wicked spears on Wyn, while the others held their weapons on Andy. A weathered, wiry man with a tiny horns and truly hairy lower body got shakily to goat hooves. Alone among the others, he seemed to carry no weapons other than a pan pipe, a mug, and strong alcohol-tinged body odor. Only her friends wore clothing.

Given their physiology, would the half-horses have two hearts? Irritated with the momentary distraction, Zita focused on finding weaknesses and getting close enough to free her friend. *Somehow.*

"Not a pace closer," Greenie said, her eyes on Andy. "Or the goddess will be no more." She moved her hand slightly, and a tiny ruby beaded on Wyn's throat.

Andy frowned and stopped, raising both hands in the air. "I'm not certain what you said, but please don't kill her."

She said she'd kill Wyn if you keep moving toward her, mano. Zita shifted to a red squirrel, matching the one she saw peeking out from a nearby tree hollow.

I got the gist, thanks, he sent.

Wyn's mental voice was high and thin. Waves of fear and worry swamped her jumble of words. *If I attempt to perform magic, I will be killed. While I could take over her mind, it is a terrible violation. Additionally, I would prefer not to accidentally lobotomize anyone. Of course, if I am too gentle, she may slip my control and kill me. Or she could murder me if her hand slips.*

Breathe, amiga, we'll get you out. How did this happen? Do your yoga breathing and get that scary brain working. Zita slunk through the tall meadow grass toward her friend.

Wyn closed her eyes, and her chest and shoulders rose and fell visibly. Her mental tone was calmer, but still far too rapid and fearful. *She was screaming and being chased by the satyr, so I let her into the bubble. At worst, he should have bounced off and run away. It seems, however, that they were in collusion, as she seized me as soon as I was in reach. The centaurs appeared immediately after.*

The satyr is the guy who looks like the devil after a bender? By the way, what's with this place? Can't a person just be a person? Do they have to be half something else? Zita half-heartedly complained, hoping it would distract her friend from the panic attack that appeared to be building.

Said goat-man wrung his hands.

Yes. Andy and Wyn answered in chorus.

Scurrying behind a large clump of vegetation, Zita paused, calculating the best angle to attack. *It makes no sense. None of these people are real.*

Wyn chewed her lower lip. *They're real here. It's like the dinosaurs in Brazil. Anything that complies with the mythic framework could exist, and I'd be surprised if we don't see more as we travel, such as sirens or cyclops.*

As she darted beneath a tree root to get closer, Zita suggested creatures to continue soothing her friend. *Or a Quetzalcoatl or a chupacabra?*

Probably not that. We're far more likely to see a unicorn or a phoenix. I don't know the extent of this realm, but my hypothesis is it's limited to Greco-Roman creatures or Indo-European ones. Wyn's usual composure settled over her body, though she still seemed poised to flee at the earliest opportunity.

After Andy had frozen in place and no one else spoke, the nymph hissed. "That's better. Where's the trickster?"

Wyn opened her eyes and cleared her throat. "He doesn't speak your language, remember?"

With a rough shake of her captive, the dryad hissed. "Then interpret for us, fairest one."

She did.

"Harpies got her," Andy said.

Still in squirrel form, Zita crept closer, darting behind another tree.

Wyn obediently repeated his words.

The satyr winced. "A harsh death. Can we not come to an accommodation? Perhaps they leave us from any wranglings with the gods or better yet, return to their homes? They've already lost their friend and we have no treasure here for heroes to plunder."

"Lies," one horse-man said. "Had a god exploded, the whole area around them would reel from the eruption of power.

Remember all those who died with Pan? The swift-winged harpies are close enough we would have felt it or seen it."

Wyn frowned. "The harpies make people explode?"

Greenie sniggered, and a couple centaurs laughed.

"Does she jest, or is she that innocent? I am myself an expert raconteur but I cannot tell. Surely the wisest course would be to wait for the Council's ruling," the satyr said. He paused. "Or to have a drinking contest. That too would suffice. I can fetch us some wine!"

"The trickster could've just been a hero, not a god," a centaur argued, ignoring the goat-man's suggestion. "They die as any other mortal. They are too ignorant of the consequences of power and too quick to deny godhood. No deity does that; their encompassing greed will not be bound. Best this ends before the Council becomes involved."

Greenie offered a cold reasoning, her finger still tight against Wyn's throat. "If we kill them all, when the greater powers return, we need not pay painful fealty to appease wounded pride. Zeus Hypatus brooked no powers save his own, or those he could control, and they have claimed him as an enemy already. Give your friend our words and see what he says."

Wyn spat out a quick interpretation.

With a final glance at the arguing centaurs, who were starting to yell at each other with loud enthusiasm that seemed split between entertainment and concern, the satyr slipped away.

Smart goat-dude, Zita thought. *Can you do an illusion to distract her?*

Wyn's eyes were very wide, but her mental voice was firm, rather than hysterical. *No, not while I maintain the bubble. And if I let it drop, the centaurs can reach me, and several have something smeared on their spear tips. However, I might be able to nudge her into believing any distraction either of you pull off. Do you think they'd enjoy our "Where's the Shapeshifter?" game?*

"Fine. You're right. I lied. The harpies didn't kill her. She's hiding over there." Andy gestured toward a stand of trees.

Wyn interpreted.

Greenie glanced at the trees, and the leaves rustled. "That's two birds, a mouse, and insects."

"No, that is the trickster you're looking for," Wyn said softly. She waved her hand at her waist.

Andy sounded half-strangled when he said, "She's clever like that." He coughed, covering his mouth with his arm. *Don't make me laugh when we're pulling something like this, Obi-Wan.*

A pair of the centaurs craned their necks in that direction. One asked, "Where?"

The nymph pointed with her knife-hand and shrieked. "She's there. The bird!"

Most of the centaurs lunged that direction.

Get away from her as soon as I get the weapon away from your throat. I'll catch up. Seizing the opportunity, Zita crept behind Greenie and then exploded into gorilla shape, seizing the wrist of the knife hand and yanking the nymph to throw her off balance and out of Wyn's protective bubble.

To her surprise, the move failed. Pulling on the arm only bent it down like exerting pressure on a tree limb, and it took all her gorilla strength to keep it there.

Greenie released Wyn to slash at Zita with the other hand, which had inexplicably grown knives instead of fingers.

Pain burned across her ribs as Zita shifted to an elephant and used that to haul the nymph off the ground and hurl her into the forest. *That works too, I guess, other than scratches.*

Andy darted forward, shoving centaurs out of his way. Spears bounced off him, and several cracked as he batted them away.

Darting through the path he provided, Wyn ran to the meadow. In English, she shouted, "Move to the meadow! She's an oak dryad, so the farther from her tree, the better."

Zita shifted back to Arca and somersaulted out of the way of a thrown spear. She took a step toward Wyn.

Andy waded among the horse-men, pulling weapons from their hands and either breaking them or throwing them to the ground.

Fleet over the uneven ground despite her lack of shoes, Greenie ran back and rushed at Zita. "You! How did you get here without me knowing?" She swiped wildly with both hands.

A pair of centaurs reared and lashed out with their front hooves, but the blows slid uselessly off Andy.

"Sheer power of awesome, I guess. Who pissed on your tree, lady? We don't want to hurt anyone, so just back off!" Zita sidestepped her. While the nymph was off balance, she seized Greenie's arms and tried to immobilize her.

Despite all of the extra time that Zita had spent lifting weights, the nymph fought back, slowly forcing her way free of Zita's hold by sheer strength.

Zita shifted to a gorilla again and growled.

"Wolverine proved any more than three knives on your hands is overkill. Let's not have any of that, now," Andy said, flicking a glance over her shoulder at them. *I can't get to you while I've got all these guys.*

Wyn shouted. "I can't convince them to stand down while we're actively fighting them. Retreat to my bubble!"

Chapter Six

"**Hold! No combat should there be!**" The words rang out in sonorous Greek.

Another centaur burst from the forest. Unlike the others, this one wore a chiton on his top half and age upon his face. Tight white curls crowned a wizened visage with a close-cropped beard, though he had the same impressive arms and shoulders of the younger horse-men. A bow bounced on one side, and a stringed instrument nestled on bulging saddlebags on the other. A trio of field-dressed hares bounced in a net bag in time to his uneven gait. On one of his haunches, an angry raised knot of a scar nearly the size of her fist stood out against the warm bay of his hide.

The other centaurs continued to try to stomp on Andy. Greenie never stopped her attacks on Zita.

In a formidable bass rumble of annoyance, the older centaur called out again. He cantered forward a few halting steps, as if the scarred leg could not quite bear all his weight. "I come as the Voice of the Council, following the dictates of Fate."

Two enormous men, easily twelve feet tall, lumbered into the clearing, carrying clubs and casting baleful eyes over the crowd.

The centaurs and nymph froze. After a second, the horse-men lowered their (mostly broken) spears and settled their forehooves on the ground.

Andy wiped sweat off his forehead from where he stood. *I was worried I'd hurt them if that kept up!*

"We have no need of you," a younger centaur called out, pointing a broken spear at the older one.

Greenie's weapons reverted to slender, uncalloused fingers. "Olympos should offer them no hospitality unless the Pyrphóros wills it. Tell me the Council has chosen the path of wisdom and will let us abandon them to the realm of the Northern barbarians."

With an assessing eye over Zita and her friends, the older centaur said, "Did you not? You weren't tempting the gods to smite you?"

"Nay, they deny godhood," another said.

The young centaur clutched at what was left of his spear. "We sought to grant them passage someplace... safer for their ilk."

"We're really not gods. Simply humans with powers," Wyn said in Greek.

Since Greenie seemed to be relying on pouting as her weapon of choice at the moment, Zita released her and took a couple cautious steps toward Wyn. Using the same language, she agreed. "What she said."

The old centaur snorted, tossing his head in a move that reminded Zita of a horse shaking its mane. "As were the so-called gods you remember. Audacious mortals stole the gods' thrones, their very names, so they might lay claim to the faithful and grow in strength, not that any of you will remember that yet. Their era has passed, and a new one begun."

"Are you certain of that?" Greenie asked. She scoffed.

Wyn blinked. "They stole what?"

With a glance at the crowd, the old centaur said, "That is an explanation for another time. For now, I speak for the Council of Creatures, and must render judgment upon your crimes."

"Wait, what? Judgment for what? They attacked us first and tried to murder us! We were just protecting ourselves and didn't even hurt anyone..." Zita's gaze fell on a centaur with a black eye... and the nymph, who had a bruise growing on her cheek. She amended her statement. "Seriously. We didn't hurt anyone seriously."

A centaur spat. "We would not have killed you. Only exiled you to another land."

Zita gestured to the wounds weeping blood where the nymph had slashed her. "From where I'm bleeding and the knife she held to Muse' throat, you sure fooled us!"

The tree nymph waved a hand in the air, anger in every tense muscle of her body. "The old gods grant no mercy to those who betray them! Has your doddering brain lost those memories, Chiron?"

"The Chiron? The teacher and counselor to so many heroes? You are the one we're seeking." Wyn's face lit. *We're in luck. He's quite possibly the best choice for us!*

Zita pressed her hand against the aching wetness of her side. *Luck?*

The old centaur bowed.

Wyn moved to Zita's side and whispered her healing spell. The pain disappeared.

"What's going on?" Andy whispered. "I still don't speak... whatever that is."

Zita hissed in his ear in English. "The old centaur wants to put us on trial for our crimes, and the ones who attacked us are claiming they didn't want to harm us, just send us far away."

He snorted. "They had me fooled. I definitely thought they were trying to murder us."

"I know, right? Oye, I almost forgot. Wyn's having a geeky orgasm because the old horse guy's name is Chiron, but I'm not certain why." Zita threw her hands up in disgust.

Andy brightened as well. "I recognize that name. Wyn said we needed someone to answer questions or give quests, and he'd be a great candidate. He knows stuff. Ask him if he knows how we can get home?"

Zita translated his question.

The old centaur chuckled. "I am Chiron. The past has ever been a closer friend to me than to others. Knowledge is one thing I have in abundance, provided you seek not prophecy or wisdom forbidden to my kind. I may know of a way you might return to your realm, but you will need the support of the Council before I may speak of it. First you must purify yourselves of the infamy you have already gained, and that is why I have come."

Wyn all but rubbed her hands together in glee.

"We haven't even done anything other than defend ourselves, and this old horse guy is claiming we're already infamous?" Zita complained in English.

Andy stared at her. "Who have you been talking to? What did you say?"

"Sometimes it's not my fault, you know," Zita groused in English.

Greenie did not let her finish speaking. "If the old ones return and find you gave succor to these, upon your head be it! I will take no punishment for you." With a final sneer, she flounced away to lean against a nearby tree.

The old centaur eyed the nymph for a moment before his calm gaze returned to Wyn, Zita, and Andy. "Our aid must come at a price. Due to your misdeeds, the Council has decreed that you must first be purified of your sins before we may render you aid beyond simple hospitality."

"With due respect, we see no council here, and are but newly arrived in this land," Wyn said.

The old centaur shrugged. "Whenever the Fates permit, the Council deems it prudent to resolve issues before they occur. We needed no testimony, as your deeds speak for themselves. It is our duty to discern culpability."

Words seemed to escape Zita before she realized she was speaking. "You make decisions before anything happens. How does that work? You had pre-existing quests set in case strangers come by and get assaulted by your people? That's crazy."

The centaur smiled. "Verily, had we not the Oracles, that would be true. When they speak, the Council listens. We heed their advice and bring all our arguments to bear so we might enact a well-reasoned and happy resolution when the time comes for the prophesied event. We have only had a few short decades since the last visitors to our realm, but that was enough for us to improve upon the mistakes we made then and better deal with all that has changed over the centuries."

"You had other guests? Who?" Wyn asked. *I have so many questions.*

Chiron's posture lost some of its tension, and he settled back into what seemed a more comfortable stance. His voice gained professorial tones. "An artificer god, like Hephaestus, and a queen of monsters. They claimed not to be gods as well, but we have learned not to be swayed by speech so much as deeds when treating with deities."

Wyn translated absently for Andy and added her own guesses. "Two of the Seventies supers? Hephaestus was the god of blacksmiths, craftsmen, metallurgy, and volcanoes. Perhaps Clockwork? The Queen of monsters has to be Dragon or an unknown. She claimed to be the 'monster of monsters' when she and Zita tangled in the Libyan desert."

"Verdad. Must be nice to have a photographic memory if you remember me telling you what she said after this long." Zita felt a moment of sympathy for any future kids her friend might have.

Andy held out his hand. "She said something similar to me. Said I was just an overgrown chicken."

Zita grinned and elbowed him. "I'm not the only one to see the resemblance, then. What about the Cambodian lady?"

"Her powers were all about plants, not monsters. The only people she's killed are those trying to enter her territory or harm someone within those confines. Dragon claimed the monster throne when we saw her in Libya, and goes on bloody, flaming rampages as the whim strikes." Wyn ticked off her points on her fingers.

"True that." Zita translated their conclusions for the gathered creatures, using both the English and Greek versions of the names.

The old centaur lifted a hand. "Yes, so they named themselves. Clockwork and I spoke through the night and into the morning when I hosted them."

"Is he still here? We know Dragon made it back. Perhaps he could enlighten us so we cause no more disruption to your fair land." Wyn flashed a winning smile, and her eyelashes fluttered.

At her comments, the mass of centaurs stirred, exchanging glances.

Chiron hesitated. "Did the great beast return home? We know not what became of them, save that they failed to return from their quest."

Andy said, "While he's talking about others, see if they've seen Tiffany and the others."

Wyn asked for him.

The old centaur shook his head. "No, you are the only strangers to walk our lands of which I've heard. If you wish to know more of Clockwork or the Dragon, we may speak more, once the expiation of your sins is complete."

"Wait, what sins?" Zita frowned.

"You struck members of our council and loosed a mad beast upon our land. We also forget not that the Harpies boil at the edge of war by your actions."

"They attacked us first in both cases! And Garm's his own person. He just likes being a wolf and left all on his own," Zita protested in Greek.

Several of those assembled scowled at her.

Wyn touched her arm and spoke quietly in English. "Hush. Don't make this harder than it has to be. Most of this audience is already unfriendly. I believe they're following a pattern. If this is a spirit realm, as I believe it to be, they may be unable to deviate from the classic heroic path."

Andy groaned. "A gift or a quest?"

Wyn nodded. "And we are short on gifts."

Setting her hands on her hips, Zita hissed, "Seriously? They attack us and we owe them? Maybe they can't break out of the cycle, but we're not part of it, so I don't see why we have to play along with their trumped-up charges."

"Because we're here and we can't leave without doing so. That's how it's done," Andy said quietly.

Wyn added her voice to his. "You can't fight against centuries of tradition, and it may be part of their essential existence."

Zita scowled but subsided. *You both recognize that this quest thing is stupid, right?*

Neither of her friends deigned to answer her directly.

After squinting at Zita, Wyn plastered on a smile and turned back toward the assembled creatures. Honey dripped from the Greek words she purred at them. "Please continue, honored council. We do regret any trespasses we have committed, though they were unintentional."

Two centaurs relaxed and returned her smile, but the old centaur let no expression cross his face. Chiron tapped his spear on the ground. "Our relationships with the Harpies will be worsened now by your actions. You injured some of ours and broke valuable weapons as well. As a result, you must quest to gain forgiveness. Once you have completed three tasks, then will we reveal what you seek."

Zita interpreted for Andy in a cranky whisper.

He rubbed the sides of his toga, where pockets would normally be. *I somehow doubt that they described themselves in such fragrant language. Zita, try not to talk to anyone. This is like the old legends my mother used to tell me, where the heroes would inadvertently annoy the spirits and either have to quest to gain their favor back or suffer under some horrible curse.*

Not returning home would be curse enough, Wyn sent.

Reluctance choking her, Zita admitted the truth. *This is a nice place that might be fun to explore at another time, other than all the creatures with recreational sticks up their butts, but I want to go home too. I'll just stand here and be quiet and supportive.*

Both her friends shot her dubious looks, but only Andy sent his opinion. *I'll believe that when I see it.*

Feeling the love here. Zita folded her arms over her chest.

Wyn inclined her head regally to the Council. "We understand. Could the number of quests be reduced at all given our innocence of the laws broken? We had neither knowledge of trespass in the Harpies' territory nor any intentions of harming anyone. The Harpies attacked my friend when she was simply flying, and the man-wolf is neither under our control nor an ally. We can take him with us when we return to our homes, if that is your preference."

The nymph scoffed. "You trespassed in Harpy territory, and it is their nature. Of course they attacked. Did you not expect them to be quarrelsome?"

Chiron broke in before Wyn could answer. "They may be from so far away they may know not the disposition of Harpies. Two of them bear skin closer to Pan's than any Grecian born." He pointed.

Andy flinched, and Zita reflexively stepped between them.

Thanks. I know the curse thing is an old superstition, and I should get over it, but... he sent.

No worries, mano. I got your back. Aloud, Zita said in Greek, "Don't point. It's rude and forbidden in some of our cultures."

The offending hand closed, and Chiron let it drop. "My apologies."

Andy's fist bumped her shoulder gently.

Wyn's brow furrowed. "Pan wasn't from Arcadia?"

The old centaur chuckled. "Nay, that trickster was both Zeus' war prize and bane." He began to say more, but one of the others coughed.

Chiron closed his mouth for a moment. His tail flicked rapidly. "Regarding your offenses, intent matters not. Three quests it must be, and mind you bring yourself no further dishonor. You may set on the first one immediately. Bring the jar!"

A twelve-foot-tall man lumbered into the clearing and set down a jar with a grunt of effort. While it seemed smaller in his massive hands, the container had to be chest-high on Zita.

Chiron cleared his throat and tapped his spear three times on the edge of the jar. "This is your first task. Seek you the bees of Aristaeus in the Vale of Tempe to the south. Return with this jar filled to the brim with their honey. Be warned, though, the bees have grown fierce since the wise beekeeper passed. His apprentice dares not harvest from them, for their stings bring death to mortals and decades of pain to immortals. Spare the queen, however, and at least some of her faithful workers, for many depend on their honey."

The nymph smirked.

"No mames, he wants us to harvest enough honey to fill that enormous chingado jar from murder-bees? Without killing too many bugs? Why were they even carting around that jar anyway? How about honey from insects that don't kill people? They've got to have nicer bees somewhere," Zita said, and then translated her last two sentences to Greek.

Andy blinked. "If they sting us, they die... and so do we."

"I believe that's the point," Wyn said softly in English.

The old centaur laced his fingers in front of his stomach. "If you wish to decline the tasks, you may, but you will find your path home obscured and hidden from you. Additionally, some may seek justice for those you assaulted."

Zita swallowed her protest. *I love how they all ignore that they sprang a trap on us and hit first.*

Be glad it's not the Aegean stables. We'll figure out something. The bees likely can't get through your skin, Andy, so much of this will be on you. With a graceful curtsy, Wyn nodded to the centaur. "Where will we bring it? And what is the name of the apprentice?"

"You may bring it here, and the beekeeper is Egidius of Aeolia."

Zita frowned. *You know, for a wise old mentor, he sucks. We have to go somewhere we've never heard of to get sweets? ¿Neta? At least my naked drunk dude didn't want us to run his errands.*

While Wyn nodded meekly to the centaur, her eyes sparkled beneath her demurely lowered lashes. *This is a sparsely-populated land. I should be able to do my tracking spell on the apprentice, especially since I have his name and a general destination to target.*

"You should go now, for it is a journey of two days if you walk as two-legged mortals do. Once you return, we will lead you to Olympos for rest and food. You will receive the second quest after the sun breaks the horizon the next morning." Chiron opened his mouth again, glanced at the nymph, and then closed it again.

Dawn? Why can't anything happen at the crack of noon? Wyn complained mentally.

All this and that's what you complain about? Sooner is better. We all agreed we wanted to go home as fast as possible. Zita tapped her foot, trying to keep quiet.

Grudgingly, Wyn sent her wordless agreement.

Zita couldn't stay silent longer and blurted out her question. "If we get done before the end of the day, can we start on the next quest instead of wasting time?"

Chuckles ran through the assembled centaurs. The nymph snickered.

Chiron's mouth bent in a smile. "That I can grant you. If you finish before sundown, I will give you your next quest so you may start."

"If they take another task before the sun sets, then they forfeit any hospitality until that quest has done. Refuge among us you may only claim between tasks, not during one. We will not have you interfering or assisting, old one, be it purposeful or no." Greenie pressed her lips together.

Another centaur, his posture shouting his discomfort, said quietly, "You are renowned and remembered for your sage advice and how freely it flies from your lips, Chiron, especially once a willing audience has sapped your ability to remain silent."

A current of agreement went through the crowd.

The old centaur sighed, disappointment on his face. "Very well, then. When your tasks are done and the sun is down, the hospitality of my table and my home are yours until you begin a new quest."

Zita opened her mouth to refuse, but someone else spoke first.

Without hesitation, Wyn said, "We would be delighted to accept your kind offer, good sir." *Hospitality was a big deal in ancient Greece. Refusing is by itself a major sin. We have to accept because, well, it's a major no-no to kill or harm your guests provided they behave themselves. At some point, we'll need to eat and rest, after all.*

Andy grinned. *So, what you're saying is that Zita shouldn't talk to anyone?*

Probably true. Wyn's voice held both laughter and pleading.

Haters. Zita grumbled under her breath.

Chiron waved them away. "Now go. We will set our camp among those trees to await you." He limped toward a section of the woods. The majority of the crowd followed him.

Wyn closed her eyes and took a deep breath. When she reopened them, she held out her hand and concentrated. A map of Greece appeared. "If we are on or near Olympus, then the Vale should be here."

Two tiny, bright flags flared on the map as she spoke.

"Sorry I can't zoom in or offer more than supposition, but cartography is not one of my interests. I haven't spent a great deal of time checking Grecian maps other than to determine our destination earlier today... yesterday?"

Zita glanced at the sky, checking the sun's position. "We arrived in Greece in the afternoon. This is the morning sun, so probably yesterday."

Before either of her friends responded, Greenie stepped out from a tree. Her flat voice made it clear she made a statement and did not ask a question. "You do not wish to redeem yourself and perform the Council's tasks."

Wyn and Andy's gazes slide toward Zita.

Greenie held up a hand. "You need not accuse anyone. Gods and heroes long ago taught we nymphs bitter lessons about inattention, and it was writ upon your faces. It is no secret I wish you gone, and you wish to leave expeditiously, yes?"

"True," Wyn said slowly, her head tilting.

"In this our desires align, so I will offer you an alternative to please us both. Speak to the hermit Arges. He and his brothers aided Hephaestus in the construction of the portals the gods used to travel between sweet Olympos and your realm. They learned much of magic and engineering, and that might speed you homeward. Of the three, he was the slowest to anger and most likely to aid you."

Her face brightening, Wyn said, "Where might we find him?"

Even though she wanted to believe it, wariness held back similar hope in Zita. *Even if I think the whole quest thing is loco, this has got to be a trap. Has to be. Greenie hates us for no apparent reason.*

Andy rubbed his hands on the sides of his thighs. *As much as I hate to agree with Admiral Ackbar there, she's got a point. The nymph did have a knife-finger to your throat not that long ago.*

Greenie gave a tight smile and admired her own fingernails. "He abides on the isle of Euonymos north of Aítnē where Typhon's couch lays. No others share the isle with his hermitage."

"One moment, please." Wyn smiled at the nymph, then took both Zita and Andy by the arm, leading them to the side. She hissed in English, "I don't trust her either, but can we afford to miss a chance to leave earlier? We talk to Arges, and if he can't help us, we do as the Council says. Arca, you didn't want to go questing anyway."

"That's true, but..." Zita shook her head.

Wyn held herself perfectly erect, her shoulders thrown back and chin tilted upward. Her lips trembled. "But nothing. My aunt lives on borrowed time, and I need to be there for her. If I'm not, her Alzheimer's will progress and she'll be left to my parents' nonexistent mercy. She'll be dead within six months. We need to at least try speaking to him."

The gleam of tears at the corners of her friend's eyes had Zita swallowing her arguments. *Ay, no. Anything but Wyn crying.* She folded her arms across her chest. Her voice was gruff, even to her own ears. "Fine, but it's still a bad idea, and we treat it like a trap. You know we got your back."

Andy nodded. "I'm in. We'll all be paranoid in this together."

"It's seriously not paranoia when she admits she's out to get you. It's justified caution." Zita jiggled her leg impatiently.

Wyn didn't wait for any further conversation. She whirled around and stepped closer to the nymph. Her map shifted, showing Greece and Italy, though no flag appeared on any of the islands.

"Can you tell me more of Arges? Perhaps his full name? What is this island near?"

While the nymph's face did not change much, Zita caught a glimpse of a smirk, quickly buried.

Chapter Seven

"I hate this part. Heights are not my thing." Despite the warm weather, Wyn shuddered where she sat in the center of Andy's avian back. An obsidian arrowhead, glowing amber with a tracking spell, patiently floated above her open palm, pointing downward.

Below where Zita perched at the edge of a wing, a potato-shaped island stretched out, lumpy with mountains. Much like the Grecian peninsula where they'd gone to rescue the hostages, sheer cliffs comprised most of the shoreline with a few rocky beaches in sheltered coves. The ground cover seemed to vary between stunted trees, stubby brush, and grasses. High on one cliff, a stone house reflected glumly above a straight drop into the brilliant blue waters of the nearby harbor, the biggest on the island. A weathered and twisted oak threw shade over benches set beneath it. A secondary building sat nearby, a massive anvil in front of it. A narrow path ran between the house and ocean with dots of still gray visible among flowering white hellebore and heather.

Zita tilted her head at Wyn. "You're the one who figured out the nymph's super vague directions and cast the spell that led us here."

Her friend did not immediately reply. After another moment of studying the magical tool, Wyn dismissed the spell, tucked away the arrowhead into her bag, and inched over to Zita. She peeked down at the ground. One of her hands sought out Zita's arm, squeezing it in a death grip. "Do you see a house?"

"Right there." Zita leaned forward and pointed out the buildings.

Leaning away from the edge, Wyn swallowed hard. "I'll take your word for it."

Zita shrugged and considered the approaching ground.

As Andy descended into the closest flat meadow, wildlife fled at their approach, as did a swarm of chickens. A herd of goats kept a wary distance. A bulbous hill hid the house from sight even though it was a short walk from their landing site.

Zita frowned. "What's with all the free-range farm animals? Chickens really shouldn't go that far from the protection of their henhouse, and somebody should keep an eye on goats. Because they're trouble. Hungry trouble. By the way, try not to cut off all the blood flow to my guns. I worked hard for those."

As she'd hoped, Wyn relaxed at the banter and loosened her grip. "I can tell. They're huge. Bigger than normal. Have you done anything but lift weights lately?"

"Today was the first day I've had a chance to do anything, and Freelance invited me snowboarding at the last minute. I haven't had much time between both jobs, including filling in for Quentin while he was on that retreat with his veteran's trauma recovery group, and the whole random helping people stuff. Most extreme sports take planning, and the mudslide rescue pretty much ate up two weeks. I did a lot of digging in that too." For a moment, she tasted mud and her nose stung with the remembered scent of the dead. Zita shook her head. Deliberately, she inhaled, filling her lungs with the fresh air and varied scents of the area.

Apparently unaware of Zita's mental wandering, Wyn made a disgusted face. "Ugh. Let's not talk about the mercenary. At least we're landing wherever this is."

"You're the one that said Greenie meant one of the Aeolian islands. This is third from the top of the chain and it's the only one with any kind of house. I don't see nobody, but your spell says he's here somewhere. The whole place can't be more than a mile and a half long." Zita helped her friend down off Andy's wing, and both women moved out of range of his huge talons.

Turning away, Zita headed up the hill to get a better view of the tower.

"It should be simple to locate Arges since he is a cyclops, a one-eyed giant. If we're lucky, he'll have our answers, and we'll be home within an hour or two." Hope filled Wyn's voice, but she wrung her hands as she followed.

Zita patted Wyn's back when her friend reached her. "No worries. It'll be cool. We'll be out of here in no time."

With a shimmer of lightning, Andy shifted back to his human form and began walking toward them.

"I meant to ask. You met harpies?" Wyn leaned forward, her eyes gleaming.

She wrinkled her nose. "I fought them, or at least tried to evade their attacks. Does that count as a meeting?"

"Were they inspiring examples of feminine power and the wisdom of experience or the usual diminishment of postmenopausal women of power by a stifling patriarchal culture?" Wyn licked her lips.

Zita blinked. "Are you writing a paper? They were old ladies with nice hair, vulture bodies, and seriously bad attitudes."

Her friend pouted.

"One threatened to poop on me?" Zita offered.

Wyn shook her head. "Not the celebration of feminine mysticism I was hoping to hear about, thanks."

"Sorry."

With a smile, Andy joined them. "Did I miss anything? Have the plans changed?"

Zita nodded to him. "I'm still checking it out first. We need to take the careful route. I hope you're right and this gets us home. I'm hungry."

Andy grinned. "Is that your secret, Z? That you're always hungry? I've got Wyn covered while you're scouting."

"I am, but that's not a secret."

He groaned. "Also, you don't understand just how awesome an Avengers reference that could have been. We'll give you a half hour head start, then hike toward the house."

"You were joking? I wasn't." Zita grinned. "Catch you soon." She changed to the familiar form of a golden eagle and launched herself skyward.

After a quick circle from high up, Zita let the wind carry her lower until the tips of her wings almost grazed the top of the grasses. Farther from the house, the goats had eaten the grass bald in patches, and it was considerably shorter, but closer to the building it grew untamed. The gray specks she'd spotted from the air were statues of animals, both wild and tame, but with surprising detail. No sign of any giant and she didn't even see the paths she'd expect if anyone or even any animals regularly passed this way. The air was still and silent, and she was the only thing in the sky, save for some gulls laughing offshore. She transmitted her findings to her friends via their mental connection. *Maybe he's sick or moved? I'm not finding any signs of life, but I'll get closer.*

Zita swooped over the roof of the building. The house itself was a series of stacked stone cubes that blended with the browns and greens of the surrounding area. An exterior stairway wound around the south end of the house, traveling to the second floor via a series of wooden terraces. Grapes canopied the walkway, so out of control that ripe fruit dripped from the vines and lay drying on the wood. Minuscule chunks of rock were scattered everywhere like tiny caltrops, but the gaps in the terraces and stairs spoke of neglect. The roof of the house itself was almost flat.

In front of the house, an abandoned vegetable garden ran thick with weeds and disrepair, though a clever barrel system seemed ready to funnel water from the roof to a dry trench that ran the length of the plant rows. Four big stone chairs sat around a fire pit nearby, but the pit itself was overgrown with grass and only visible thanks to the ring of rubble around it. Beside it, a huge metal cauldron was tipped on its side under the only tree, a holm oak. The building she'd pegged as a forge seemed equally forgotten. A foul, vaguely reptilian odor underlaid the scents of the Mediterranean shrubs and fruit.

Zita sent a brief description of the place to her friends and then added her opinion. *Well, this place screams wrong, and it's definitely a trap of some sort. However, I've seen the soup pot of my dreams. It's big enough I bet you could feed a squad of Marines fresh off a mission and have leftovers.*

What's wrong about it? We were coming toward the house and ran across some of those statues you mentioned. Wyn said they're magic, but she's trying to determine what exactly before we come any closer.

Pues, that's a good idea. Everything's all abandoned but something moved inside the house. I don't think the cyclops is here. The statues probably all come to life like that one in the museum or something else creepy.

After a brief debate with herself, Zita shifted to a squirrel and began checking the rooms, starting at the top. While there weren't many rooms to check, they were all built on a large scale, with ceilings twenty feet high. *I guess that makes sense if you're giant-sized. Weird that none of these rooms connect unless you're willing to walk on the terrace or fly.*

The thought must've leaked to party line, as Wyn absently replied to it. *The lack of connecting rooms was a defensive feature in ancient times. It made it harder to raid rooms if the walkway was destroyed.*

The last of the rooms on the second floor seemed to be a dining room, based on the giant wicker seat and table set as if for a meal. If it had held food at some point, it had long ago disappeared, leaving the clay platter and smaller bowls empty except for dust. A statue of a homely giant, fifteen feet tall, held a matching cup beside it. *How vain do you have to be to put a statue of yourself in your house?*

Fur on her back rose in an instinctual warning, and she teleported, diving into the mug. From outside her hiding place, she heard a strange noise, like a combination of a slow walk of a four-legged animal, a slither, and a hissing sound.

The noise passed by, never entering the room, so she poked her head out of her hiding place.

Silhouetted in profile, the strangest creature she'd ever seen clucked, then pecked at the ground just outside the room. Something crunched in its beak. The curious reptile had the length of a dachshund, but none of the appeal. Reptilian legs ending in talons like those of a hen propelled a barrel-shaped body, matched by a scaly rooster's head that it carried upright, while the tail was that of a snake dragging on the ground. In the center of its head, a white spot glared from its forehead like a malevolent third eye blinded by cataracts. The beast stalked forward a few more feet, clucking, and ate a rock.

What is with the Greeks and their thing about mixing up animals? Nobody's here, except for this thing that looks like a chicken and a snake got it on and had this weird-ass, pebble-eating rooster-snake-lizard child with a big white polka dot on its head.

A what? Don't get close to it! Worry filled Wyn's mental voice.

No sé. I don't have to know what it is to know it's bad news.

Andy asked, *Does the reptile have wings? Don't let it see you. I think I know what's going on. These aren't just statues; they're animals that have been turned to stone.*

Zita ducked back down into the mug, glad it was long dry. *No wings. What's the deal?*

Wings would mean it's a cockatrice. No wings means it's probably a basilisk. Andy's voice was matter-of-fact.

Curiosity accompanied Wyn's words. *You've read Pliny? The description does fit a basilisk, but they were known for their poison.*

Not in my college D&D games, they weren't. The reason the place seems deserted is because the basilisk turns everything it looks at to stone. Except plants, apparently, Andy sent.

It doesn't change metal or stone either. The statues don't match the local rock formations. Some of the stuff you two know is bizarre. When is it useful to know about ancient Greek killer chicken-lizard-snake hybrids? Zita sent.

Andy's mental voice was wry. *Right about now, for one. Given how little moves near the house, I'm guessing the guy we need is probably a huge statue in there.*

His theory does support the evidence. Wyn's words were slow, as if she were distracted.

Zita curled her thick tail around herself, grateful for the safety of her hiding place. She pushed aside a pair of tiny petrified flies, careful to keep them from rattling in the enclosed space, and eyed the bearded, surprised face of the statue above her. It only had one eye. *In which case, I found him. And yes, he's going to be a hard man to make talk because he's currently granite. Should we put up a sign or something to warn people away?*

We should definitely post warnings. Somehow. Thanks for the puns, though, they do make it all a little better. Andy sighed mentally.

Sympathy colored Wyn's reply, but she still seemed absorbed in something. *Poor Arges! Do you think the nymph knew what happened to him when she sent us?*

Zita remembered the sly glint in the tree woman's eyes. *Wouldn't surprise me if Greenie knew. Let us know if you'll need any special stuff to reverse it, Wyn, but the island's pretty sparse. You might have to just magically tell him not to play garden statue anymore.*

What, in case of accidental petrification, break glass for a counterspell? I can't just whip up magic on demand like that. I don't have an anti-petrification spell memorized, nor do I dare get close enough to the house to study Arges. It's unlike anything I've ever encountered before. It's almost alchemy—magic chemistry—more than ritual or spells.

Zita considered her friend's tone. *She's freaking out, but she also sounds intrigued.*

Fantastic! Arges might have a chance, Andy sent back.

Wyn inserted, *You know I can hear you both.*

A chuckle preceded Andy's answer. *We wouldn't tease you if we didn't have faith in you. If they were living creatures before they got turned to stone, it's an effect like poison or a curse. You know how to handle both of those.*

Wyn's tone brightened. *True. If I treat it more like those and mix that with a counterspell, perhaps I could do something? However, I don't know if Arges'll be alive once he emerges.*

Zita stayed very still within her cup as she heard the tap of claws on hard ground and a soft hiss nearby. *You can do it.*

Andy added, *We can backtrack to a chicken statue, and you can use that to test your spell.*

Horror laced through Zita. *If they're already dead though because of the spell, do we need to try? Then again, if they're alive and trapped in their own body, how horrible is it to be stuck there, unable to move? Especially if they're conscious. They could all be mad.*

Party line went dead.

Guys? Guys? Please don't be dead. Or statues. Zita wove her paws together and fought to stay still.

Warmth flooded her as the link returned.

Softly, Wyn sent, *Sorry, I needed to scan the closest stone animals to see if I could detect their minds. Now that I'm inspecting them up close, I can see a faint glow of a living aura beneath the outer veneer of magic. Before, I thought it was all one spell. When I attempted using telepathy on them, I couldn't find them, so hopefully they're in stasis.*

So, we have no choice then. We have to rescue the cyclops. We can't leave him like that forever, Andy sent.

You're right, but I'm pretty certain the whole house is the basilisk's den. I've only heard one so far, but they're quiet enough I could've missed one. From what little I've seen, its primary hunting ground is the balconies and stairs you have to use to get between the different rooms. Why don't you grab one of those stone chickens and use it to figure out what you'd need to do to reverse the spell? I'll get out of here as soon as it's safe. If I suddenly drop off party line, I'll be the most awesomely fit rock animal in this place. The sound of the basilisk's movement receded and Zita peeked out of the top of the mug.

The animal had not gone far, simply retreated to a leafy nest by the grapes.

A bee buzzed toward a particularly ripe bunch of grapes fermenting in the sun.

Evidently, the basilisk saw the insect as well.

A pebble shaped like a bee fell.

Waddling forward, the basilisk trundled over and ate it, then retreated to a spot outside Zita's line of sight. It clucked.

You'll need to neutralize the basilisk so we can get close enough to retrieve Arges. Anything this woven into the fabric of the victims will take time, Wyn sent.

Zita ducked back down and snorted. *Sure, I'll jump right on that, if you can stop the basilisk from petrifying my culo while I do.*

It'd have to find your rear to do that. Better friends of Quentin have tried to do that and failed. For all his light words, a tremor ran through Andy's mental voice.

Verdad, but I don't want to spend my life as a garden statue. I have people I care about and things I want to jump off or onto. Zita carefully did not think of Freelance, stuffing that thought into the darkest closet of her mind before it could leak onto the communication with her friends.

Andy asked about the escapes she'd already discarded. *Can you fly to us? Or teleport?*

I can't fly because the odds are too good it'll spot me. I might be able to teleport, but I'm not certain I can do that with Arges. He's really big, and I don't want to risk teleporting just part of him. All the doors I've seen are either broken or rotted through, so it's not like I can shut it in one room. Zita controlled her breathing, keeping it quiet while her mind raced.

Wyn's voice was hesitant. *The ancient Greeks believed that everything in nature had its antidote. It's risky for you, though, Zita.*

Me? Why? She squirmed onto her back and scratched her stomach as she mused ways to handle the basilisk. *There was that big-ass pot.*

I have a feeling that is beyond bad about this, Andy sent.

After a mental sigh, Wyn admitted, *As do I, but we have little choice. For a basilisk or cockatrice, the traditional antidote was a weasel.*

I have to fight it as a weasel? Won't that be a problem if I'm a rock? You know it eats at least some of the things it petrifies, right? If weasels are immune to petrification, I could maybe take it since they're tough little things. Wishing she could tap her fingers or pace while she thought, Zita considered fighting strategies in rodent form.

Supposedly, you just need to get near it and... err... stink. They object to something in a weasel's scent, and it should be safe for you. Theoretically. They're the only creatures said to be immune to the basilisk. That said, avoid fighting it directly, as typically both die after a confrontation.

Inside her hiding place, Zita closed her eyes and shook her head. *Sí, by all means, build my confidence about surviving with important little details like that.*

When have you ever had confidence problems? That said, can we come up with an option that doesn't end with Zita dead? Although he tried to keep his tone light, worry clouded Andy's voice.

Zita's mind whirled, settling on a plan. *You're right, that's usually not a problem for me. I generally take calculated risks, but I don't see a way around handling the basilisk. Pues. I think I have an idea. It won't be a permanent solution, but if we're not fighting it directly, it'll have to do. Are you close enough to make a distraction? It's parked right outside the room I'm in, and I need enough time to set a trap. Let me know when you start.*

A few minutes passed.

Simultaneously with Wyn's mental voice and the sound of a crowing rooster, the basilisk hissed, an angry sound. *Distraction ongoing.*

Greenery rustled, and the distinctive slithering gait hurried away.

Zita vaulted out of the mug, transforming in midair to land as a weasel, just in case the form conferred any immunity. Each step cautious, she snuck to the door and listened for the sound of the basilisk. While the sunlight seemed harsh, her vastly improved hearing and scent enabled her to track the departing creature. On the downside, her stomach grumbled at the rich odor of the fruit, fermented and otherwise.

No time for food. That's got to be among the top-ten saddest phrases ever.

She scampered over by the tree, checked once again to see if the basilisk was returning yet, and began constructing a pit trap. As a badger, her powerful claws tore through the ground, digging a deep hole. After a few judicious teleports to grab necessary items, she shifted back to Arca and fitted the cauldron neatly in the hole. *The smooth walls should keep the basilisk from climbing or digging out of the trap.*

She was halfway done hiding the opening with a platter, vines, and leaves when a wave of surprise and pain blasted through the mental connection, and both of her friends exclaimed.

Her stomach clenched, and she crouched low. *Guys? Are you okay? Dios, please tell me there's only one of those things and my friends aren't art now.*

We are unharmed. Wyn answered first.

Zita let out the breath she hadn't noticed she was holding.

It would be best if you don't let the basilisk see you, Andy said.

Ruefulness accompanied Wyn's agreement. *Agreed. Avoid if at all possible. If it does petrify you, I won't rest before I return you to flesh, even if it requires the explosion of every chicken here. Once we figure out a way to get close enough without being petrified ourselves, of course.*

Wait, what happened to the chicken? Zita stopped.

Let's just say she's still working on how to reverse the petrification, Andy sent.

Wyn ignored both comments. *Are you done with your construction project? I think it's headed back your way.*

Zita lifted her head.

The only sound was the soft rustle of the tree, and she couldn't scent the basilisk. Since it seemed to be away, she hurried to finish her preparations.

For her hiding place, she put a bowl over a second, smaller hole, ensuring it had enough of a gap for air and for her to see out. *Now I can hide without it seeing me. Time to bait the trap.*

In the shape of a weasel, she placed petrified bugs on the leafy cover over the cauldron mouth.

Something clucked nearby and the salty breeze carried a distinctive reptilian stench.

She darted beneath the bowl. Her rapid movement knocked the insects into the cauldron with a rattle.

After a quick glance around—the basilisk wasn't visible yet—Zita darted back and reached into the cauldron. Her paws touched only air.

I don't have time to find more!

Moving the leaves aside enough for her weasel form, she jumped into the cauldron. Her front paws had just claimed the stone insects when she heard the tell-tale movement of the creature.

Zita stared upward. *Run? Or hope it's not stupid enough to fall into my trap with no lure?* Abandoning the flies, she leapt, shifting to a lemur, and clung to the edge of the pot.

The basilisk was headed back to the stairs.

Zita started to relax. *Once it gets far enough into the building, I'll teleport into the tree and then back into my bowl. If I make a noise from there, maybe it'll come check it out and fall in. It's too close to risk it right now.*

A branch snapped and twigs showered down onto the trap, bringing down some of the grape leaves.

The basilisk turned around.

Zita dropped back down, returning to weasel shape on the way. *Guys? Stay back. It's here.*

Puzzlement accompanied Andy's reply. *We're still on the other side of the hill. Some cleanup was necessary... and we need to collect a few chickens and other creatures for Wyn to test her de-petrification spells on before she tries to help Arges. Unfortunately, we can't find many lizards or mice so it's mostly livestock.*

The clucking drew close.

Oh, okay. Pressed against the iron wall of the cauldron, Zita inched along it searching for a location where she could see the sky at an angle that wouldn't be visible to the creature. Since it had a rooster head, she assumed the basilisk had the same excellent field of vision as a chicken—300 degrees around itself. She tried not to think about being petrified in midair or caught in her own trap if she failed to locate the right spot.

Wait, you trapped yourself? Wyn sounded panicked.

The basilisk alerted again from far too close.

Recognizing the sound, Zita tensed, and prepared to teleport or fight as necessary, praying she'd be faster than the creature.

The sound drew farther away, and Zita relaxed slightly. *I'm fine. Everything's fine. All good.*

Another twig snapped, showering oak leaves into the cauldron. Little of the leafy canopy remained above her, and the platter only covered part of the opening.

The creature's retreat stopped, and it hissed. Its steps drew closer.

Zita held her breath.

Suddenly, the basilisk shrieked, a high-pitched, enraged squawk as loud as an air-raid siren, and the slithering sped up.

She winced. *Carajo.*

The tip of its beak speared through the few remaining leaves.

Her heart thundering, Zita teleported into the narrow strip of sky she could see and switched to an eagle. Wings burning with effort, she pumped them hard to rise high and hopefully outside of the basilisk's line of sight. *Dios, please don't let it see me.*

She glanced down.

The tip of the long snaky tail disappeared into the trap.

Seizing her chance, she teleported next to the trap. After shifting to a lemur again, she pushed and shoved until the platter slid over the opening.

From the hole, hissing mingled with fowl fury.

She pushed harder until the hole was covered, save the slight gaps where the oval platter was unable to cover the round cauldron. Careful not to approach too close, she threw leaves at those spots until they were covered as well.

Zita exhaled, shifting to Arca. *Somebody ordered a giant stone cyclops? Basilisk should be trapped for a while, but I wouldn't bet on the trap holding forever.*

Thank the Goddess you're safe! Relief poured through Wyn's voice.

One of her feet felt numb as if it had fallen asleep, and Zita tapped it against the ground. When it didn't seem to make a difference, she glanced down. *Carajo.*

Andy responded. *Z? I'm flying us, and we'll be there in a minute. Everything good?*

Her toes refused to wiggle. Stomach churning, Zita stared down at her gray left foot. *Things are a little rocky. You've got that anti-petrification spell figured out, right?*

Chapter Eight

As Wyn had not figured out a way to reverse the petrification, they took Arges and retreated from the island before the basilisk could free itself. They returned to questing. Retrieving the honey took all of three hours. Most of that time was spent trying to locate the Vale of Tempe and then find the correct meadow again. Wyn put the bees to sleep, Andy cleared the massively overgrown path, and the assistant beekeeper had extracted the sweet without harming many insects. As she had nothing else to do, Zita settled for familiarizing herself with the changes to her balance created by her foot, which was granite from the tip of her toes to the ankle.

Their return seemed to alternately startle or annoy those waiting. Whatever the creatures waiting for them had been expecting, it was not to have a gigantic, glowing golden eagle carefully set down an oversized, one-eyed garden statue and an enormous jar of honey only hours after they'd left. They'd clearly prepared to spend the night under the trees, in an orderly campsite ringed by giant torches stabbed into the ground. The crowd buzzed with several conversations at once as they began disassembling their camp. Chiron's face was a study in thoughtfulness. While he considered their return, the young satyr and centaur, who had been listlessly standing beside him, disappeared into the crowd.

Prior to their landing, Wyn had redone her lopsided turban and mummy-like mask. Now, a half-veil hid her lovely face but left her eyes exposed, and her hair hid under a wimple made of the remains of Andy's cape. She glanced back, wringing her elegant hands as she paused at the edge of an enormous wing.

Zita hated that look. Had hated it as a teenager with cancer, and still loathed it. "Go on. Go talk to them. Find out the next quest so we can check it off and be on our way as soon as possible. I'll watch your back from here so they can't claim my foot disqualifies me or something else ridiculous."

Her friend still hesitated.

"Órale, I screwed up. My foot's a rock now. It doesn't hurt and is stuck in the one position, but it doesn't feel any heavier than usual. So, I can hobble along fine until you fix it. We don't need to talk it to death. End of discussion. Just go." She folded her arms over her chest and forced a nonchalance she didn't feel.

Wyn finally bowed her head and descended to speak to the assembled crowd.

Exhaling deeply, Zita peered over the wing. Her fingers tapped an impatient staccato on her hip. She focused on what was happening below, in part so she could avoid thinking about her foot.

Wyn wafted over to Chiron, who wore a small tight smile. After some gesturing and conversation, the old centaur banged his ceremonial spear and spoke.

Since Wyn's body lost some of its tension at whatever he'd said, Zita smiled. "I think they accepted the first quest as done. Only two more left! We could see home tonight!"

Wingspan did not reply.

Greenie pushed her way to the front of the crowd, along with an unhappy giant and another centaur. They spoke, and Wyn seemed to argue something with them.

After a few moments, Wyn climbed back up.

"What's the verdict?" Zita said.

Her friend smoothed her toga and straightened her veil. "Chiron has informally accepted the first quest as complete. We're going to stay at his home overnight at Olympus, which I'm told should take a couple hours to reach. The Council needs to verify the honey before it is officially done. We'll have to wait until tomorrow for the second quest. I'll ride Chiron—"

Zita opened her mouth to tease her friend, but Wyn sped ahead first.

Waggling a finger, she narrowed her eyes. "Do not make that joke, Zita. Given Chiron's injury, it would insult him if I refused. Andy needs to carry Arges, as they don't have anyone who can handle his weight without risking injury. Most of the crowd will disperse once we get closer to Olympus, so we'll have fewer people gawking at... your issue when we reach the outer gates."

"I don't care what they think about it provided they don't use it as an excuse to stop us from going home. We'll do the other two quests tomorrow and leave. If I have to claim my foot's broken and wear a plaster cast over it for a few weeks, eso es la vida. It's not cancer and doesn't hurt, at least." Zita shrugged, her stomach roiling at her own statements.

"Very well. We will depart as soon as they've taken down their camp unless Andy has any issues."

He remained silent.

***

After a couple hours' journey up the mountain and into a sheltered ravine, the remaining members of the delegation arrived at Olympus at twilight. In the center of a wide, grassy area, a steep ramp led to a thick wall liberally decorated with arrow slits. A huge white marble gate, inlaid with and lit by glowing gold in the shapes of eagles and lightning bolts, ground open at their approach with a low rumble.

Andy circled overhead, having flown at a pace matching the ground travelers. In the anguish of impatience, Zita had started working out, finding the limits of her new condition.

After a satyr helped her dismount from the centaur, Wyn stared upward. Her mouth moved, but the words were only audible over their mental connection. *Chiron says you can only pass the gates in your man form, Andy, and requests that you carry Arges, if possible.*

After Wingspan landed, Zita climbed down. A shimmer of lightning raced over the avian form, and Andy stood beside her, Arges, the honey, and an assortment of small petrified animals, mostly chickens.

A giant, his gaze averted from the petrified cyclops, claimed the jar and walked ahead of them, his much longer stride carrying him away at a rapid pace.

Chiron nodded to them and then paused, his gaze stopping on her foot. His forehead wrinkled.

Zita lifted her chin and walked over to Wyn.

Without speaking, the centaur and his entourage swept through the gates.

Andy picked up Arges and an armful of statues and followed. With the smallest statues in her arms, Zita kept to his side, and Wyn joined them. A pair of giants carried the remaining stone animals. Thanks to one of Wyn's spells, diamonds of light floated above the procession, one for each individual, illuminating their path and immediate surroundings. The huge gate clanged shut behind them with a harsh finality once everyone was inside.

Foliage ran wild within, with no visible structures other than the walls they'd passed through and another set ahead of them. Elm, cherry plum, yew, and hazel battled with holly, ash, maple, and a variety of colorful shrubs and greenery for dominion. While smaller and thinner, an inner gate groaned under even more glowing embellishment. Thinner secondary walls shone a spotless white. Willows and alders whispered over the reeds that lined a cheerful river circling the interior city like a natural moat. The fresh scent of the water and plant life perfumed the air, undisturbed by any fires or signs of civilization.

"Did we already meet the whole town?" Zita whispered to her friends.

They passed through the second gate and finally saw buildings. All were in ruins, save two. One was a huge building with soaring pillars and ornate stonework accented with gold, as if someone had built an expensive museum in the center of the town. The other was modest in comparison, the size of a small mansion, notable only for the wide entry and the way it huddled in the shadow of the inner walls. Old boundaries were still visible, delineated by the type of plants dominating that property as each seemed to favor different flora.

While Chiron and most of the others continued on to the museum-like building, they secreted Arges in the most complete of the ruins, a tower with only one side missing. Yet another nymph grew a curtain of ivy over the open sides of the tower, obscuring the contents from view.

Once the cyclops had been safely stored, the ivy nymph and a faun led Zita and her friends to the smaller mansion.

When the goat-man tried to spirit Andy away, they protested being separated.

With the same horrified glee as if they'd handed her a delicious bit of scandal, the nymph explained that as gods, they would eat together, but that men and women had quarters in different sections of the house. They were also expected to bathe in separate hot springs before the evening meal.

A quick mental discussion had Zita and her friends agreeing to separate, but to keep party line active in case anyone needed aid.

As the chattering faun led him away, despite being warned that Andy spoke no Greek, Zita's friend had a polite, frozen smile on his face.

The ivy nymph led Zita and Wyn to another part of the house, with Wyn enthusing the entire way about the hot springs.

Zita was far happier to hear that dinner would follow their baths. She sniffed the air, and her nose wrinkled. *Much-needed baths.*

***

Following a copper-haired nymph and wearing masks and borrowed togas—or chitons or bedsheets or whatever they were—Zita found herself in a wide hall, with Wyn beside her. Wooden benches, decorated with linen and pillows, were arranged around shorter tables. At a nest of three couches, a taller table claimed center position with a pile of rugs and blankets beside it. Candles in elaborate metal holders were everywhere. Aromatic woodsmoke accented the cavalcade of tantalizing food odors and had her stomach rumbling. From the dishes, finely spiced meat and fish summoned her, with subtler odors from the nearby baskets of bread and vegetables teasing her. Spoons were the only silverware, and no cups graced the tables.

Why do they even have spare clothing anyway when almost everyone's naked? This place is so bizarre. Would diving face-first into the food be rude? Or make them laugh like offering to help with the cooking and cleaning did? Sweat beaded Zita's forehead as the nymph led them past the blazing hearth and gestured to the bench closest to the tall table. She fidgeted with a pin from her original toga, now holding her temporary clothing in place.

Wyn's eyes grew distant for a moment before they sharpened again. She seated herself at one end of the couch in a partially reclining position. *Follow my lead.*

"Please, sit where you will." The mellifluous alto of the nymph was studied, neutral. Tumbling copper tendrils escaped a fancy braided hairdo studded with tiny semiprecious stones. Unlike Greenie, this nymph was impressively muscled, with broad hips and shoulders. *She swims or wrestles. Given the way she plants her feet solidly with each step, it's probably the latter.*

Unsure what to pick, Zita sat on the same couch as Wyn, scooting to the very edge of the seat so her feet could rest on the floor. *Well, at least I'll be closer if anyone tries anything.*

The server flashed her a smile and joined the only other person in the room, a slender nymph with no muscle tone and purple curls accented by deeper purple flowers. Nonetheless, neither seemed to have trouble hefting the platters that groaned with food.

Zita's stomach gurgled, and she lost track of what she wanted to say momentarily as a nymph set a dish nearby.

Once both of the servers were outside earshot, she lowered her voice, even though she spoke in English. "Do you find it suspicious that Chiron showed up just as we were going to fight those centaurs? Don't tell me I'm being paranoid. This is a couple hours' hike from where we were, and they appeared out of nowhere."

"I could've used another hour or two in the baths. If I didn't want to be polite, I'd stand for the duration of supper. It has been far too long since I've ridden a horse." Wyn fussed with the fabric concealing her hair. A graceful wimple hid every curl in a fluid wash of fabric that framed her face. Instead of using a veil, she had followed Zita's example and crossed a couple strips of cloth to form an X-shaped mask that let her see and eat. *While he has been propitious to us so far, I do agree about Chiron's timing. I'd rather not mention any qualms aloud, however. In a land filled with magic, it's possible someone might understand what we say.*

Zita snickered. "The old guy likes your pretty butt. You should've just let Wingspan carry you."

Toying with the fabric of her wimple, Wyn huffed. "It would've been rude to refuse his generous offer, especially when we require their aid to return home. Also, he complimented my seat, not my derriere. An experienced equestrian knows how to sit to make it easier for their mount. He simply meant I comprehend how to properly ride a horse."

Not bothering to hide her amusement, Zita said, "Oh, is that what the kids are calling it these days? The dude's a centaur. How is that not dirty?"

Her friend batted at her with a hand and smiled sweetly at the server as another dish was delivered. Once the nymph moved out of earshot, Wyn changed the subject. "Speaking of suspicious, what's going on with the mercenary? You seemed shell-shocked on the way to Greece."

Zita started. "Oh, that. Nothing important." She scratched the back of her head and seized the opportunity to change the subject when the scent of hyacinths and spiced meat announced the presence of another dish and the purple-haired nymph. After muttering a quick thanks in Greek, she pointed to the new bowls and addressed her friend in English. "Hey, is that rabbit stew? I'm starving! You want to try some too?"

Wyn's head tilted back, and she sighed a long, dramatic exhalation. "Now, I know you're hiding something. Aren't we past this sort of elementary deflection? We both know you'd recognize food before I would, with few exceptions."

"Practice makes perfect," Zita said, hoping Wyn would take the bait.

His expression that of a hunted man, Andy slid onto the couch closest to the women. He also wore a borrowed toga with his thunderbird pins holding it in place. "Hey, what'd I miss?" Tension left from his shoulders as he spoke as if the presence of his friends soothed some secret worry.

"Arca's being difficult." Wyn pursed her lips.

"Well, sure, that's kind of her thing. She's short on social graces." He grinned and nudged Zita.

Wyn's eyes gleamed. "One could argue she is simply short."

"Height jokes, really? Feeling the love here, guys." Zita glanced at the food, wondering if it would be polite to start eating. *Or to stuff food into other people's faces to shut them up.*

Chiron trotted into the hall, the stutter in his walk announcing his identity before he was visible. "I fear Council matters delay me, but welcome to my home! I bid you, please break your fast! I will join you when I can." He gave a partial bow, murmured to the sturdy redhead, and left, tail swishing behind him.

"Freelance said something that shocked her, and she's reluctant to discuss it. Did he tell you how many people he's killed?" Her voice low, Wyn lifted an eyebrow. Her fingers hovered over the dishes of chopped meat, before changing course to steal a slice from a bowl of roasted leeks and apples.

As she picked out a roasted chunk of what was definitely rabbit from a dish, Zita took a moment to reply. She lowered the meat. "Oh, right. First off, no peeking, Muse."

"Food down! Food down! Something must be wrong," Andy whispered, a half-smile on his face. He perused the offerings and claimed a piece of flatbread smeared with a soft cheese.

Wyn blinked. "He told you that? If I'd peeked, I'd have little need to question you."

"No, nothing like that. Apparently, he thought we were dating or something? And now we're either broken up or secretly dating? It's not upsetting so much as confusing." Zita frowned at the rabbit chunk, then popped it into her mouth.

"What?" Wyn leapt to her feet. Her hands clenched into fists. "You've been doing what? His assumption that you were dating moves him from creepy android to creepy sociopathic stalker territory. We need to avoid him forever."

Andy opened his mouth, paused, and held out his hand. "Calm down, Muse. Why would he think that?"

"Did you miss the part where she said he assumed they're dating when she never encouraged him?" Despite her angry tone, Wyn did settle back into her seat.

His words slow, Andy eyed Wyn. "Subtlety is not one of Arca's talents. He might've noticed her ogling him and slobbering. Let's get the whole story before we condemn him."

After finishing the morsel of food, Zita had to defend herself. "I don't fawn over him or nothing, and I try not to stare at him even when he's not looking. There's no drooling... unless I'm a dog or some other animal at the time, and he's holding a sandwich." Sorrow filled her. "He's never holding a sandwich."

Andy snorted. "I'd be surprised if you fell all over anyone. What have you been doing?"

Zita shrugged. "We've been hanging out some, doing cool stuff. You know, climbing, jumping off high things, sports... I guess since we never said otherwise, he assumed we were dating. I never thought anything of it. Pues, I even tried to pretend like I wasn't checking him out to keep from making him uncomfortable."

"How much is hanging out some?" Andy's expression was speculative.

She had to think. "Maybe eight times since the thing with Dmitri in February? Possibly ten? Things happen, so sometimes we have to quit partway through or reschedule."

Wyn leaned forward. "Eight to ten times?" Her voice rose in both pitch and volume.

After lifting her hands in the air, Zita said, "I wasn't counting until you asked. We just kept coming up with more to do. Since I've been stuck mostly working out at home, why wouldn't I agree to go? A woman can only do so much cardio and weights in a small room, after all."

Andy's eyebrows rose, and he shook his head at Wyn. "Were your meets in public places?"

While waves of disapproval pulsed over party line from her, Wyn stayed quiet.

"No, that'd be hard to do with the masks and notoriety and all. Plus, a lot of the public places require money, and you know my budget," Zita said.

Shaking his head, Andy said, "Was it just the two of you doing stuff? I can't believe I'm asking but was there kissing or more?"

Wyn's expression promised nothing good.

Zita wrinkled her nose. "Yes, we were alone, but no kissing or naked fun times. Like I said, I even tried pretending like I didn't notice all that sexy competence. There was nothing to tell, so I didn't mention it. Mano, I invited you to some of our get-togethers. You weren't interested or were busy. And before you get offended, Muse, I figured you wouldn't want an invite since you're not into extreme sports. Between that and your weird fear of the guy, I figured you'd be happier not joining us."

Wyn touched the pendant at her throat. "Thank the Goddess for small favors, though you should've mentioned that's what you've been doing."

His ears red, Andy nibbled at his bread. "To be honest, I can see why he thought you were dating, though it would've been better if he'd said something. I mean, think about it. You have two jobs, hang with us, work out like a maniac, and do superhero duty as well as that week dealing with the mudslide, but you squeezed in that much time with him?"

Zita lifted her hands in the air. "It was fun! I do stuff alone with people all the time without it meaning anything. Pues, mano, we go bouldering on the regular, and the thought of dating you makes me want to barf."

"Flattering as always, though I feel the same way. Based on the practically nothing I know about him other than he doesn't talk and he's scary, I'm guessing other people don't just hang out with him." Andy grinned.

Their loss. Zita bit her tongue to keep her opinion from escaping.

Wyn took a deep breath. "I can't believe you didn't tell me. Tell us. We're both crushed that you kept it from us. But you're broken up now?"

After a quick glance to confirm that Andy seemed more interested in his cheese bread than in being distraught, Zita admitted, "Not sure. We might be? He said something about my reputation being protection for me, and him screwing that up. And I said maybe or agreed or something. So, I don't know if we're secretly dating or not dating or what."

A snicker came from Andy. "I know I shouldn't laugh, but this is so you. So, what are you going to do?"

An olive met its demise in Zita's mouth. "Talk to him about it when I see him next, I guess."

"And make certain he knows you're not dating?" Wyn leaned forward.

Zita licked her lips and braced herself. "Actually, I don't know. It would be complicated, and I'm not real good at people stuff. Then there's the masked aspect to consider. On the other hand, he's the best extreme sports partner I've ever had, fun, and... nice in a nonverbal way. Even kind of funny with these dry little jokes. If you blink, you miss them."

"Nice? He shot you the first time you met! Are we still talking about the same man who also shot Wingspan and me in Brazil?" Wyn's voice rose.

The nymphs paused and glanced at them, but when none of them said anything in Greek, went back to whatever arcane thing they were doing arranging food.

Andy's expression also seemed dubious.

"He didn't kill us, though, and he could've. In April, I mentioned I wasn't familiar with skiing or other winter sports, and he set up a snowboarding lesson in Colorado in May. Not to mention, he's all capable and sexy and stuff. I'd have to be loca to not consider it. Him. Us. Or whatever. Can we just eat?" Zita seized a piece of bread and stuffed it in her mouth.

Wyn gagged.

Andy eyed Zita. "If you do date him, how are you going to sabotage something with a man who doesn't talk?"

After finally swallowing, she rolled her eyes. "For the last time, I don't do that. Most relationships just don't work out. Whatever it is with him probably won't last either, but I might give it a try. First, though, we'll have to straighten the whole dating/not dating thing out, so I'll see if we can figure out a bunch of rules or something."

"Ah, that's how," Andy said.

Wyn shook her head. "Rules? Like no murdering while dating you?"

Zita wrinkled her nose at her friends. "Neta, guys. The man's a mercenary. I won't ask him to do something that might get him killed. I mean rules about dating other people. It's not like I can tell my family to stop fixing me up because I'm dating a hot dude whose name I don't know and can only communicate with via a stolen phone."

Andy nodded solemnly. "That's right, your oldest brother would have a heart attack. Poor guy, I can see it now."

Careful to avoid mentioning her brothers' names, Zita nodded. "Exactly. Though he's been dating that vet now for a few months so she could give him CPR or something. Not to sound like an awesome but cheesy kung fu flick, Middle Brother said that Mamá told him that Eldest Brother is getting serious enough about his girlfriend to scout out other jobs to avoid conflict of interest issues. Plus, his current... company... blows."

While Wyn's folded arms and glower did not abate, Andy smiled. "Think he'll invite you to the wedding?"

Zita waved a hand. "Of course. I'm family. Plus, someone's got to keep Middle Brother from sexing up all the bridesmaids and some of the guests if he falls off the no-sex wagon. Let's not get ahead of ourselves, though. She still needs Mamá's stamp of approval. Eldest Brother would never marry without that unless a baby was in the works. If I understand it right, a grandchild is like a super free pass for anything short of assassinating the Pope."

"That's lovely for him, but—" Wyn began.

Zita interrupted her friend as she had a wonderful thought. "In fact, if he gets the vet pregnant and they elope, there won't even be a wedding to sit through! That'd be awesome!"

"Yes, it would be very convenient for you," Andy said. He snickered.

She bounced in her seat. "I know, right? Skipping the wedding and getting a niece or nephew!"

Wyn cut into the conversation. "Aren't either of you taking this seriously? I don't like Freelance. He's dreadful and kills people. I think you should go back and tell him you're definitely not dating and not interested. He's unnatural." Wyn scowled.

Zita blinked. "You're a witch, sitting with a pair of shapeshifters in the house of a centaur in ancient Greece. Today we dealt with man-killing bees, tricked a cranky basilisk, and were attacked by multiple non-human creatures. Are you real sure unnatural is the word you meant, book girl?"

"This isn't actually ancient Greece," Wyn said. "It's more like... Hollywood's version, where Roman practices are mixed with Grecian and with what works on camera. Close, but not quite. Our clothing, for example, seems to be an odd combination of togas and chitons. The candles are too perfect to be authentic rushlights and never actually burn down. I spent some time in the bath rummaging through my memories of such things." She left out the fact that her photographic memory gave her a lot of material to peruse.

"And here I thought you were just complaining about your sore butt and taking forever with your hair and mask," Zita muttered. She sniffed at her cup and took a cautious sip. Finding nothing but a shake-like drink of barley water sweetened with honey and some herbs, she drank deeply.

Andy hummed. "Given our earlier discussion, my avian half seems to consider this just another spirit realm, another world above or below our usual one, like the layers in an onion or the many worlds of the Diné creation myth."

Wyn narrowed her eyes at Zita, but her expression lightened when her attention turned to Andy. "That would make sense, but it's a difficult conjecture to prove. You know, perhaps one of the ladies over there will reveal additional information to a friendly face." Rising, she drifted across the floor to the purple-haired server.

Andy watched Wyn walk away and then leaned closer to Zita. His voice was quiet. "Listen, no matter what Muse thinks, you need to decide for yourself what you want with Freelance. Personally, I think you should go for it if you've enjoyed being with him and think he might eventually be trustworthy enough to unmask for. If you don't feel that, don't coast along like you've been doing. It's not fair. He's not the kind of guy I'd hang with, but it's not fair to string him along just so you can do extreme sports with an attractive person. It's pretty clear from what you said earlier that you still think he's hot."

Zita nodded slowly.

Andy cut her off before she could reply. "Please don't elaborate. I feel girly enough just having this talk with you without it turning into an extended description of another man's body. Where do you see this thing with Freelance going?"

"Probably nowhere. Regular relationships are complicated enough, assuming you find one worth the time. If you add in both of us wearing masks, it's probably more trouble than it's worth."

"When did you ever go for easy? I'm pretty certain you do things the hard way for giggles. Look, we both know that neither of your brothers is ever going to find someone for you. Eldest Brother picks guys that'd be right for the woman he wants you to be, and Middle Brother chooses men he'd date were he a girl. All jokes aside, you're not your brothers, or Muse, or even me. What do you want? Don't answer, just think about it, okay?"

"I can do that," she said.

He took a deep breath. "While we're on this awkward subject, I should tell you... that is... I've been seeing..."

The burly nymph who had shown Wyn and Zita to the hall earlier sidled onto the bench beside him, cuddling up to his arm. She brandished a pitcher of the barley drink at them. "More kykeon? May I please you with anything else?"

Andy leapt out of his seat as if she'd set his toga on fire. He didn't ask for a translation. "Nymphs! They kept popping up and getting handsy while I was bathing too."

Zita glanced at him. "You want me to tell her no for you? I'm good at it."

"That's true. You're also good at saying how things wouldn't have worked out anyway," he said, rubbing his arms.

"Because it's usually true." Zita crossed her arms over her chest.

"Is it, though? Think about it. What do all your failed relationships have in common? I'll give you a hint, it's your refusal to budge on that assertation." Andy said. Even though he kept his face away from the nude nymph, his ears burned red beneath his olive skin.

Rich copper hair glinted as the nymph stood and stepped close to Andy. She ran her hand down his chest. "For a mighty god, you seem distressed. I am known for my skill with my hands and could ease your tension."

Andy jumped away with an inarticulate cry as if she'd poured acid on him. His hands flapped in the general direction of the men's quarters, and then he all but ran there. "Telling her no is good! You know, I forgot something in the bathing chambers. I'll be right back."

If his voice was higher than its usual register, Zita refrained from mentioning it when she called out after him, her brain still chewing through his advice. "Sure, I got this, and I'll have her tell the other nymphs. In the meantime, I'll be here. With the food and the food. Hurry back if you want to eat."

Chapter Nine

Her hand still outstretched, the sturdy nymph blinked after Andy's retreating back. "Have I angered you both? What troubles him? He will not even gaze upon me. Is he ill?"

"Sorry, tree girl. He's a big baby about nudity and doesn't speak your language. He also doesn't like people touching him without permission. Actually, all three of us all like people to ask first. If you could pass that along to the others, that'd be good. You're fine." After answering in Greek, Zita rolled her eyes and stuffed in another mouthful.

"Are we nymphs fallen so low that we are no longer mentioned in the studies of children? Clearly, I am of the mountain, not the trees. I would have thought you would know that, given your resemblance to my kind," the nymph said as she gestured to Zita's arms. "Do his preferences turn toward green bounty rather than the earth's kindness? This is my mountain, you know, but I know the Anthousai there would welcome him. I will tell the others that they must ask before touching." She nodded toward the purple-haired woman.

"Sorry, I didn't mean to be insulting. Nobody bothered to tell me anything about nymphs other than some live in trees or as trees or something like that." Zita nodded toward the approaching Wyn. "Muse over there would know what you're talking about, but I don't. Not to mention, the only other nymph we've spoken with has been a real bitch."

Her belligerence fading, the copper-haired nymph's head tilted. "Oh. Her. That is the way of it for us. Half of us, including that daughter of the oaks, wish no godly contact lest they are charged the penalty of womankind. The rest, including me, choose instead to pay, willing or no, but on our own terms. It is better to gain some control and perhaps even pleasure from it, rather than suffer the hunt and punishment. Now, all of us must choose whether we would risk a new pain or cling to a familiar one."

Wyn joined them in time to hear the nymph's reply. Behind her mask, her lids lowered to hide her eyes, though sorrow spoke in the graceful downward slope of her head. "We have no interest in the unwilling, especially when there is an imbalance. One of the things we do back home is stop those with power from harming those without," she said softly.

The nymph spared her a smile. "You are young in power yet, with choices to make. What I've seen so far is why my father and I—"

"Father?" Zita questioned. "Did we meet your dad?"

"Chiron. I am Melanippe, nymph of this mountain."

Father? How can a centaur have a human kid? Or nymph. Or any kind of non-horse-body kid? Zita managed to keep the questions from spilling out aloud only because she'd taken too big a bite in her surprise.

Mythological genetics. In most cases, you don't want to know. Wyn replied. Her eyes sparkled, a sign that she'd heard something interesting as she gracefully sank back into her seat.

Andy's agreement was brief from wherever he was hiding. *Believe Wyn.*

"Legend has it that you know almost everything that happens on your mountain. Before we came here, we were in a cave with several other people, criminals we were chasing. A woman with scars on half her face, a blond man who talked a lot, and several others. Have you seen any of them?" Wyn delicately plucked a grape from a dish and ate it.

Melanippe paused before answering slowly. "Anything that affects my earth is known to me, but sometimes the mountain does not notice the same things as mortals. The three of you and your wolf are the only newcomers to my mountain—unless these others hide in the shapes of trees or animals?"

Zita shrugged. "As far as we know, they don't have shapeshifters other than Garm, but they had guys I didn't recognize."

Wyn concurred quietly.

"Then none of the nymphs of the land or trees have seen them, for word would have spread quickly of strangers in our midst, especially any that would wear the mantle of a god or hero."

"Speaking of your mountain, why didn't we see Olympus from the air when we were searching for it? I know Wingspan and I both passed over this section. How did we miss it?" Zita said.

The nymph chuckled. "If you live here or are a god attuned to this realm, you can see it. Otherwise, you can only come to Olympos if guided or granted a quest to do so. I can also permit people to find it, as I will do while you are cleansing your names, though you will require a guide to pass through the gates. Do not fear, we shall know when you are here and have someone stand ready to aid you."

Zita sighed. "Right, more magic stuff." She ate.

Amusement danced on Melanippe's face, and she patted Zita's shoulder.

Wyn tilted her head, curiosity on her face. "So, gods who weren't attuned... who were they?"

The nymph shrugged. "I do not know. The ones who are can find it and allow others to become attuned. The ones that are not, cannot. In times long gone, when Zeus angered the snake-dragons of an eastern land, they chased him here until they lost him behind Olympos' concealment."

"What did he do?" Curiosity lit Wyn's face.

Melanippe grimaced. "The more he held, the greater his glory. With that came more power, so he left to conquer. Fortunately, other lands were not so easily subjugated as he hoped, even though he ranged quite far. My father could tell you more. For most of us, man's legends obscure true history, but Chiron retains more as he has ever been the teacher."

Hooves clattered on the marble floor. As if summoned, the centaur entered the dining hall from the men's quarters, one hand on Andy's shoulder. With one last pat on Andy's shoulder, the centaur settled his equine bulk onto the blankets and pillows of the largest table with a pained groan.

His eyes avoided the nymph, and Andy returned to his old seat. He gave a little wave.

Behind him, Greenie and a pair of satyrs strolled over to another set of benches nearby. The nymph claimed one for herself while ostentatiously keeping a level stare on Chiron. The satyrs shared another and set to eating.

Chiron dipped a hand into a bowl and began to eat. "Forgive my absence. I fear matters arose that required immediate handling. However, I found good Wingspan when I returned, and we had a lovely stroll back in together. Is that not true, my friend?"

Andy returned a weak smile and bobbed his head. *I have no idea what he's saying. Or what he said earlier.*

One of the goat-men raised a cup to his lips and nearly spat out the liquid within. "Could I get some wine?"

Melanippe rose to her feet and topped off drinks. She narrowed her eyes at the satyrs. "Nay, you know spirits are banned in the homes of civilized centaurs. Only the wildlings still drink. "

The satyr stared at his beverage, and his shoulders slumped. "I hoped the kykeon was a fever dream, but thank you, even if the drought kills my companion and myself."

His mouth full, the other goat-man nodded with a lugubrious expression.

Greenie purred, "The mountain is most generous to guests, is it not?"

"More so than any of the acorn-flinging weeds who flee from hospitality as if it would poison their roots." Melanippe flounced away.

Chiron stared at his own drink but made no attempt to touch it. After a moment, he straightened and smiled. "My apologies again for missing the beginning of the meal. When the Council calls, I must answer. Our new companions are here to witness that you receive no gifts outside my hospitality that may aid in your quests."

Andy shot Zita a questioning look.

In English, she whispered, "The new guys want booze. Melanippe said centaurs don't drink, and then she and Greenie were getting all up in each other's faces. Chiron apologized for the Council making him late and saddling us with the spies over there to make sure he doesn't tell us too much." She shrugged and took a swig of water.

He grimaced. "Ah. Politics."

Apparently, while Wyn's attention appeared focused on Chiron and the new guests, she had heard the summation. *You are aware that's not exactly what he said, right?*

It's called a summary. You know you can get those for books, too. They're faster than reading the whole thing. Huge time saver.

Hush your mouth, foul blasphemer. A laugh carried across the mental connection, lightening the librarian's rebuke. Wyn smiled and spoke aloud in Greek. "Do your duties as a Council member take a great deal of your time?"

"No, sometimes it would be decades between meetings, but the land seems to have been awakened from its long slumber recently, perhaps with your presence?" The old centaur's eyes twinkled, and he ate something green.

A discreet, feminine cough came from the nearby benches when Chiron began to speak again.

Whatever else he had meant to say, Chiron kept to himself.

Her face as serene as if nothing had happened, Wyn changed topic. "You mentioned previously that others came before us. Who were they?"

The centaur brightened. "Ah, history, a great favorite of mine! Which did you wish to know of? The long-ago mortals who claimed the thrones of the gods or the more recent ones?"

Greenie cleared her throat. "Not too much about either, revered teacher, until such a time as they have shed their dishonor."

Chiron's tail flicked several times, but his expression did not change.

Zita didn't know whether to be pleased that an in-depth history lecture had been averted or annoyed at the cause. At the visible frustration on Wyn's face, she buried her glee. She pressed a succulent bowl of honeyed figs into Wyn's hand and grumbled in English. "Told you the quests were stupid. At least they're feeding us."

Her friend gave her a half-smile and determinedly tried again. "We would love to hear what you can tell us of both, without going against the Council dictates, of course."

The centaur gave her a paternal smile. "I would be delighted to speak with you. As I am and have always been the teacher, less of the past is lost to me. Most here tend to live in the present, remembering only the major insults and glories of history rather than the trivia. Let us begin with the distant past. While I do not clearly recall the time before, select humans fell into long slumbers during the same week or two. Those who survived awakened as gods and heroes."

Zita and her friends exchanged glances.

Wyn said, "Were they all equally powerful? How many times did this happen?"

Chiron shook his head. "Once only, and nay, many had merely slight tricks, like the curly-haired Boreads or fleet-footed Atalanta. Some had power enough, like Orpheus with his enthralling music or Circe with her cursed swains. Only a few shall we name as gods, such as he who claimed the mantle of Zeus. Or yourselves, though it is strange that our last guests made no mention of you and said new gods were surpassingly rare. Tell me, has the invasion of the sky monsters begun again?"

Without him needing to ask, Zita summarized for Andy. "Supers happened a long time ago, pretty much the way they did with us. Then Chiron asked if sky creatures had attacked again."

"Do you know why or how it is that some have abilities and some do not? And how can you tell which is which? What do you mean, an invasion?" Wyn's eyes were wide and bright.

Greenie cleared her throat loudly.

Chiron's tail flicked. "We know the mightiest of mortals, those we term gods, when we see them, if they do not take pains to hide their abilities. The heroes, greater and lesser, we cannot tell from ordinary humans. Or wolves. Had the wolf not spoken, we would have thought him merely Arca's pet."

"Boy, that would've cheesed off Garm," Andy commented when he got an interpretation.

Zita chortled. "I know, right?"

Wyn had better focus. "Is spotting gods something we could learn? And you never answered what you meant about the sky creatures?"

"With time, you may learn if you will it. Heroes never grow in power, only in their skill with that which they've been given. A god such as yourself may grow in ability with age and desire. The abilities closest to their hearts come first and most gently. She who was Athena—"

Greenie interrupted. "Tread carefully."

The old centaur glared at the nymph. "She who was Athena learned battle styles with but a simple demonstration. However, she struggled to cast magic to change her appearance so much that she frequently used the same tricks as mortal actors."

The nymph cleared her throat. "Enough said on such things."

Excitement and exasperation ran through Wyn's mental comment. *That explains why flight in human form didn't hurt Andy, but language acquisition hurts you, Zita. Bless her heart, Greenie is ruining what would otherwise be a lovely educational discussion.*

Chiron continued speaking. Only the persistent flick of his tail betrayed any kind of reaction; his face was placid. "As for the invasion, clearly it has not happened, or you would understand. Once you've emerged victorious from your quests, I will be free to speak of anything we wish. However, as I would not ruin the sanctity of your quests, I will speak of history in only the barest of terms. Even the esteemed daughter of oaks might allow that, as the present is constructed of the materials of the past."

"You said something about mortals with powers stealing from the gods?" Wyn settled into questioning him, with Zita interpreting for Andy quietly.

His face and body relaxed as the old centaur warmed to his topic. "Yes, the most powerful found each other—for the Fates bind like to like—and claimed the worship owed to the true gods of Olympos. I know not how they did so, for it was a secret known only to them. One day, they were there, and we were vassals."

Wyn couldn't help but comment after interpreting for Andy. "Fascinating. He may be unable to conceive of anything outside of his theological framework, and hence it's all hazy to him."

When she was done speaking, Chiron said, "The new gods built upon their conquest here, reshaping it so that none in the mortal world and few here, on pain of death or suffering, knew of their mortal origins. However, even their might could not escape that which befalls all save true immortals. By the time Aléxandros ho Mégas rode out in conquest, the gods could no longer sustain their reign or their lives. Despite that, their names must have lived on in glory, or we would no longer be here."

Wyn's eyes were distant. By the time Zita finished filling in Andy, her attention had returned to the present. She added to the interpretation, "His reference implies the first wave of metahumans died out around the time of Alexander the Great, so it's been a very long time."

The centaur leaned back against his seat and ate a mouthful. "The world has undoubtedly grown fascinating and wild without the fickle guidance of the gods. Humanity's view of such must've changed, though I see that many of our old concepts remain. We met the Craftsman and Monster before, and in you, I see the Witch, Trickster, and—" his voice trailed off for a moment as he considered Andy—"the Protector?"

When he had been told what Chiron had said, Andy scoffed. "I'm just a man who turns into a bird and is a little extra tough."

"That's like saying the sun's a little bit warm. Buey. Who's in denial now? If any of those descriptions are wrong, it's me. I'm honest and shit, not like a liar or stuff." Zita scoffed, keeping her comments in English.

Wyn was gentler. "Your avian form does resemble some of the legends of Thunderbird, and you have mentioned that spirit was a protector in the stories you were raised with."

Around another mouthful of food, Zita said, "Not to mention, mano, you get all squiggly when people are in danger. Remember when we had to go to Vegas because your... someone... was in danger? You said it's like an 'other people in danger sense' or some shit like that makes you all tingly when there's a fight. That last bit might've been a euphemism."

Andy's response was pained. "Nice, Arca."

Wyn turned back to the centaur. "Fascinating! We do have concepts of superheroes, mortals with abilities beyond those of the common man. They're merely human, though."

The centaur sounded out the English word. "Whether you are one of these 'superheroes' or gods, you must purify your names before I may say much more. It would be my greatest delight to speak with you on any topic." He glanced at Greenie, and his tone turned dry. "I do enjoy civilized discourse."

"Who doesn't? What about the more recent past? You mentioned Clockwork and Dragon?"

Chiron inclined his head. "Yes, it was... not long ago. Less than a century, more than a decade. Clockwork had found an artifact that intrigued him, and he used it to trigger one of the few remaining gates to Olympos. He stayed with me, and we had such fascinating conversations! He was particularly interested in the previous invasion and the passing of the old gods. Dragon accompanied him, though she never entered Olympos proper, preferring the meadow outside. One day, Clockwork chose to explore a site that had been a subject of some conversation. She went with him. Neither returned, and while we knew of no explosions, we assumed them both dead until you mentioned seeing Dragon. They were here for perhaps a week."

Zita couldn't help but ask. "Where did they go?"

"He can't say," Greenie interrupted.

The old centaur chewed his food very deliberately. "I fear I may say no more. Perhaps you could regale us with tales of your adventures? Arca, what thrilling adventure left you with a stone foot? I confess I missed it when first we met, but it must be quite the tale!"

The otherwise delicious food turned to ash in Zita's mouth, and she had to take a swig of the barley drink to wash it down. "We went to an island with a basilisk on our way to the bees on some incredibly bad advice. It didn't work out as well as we'd hoped."

Proving that everyone was listening in, all other conversation in the room stopped.

A goat-man frowned. "Does not one among you claim to be a witch? You didn't curse the beast or charm it or work a spell upon it to kill it?"

Her face paling, Wyn stared at her hands. "My magic is a part of my faith. It works with the natural order, not against it, and any harm I wrought with it would return to me threefold. I..." Shoulders slumping, she finished in a whisper. "I would've stopped it if I could've."

"I was too slow when I sprang the trap on it. Muse did her part of the plan perfectly," Zita cut in. She fought the urge to bounce her leg up and down—no use drawing more attention than she already had.

Chiron frowned. "That is from the basilisk? But it did not turn you completely? Such a thing has never happened. Either one becomes stone or does not. A god should not be afflicted so." He gave his daughter a look.

Melanippe shook her head slightly.

"We told you we aren't gods. Is there a cure?" Zita blurted. Her question must've held more of a bite than she thought because Wyn set a hand on her shoulder.

"The Council willed you give them no aid," Greenie snapped out.

With deliberate slowness, Chiron took a long drink from his cup and set it down. "The Council need have no fear of me overstepping my bounds. Unfortunately, even could I speak, I have no aid to give. None of the gods ever suffered such a fate before. If our magic affected them, they would always use their power to drive away the effects and then punish their attacker, whether the insult was intentional or not."

The two satyrs stopped eating and craned their necks to stare at Zita. "Didn't one northern god have a false hand? Perhaps it will be the symbol of her godhood?"

Eyes wide, the purple-haired nymph nodded. "So it could be!"

They're talking about the Norse god Tyr, who sacrificed his hand to bind the evil wolf Fenrir. Fascinating that they can be aware of other spirit realms enough to have heard of him. Fascinating! Wyn leaned toward the satyrs, her mouth opening.

Greenie began, "Petrification is always permanent. Perhaps she lacks—"

"Enough!" Unable to sit still any longer, Zita exploded to her feet and began pacing.

Everyone in the room fell silent and stared at her. The loudest sound was that of her petrified foot hitting the floor.

A sound I might have to get used to. Zita ran a hand over her hair and fought to drag in air.

"Arca…" Wyn began, half-rising from her seat.

Andy was already on his feet, face stricken. *Z?*

Wyn whispered a quick summary to him.

Hearing it all again increased Zita's restlessness threefold. Aware she was overreacting and unable to help it, Zita straightened her shoulders and smiled, forcing her body into a casual pose despite her need to move. "Muse will fix it when she gets a chance. It's late for me, so I'll just take a walk and go to bed." She waved and left the room. Her steps sped up with no witnesses. *Stay and enjoy the meal, guys.*

We'll come with, Andy sent.

Wyn sent agreement and added more. *We need to talk about the petrification. You've been avoiding the subject.*

Before they could catch up, she switched to a jog, escaping into the fragrant summer night outside. Her attention caught on the bulk of the tower, dark against the moonlight. *Don't. It's not that big a deal, but all this has been a lot to... uh, process or some shit like that. Get your eat on and relax. See you tomorrow.*

Is climbing in the dark wise, considering? Wyn's comment accompanied a thick wave of worry.

Andy was only a second behind her. *I'll come spot you while you climb, so you don't fall.*

Zita paused. *How did you know that's—never mind. I promise I'll just run around a little and then go to bed. No climbing. I'm fine, just tired.*

Party line buzzed, and she suspected her friends were conferring behind her back as she began free running through the ruins, sticking to moonlit areas as she vaulted over obstacles and bounced off trees. Her foot unbalanced her, sending her tumbling a few times as she tried to compensate for her condition. *Can't have them fretting all night.*

Careful to lighten her tone, Zita sent, *I'm for real fine, not like Wyn needing ice cream fine. Though if you find any of that, I wouldn't say no.*

Her friends' relief flowed across the link as she'd hoped with the joke, even though the words were a lie.

Chapter Ten

The next morning, Zita and her friends followed a young satyr from the half-crumbled tower holding the stone cyclops back to Chiron's home. Their original togas had been returned, cleansed and sweetly fragrant from air drying.

Their guide seemed to feel the need to fill the silence with his many and varied opinions on inconsequential matters, including breakfast. "I've never seen anyone but a giant eat that many tiganites."

Andy leaned in. "What'd he say?"

Zita told him.

He nodded. "I have to agree with him. Watching you down all those pancakes was pretty impressive, and I've eaten with you before."

She rubbed her too-full stomach. "Órale, I was hungry and figured I should eat while I had the chance. It was good though. Not to mention, I got up early and talked to Chiron about javelins and other sports stuff. Real old-school Olympics and all that." Her new, uneven gait held a bounce as she was unable to contain her jubilation that the stone had not progressed overnight.

He grunted. "Figures."

The satyr continued the stream of chatter, most of which Zita tuned out.

Wyn said nothing and picked her way to the building. Her shoulders slumped, and her lip trembled.

Andy and Zita exchanged glances. He said, "I'm sure you'll get the spell to remove the petrification right next time. I mean, you did manage to turn the statue back into chicken."

"But it was dead. It shouldn't have been dead," Wyn said softly.

Zita patted her back awkwardly. "But at least it didn't explode like the one on the island?"

Her witchy friend winced.

Andy grimaced and gave Zita a curt shake of his head.

She held up her hands in surrender and mouthed, "I tried" to him.

He patted her shoulder.

Chiron, Greenie, and a handful of others stood on the steps of the old centaur's home. Melanippe's coppery hair shone in the sunlight among them.

Right before they reached the crowd, Wyn lifted a hand to stop and turned to Zita. "Are you certain you want to come along? We wouldn't blame you or think less of you if you wanted to stay here while we go questing."

Andy nodded. "What she said."

Zita snorted and waved a hand downward. "My foot won't be any less rock if I sit around and stare at it. I just have to work harder to accomplish things, and I've never been afraid of a little extra effort."

"We still should talk about it. You can't avoid the topic forever," Wyn said.

She cocked her head at her friend. "There's nothing to say. My foot's granite. You'll figure out a way to turn it back eventually. If we get home before you do, I'll just claim it's broken and not explain how it happened. Everyone will assume I did something foolish. Topic done."

Wyn opened her mouth, glanced at Andy, and then her shoulders slumped. "It's your choice. I swear I'm doing my best."

Frowning, Zita clapped her friend on the shoulder. "I know. You'll get it. I have faith."

The young satyr reached the crowd and turned around. Surprise shone on his face when he noticed they'd stopped following him. He called out, "Did you need help to walk up the stairs?"

Zita almost growled at him. "No. We're all good." Without giving her friends time to say otherwise, she stomped and hobbled to the group of creatures.

Wyn and Andy hurried after.

Once they were there, Chiron tapped his spear twice against the ground. "For your next labor, you must retrieve one of the golden apples that grow in the Garden of Hesperides and bring it here."

Greenie smirked.

Wyn pursed her lips, her eyes distant.

"It's not apple season. Do we got to wait for the fall to get an apple? We don't have that kind of time. Maybe we could find some late-season ones in the southern hemisphere, but apples weren't native there, so the odds of finding any..." Zita frowned.

"Truly, whatever animal suckled you was an ignorant one. The Garden was sacred to Hera, and the apples therein magical. They grow year-round." Greenie sneered at her.

Folding her arms over her chest, Zita scowled at the dryad. "Don't insult my mother. She's a saint, not an animal. I'm surprised you don't know how trees work being part tree or something and all."

Beside her, Wyn straightened, her long lashes lowering. "Magic trees and unnatural seasons, Arca. May I ask one question?"

Chiron nodded.

Greenie held up a hand. "You may, but we will not allow him to answer should it be too much an aid."

Inclining her head to the nymph, Wyn said sweetly, "Which of the homes near here belonged to Aphrodite?"

Blinking, Greenie said, "The one to the south, with the reflecting pool."

Behind her, Chiron's face was curious for a moment, and then he smirked.

"Thank you. Bless your heart for answering." Wyn switched to English. "Arca, Wingspan, let's get this quest done." With those words, she swept out of the temple, toga swirling around her legs.

After exchanging shrugs, Andy and Zita followed. Greenie, the centaurs, and the other assorted creatures trailed after them.

Wyn leaned close to them and said in English, "I have an idea. Which of these piles of rubble are to the south?"

Zita pointed, turning it into a gesture when Andy winced.

"Excellent," Wyn murmured and strode that direction. She paused in front of a rectangular pool, mostly filled with rock, tilting her head as she surveyed the palace ruins. "This one, I think. Arca, would you see if you can detect an apple beneath the rubble?"

"What makes you think I'd be able to sniff one out under all that?" Zita's eyebrows shot upward as she eyed the collapsed building.

Wyn giggled. "It's food. You're you."

"Good point." Zita shifted to a bloodhound and inhaled as the world suddenly sharpened into olfactory brilliance. Her petrified paw was easier to manage with three others to help her balance. Smacking her lips, she began picking her way through the rubble. *Rock, mold, rock, gold... oye. That smells as good as fresh-baked apple pie appears in commercials! Now that's some magic.* She sat and bayed for the sheer joy of noise. Her tail may have thumped.

"I do believe we have a winner. Wingspan, would you do the honors of removing the debris from atop our prize? Arca, would you watch for the fruit?" Wyn smiled sweetly and waved to the crowd as if she were in a beauty pageant.

His brow furrowed, Andy strode over to Zita. Obediently, he lifted heavy chunks of marble aside.

Memories of digging through the mudslide brought a sour taste to Zita's mouth. She shifted back to Arca rather than continuing as a dog. Determined to ignore the increasing stiffness in her bad leg, she helped him move smaller pieces of rubble.

When yellow gleamed after a few minutes of their joint effort, Andy bent and passed it to Zita. Despite its time buried under the ruins, it was lustrous, unbruised, and perfect, other than a thin layer of dust and a phrase carved into it. Her mouth watered at the smell, even in human form, and she couldn't help polishing some of the dust off. She carried it over to Wyn. "Don't know how you knew that was there, but good job."

"Thank you. I do enjoy reading a nice bit of mythological history sometimes." Wyn clasped her hands together, a pleased smile on her lips. After accepting the fruit, she turned to the assembled crowd and asked, "Now, we have a magical apple from the Garden of Hesperides. To whom should we give this?"

Greenie's strident voice rose over the movements and quiet exclamations of the crowd. "It should not count. They did not go to the Garden nor deal with the dragon! How do we know it is not merely a trick or one they hid among their belongings?" She shoved her way to the front and scowled.

"We don't have pockets," Zita muttered but kept her words in English.

Andy elbowed her and then brushed dust off his spare cape. *Diplomacy, Z.*

Why does that always seem to involve me keeping my mouth shut? She harrumphed but bit back any further commentary.

Wyn turned over the apple and showed Chiron an inscription on it. Her eyes sparkled. "Is this not the Apple of Discord that sparked the Trojan War?"

The centaur examined it. "So it is. Clever of you." He held the apple above his head, and his voice boomed out over the crowd. "The fruit holds the inscription of the fateful contest. I declare this task complete."

Andy and Zita exchanged a quick fist bump.

"Do you all not believe me now? While I hold no power to bid the mighty Council to do aught, I am certain they have much to discuss," Greenie called out.

A giant grunted. "Very well. We will convene in the megaron immediately."

Surprise flashed across Chiron's face before his expression fell into businesslike lines. "As the Council wishes. Shall I give them their next quest first?"

The giant who had spoken shook his head. "No, for this concerns them."

With a pinched expression, the old centaur addressed Zita and her friends. "Walk Olympos freely but stay within the inner walls. We shall send someone to fetch you once consensus has been achieved."

"Pues, a government body reaching agreement in a few minutes? Guys, we'll be here forever." Zita groaned and rolled her eyes. "Well, at least I have ideas for how to pass some of the time. Where'd we put those javelins? You guys want to learn how to throw them, right?"

"I should concentrate on interplanar travel and reversing the petrification effect while you two throw sticks around," Wyn said.

"Nice try," Zita said. "Don't worry, you'll love it once you try it. Or hate it." She tried to keep her thoughts quiet and off the shared party line. *In any case, hopefully, it'll distract you from being upset about the delay. I'm not thrilled, but my family's sanity and life isn't at stake this time.*

Wyn sighed and trailed after. "I know which of the two is most likely."

With a laugh, Zita headed back to the centaur's home.

From behind her, she heard a gasp. "Your leg!"

"Did I step in something? I don't have feeling in the one." Zita glanced down and froze.

Her leg was now stone to her knee.

***

After her friends had given the javelins a few cursory throws, they returned to the ruins that held the stone cyclops. Wyn had seated herself near Arges and the few remaining stone birds, sketching runes in the dirt and then erasing them. Andy alternated between standing protectively near the witch and hovering at the base of the crumbling tower. Zita was exploring the necessary changes to climbing, given the stone leg, using the sturdiest wall in her Arca form as a test subject. All of them ignored Wyn's latest failure, a living goose of gray stone and volatile temperament, currently distracted by a cloudy mirror Zita had borrowed from Chiron's home.

She had refused to discuss the change to her leg, instead throwing herself into the climbing, even if all her skill could not completely override the inflexibility of her petrified limb. When she paused halfway up, enjoying the light burn of exertion and view of the ruins, a young faun emerged from the museum-like building and ran to Chiron's house. A moment later, he ran out and shouted, but the wind tangled his words into incomprehensible knots.

"Guys, I think they want us," she called down.

After a rapid mental conversation, Wyn strolled out of the tower and over to the goat-man. When she returned, she collected her belongings from the rock she'd been working on, stowing them in her bag.

Taking that as a hint, Zita began a careful descent.

Wyn glanced up and shuddered. *We've been summoned for our next quest. Even with your propensity for heights, I don't know how you can stand climbing that. It could collapse at any moment! Is it wise with your leg, anyway?*

Zita scoffed. *The blocks are solid, undamaged stone, and their sheer weight is holding this wall together. That's more than enough structural integrity to handle my weight and then some, though I wouldn't suggest Birdy McLardbutt perch on it until someone does maintenance. With the exception of Chiron's place and the fancy-ass palace on the hill, none of the other buildings or even the other walls of this tower seem sturdy enough to climb at all. They've got too many pieces missing. As for my foot, I've got things to do that won't wait, and climbing is one of them. Andy's there to catch me if I fall.*

When she reached the bottom a few seconds later, she bowed.

"Show-off," Andy said, but his smile took any sting from the insult.

Wyn led them to the museum-like building. "He said they're waiting for us in the megaron inside."

"What's a megaron?" Andy asked.

Wyn paused. "It's a combination of a throne room and feast hall, I suppose. Like Chiron's dining hall, but grander. It seems to be where the Council convenes."

As they passed through the antechambers of the only other intact building other than Chiron's home, Zita eyed the high, ornate walls. "This place might be a fun climb, but hopefully, we won't be here that long," she mused.

Wyn sent a single word. *Focus.*

"Oh, that smile says we're in trouble." Andy came to a sudden stop in the vestibule doorway, blocking entry into the room beyond. After a long moment, he stepped aside to allow the women entry. *Greenie is way too happy.*

Wyn murmured her thanks, and the three paused to survey the chamber that served as the main gathering place of the Council that Chiron had yet to explain to them.

The megaron made Chiron's dwelling seem modest. Within it, a variety of creatures, with no more than two or three of each kind, stood in small, awkward groups around the room, as if having more of any one type had been forbidden. Unhappily, a familiar green-haired woman stood among them, a mean smile on her face. The room was configured oddly. A hearth claimed the center of the room, surrounded by four columns supporting the roof. Sub-chambers led off on all the sides save the one through which they had entered. Benches and low tables were scattered throughout. An exquisite tile mosaic of sea life glowed from a pool scented strongly of salt and housing two fish-tailed men. On the opposite side of the hall, an empty pool smelled of freshwater and was decorated with reeds, frogs, otters, and similar imagery. Silenus snored on a chaise by the water, his cup cradled close like a beloved stuffed toy. A battered purple fleece covered him like a blanket.

I guess the empty one is for freshwater fish-men? How did they get in there anyway if they don't have legs to walk from the nearest river? More magic crap, I bet. Are those just there for them to lounge around in? They're too small to do laps without a bar. If it bubbled, it could be a hot tub, but it's just about the size you'd want for a walrus to take a nap, or several frogs could have a good time. Maybe a koi pond? As they moved forward, she glanced in the water. *No actual fish other than the dudes.*

Next to the fire, Chiron waited at the base of a set of steps up to a raised dais. Two piles of black marble rubble covered the top of the platform, one significantly larger than the other. Both glinted with hints of twisted gold, echoed in the trim of the stairs to the raised platform, each of the seven steps a different color of the rainbow.

His tail flicked, and his face was sober as the old centaur gestured them to come closer.

"If they think we smashed whatever used to be on the platform, I'm not taking the blame for that too," Zita warned her friends. They nodded, and the three approached as a unit. Without needing to say anything, Andy and Zita kept Wyn sandwiched in the middle.

One of the fish-men blew them—most likely Wyn, but it was hard to tell—a kiss. The other flashed them a coy smile and tossed his soggy hair.

Wyn smoothed the front of her toga. Her chin hitched upward, and her shoulders set. "This too, we shall handle with aplomb and grace." As the warmth of party line connected the three friends, she continued mentally, *It's not like we have another choice. Zita, try to be quiet and appear less like you think they're going to backstab us unless you punch them first.*

As entertaining as smacking obnoxious people can be, I'd rather go home, Zita sent back. She tried to school her expression to blankness or at least a neutral expression that hid her frustration.

Andy frowned at the women. *Whatever's going on, Chiron's not thrilled. Z, are you okay? You have this constipated expression on your face.*

She huffed out a breath and abandoned attempting to be inscrutable. Her gaze caught on an eagle-headed, winged lion that appeared to be holding a soft, one-sided conversation with a knitting minotaur. After a blink, she refocused her attention. *So bizarre.*

When they reached the centaur, a long moment of staring passed with no one breaking the silence.

Unable to wait any longer, Zita blurted out, "We've finished two quests. Now, what's the last one?"

The green-haired nymph practically skipped over to the old centaur, carrying the long spear that Chiron had used earlier. She poked Chiron with a twiggy finger. "Speak now, old one, or risk losing all."

"Oh, joy. Greenie's playing prompter. That can only mean good things for us." Zita rolled her eyes but kept her commentary in English.

Andy murmured, "Perhaps we'll get to go throw the One Ring into the volcano this time."

A startled giggle erupted from Wyn, and she covered her mouth with her hand. "Shush, you two. You're not helping."

Andy grinned when Zita frowned at him. "Never mind, Arca."

The centaur trotted a few steps forward. "My friends. I regret that our deliberations took so much time. I again give you my apologies, but dire things have happened that must be rectified, and I fear your quests must be stricken from the records."

"What?" Zita squawked. At a sharp elbow to her side from Wyn, she closed her mouth with a click.

Diplomacy, Wyn sent, though her knuckles were white where they clenched the delicate linen of her toga. "Can you clarify what you mean?"

Guilt flashed on Chiron's face before his normal stoic expression hid it. "Since your return from your quests, the Council verified your deeds, and they have decided that you may claim no glory from your first quest as you sought and received aid."

Zita exploded on party line. *They've been fact-checking us? And we failed? What the—*

Wyn cut her off. *The ancient Grecian gods were not known for their veracity, so I can't blame them.*

Do they get to do that? Are you certain punching someone is out of the question? Zita swore internally.

Wyn folded her hands in her lap. "That we could receive no aid was not specified when we accepted the tasks. We requested the beekeeper harvest the honey to keep the maximum number of bees safe, per the conditions actually given to us."

The dryad couldn't wait for the centaur to finish speaking and gestured at Zita. "Additionally, one among you stole honey for themselves, so you gain no glory from your second quest either."

Wyn and Andy groaned and turned to Zita.

She lifted her hands in the air. "What? It smelled delicious, and I didn't steal it. I asked permission."

"Is this truth? Did any approve the gift?" Chiron turned to face the other creatures.

A low murmur ran through the room.

Zita folded her arms over her chest. "I'm not a thief. The beekeeper was cool with it and even put it in the jar for me. Go ahead and ask him."

Greenie's lip curled. "He has no authority to give honey to anyone."

"Then he should've said so! I can give it back if it's a problem. Muse, it's in your bag."

Frustration visible in the stiff set of her shoulders, Wyn dug through her bag and pulled out a fist-sized jar. *I knew I should've asked what you needed the container for. Why would you do that? You should never take anything unless it's explicitly given to you here.*

Nobody mentioned that to me! Zita accepted the jar from her friend.

It's a standard rule when visiting a spirit realm! Wyn scowled at her.

I asked first! And is someone going to fill me in on everything I don't know? It was meant to be a birthday present for you. Organic magic bee honey for your tea.

Andy set his hand on Wyn's shoulder. *Relax, it was an honest mistake. For future reference, Zita, take only what they offer, and nothing more.*

Wyn sighed. "We apologize for the misunderstanding."

"What's done is done, and you must suffer the price of it." Glee infused Greenie's words.

Tapping her chin, Zita asked, "If we're being penalized for taking it, do I get to keep it?"

A fish-man splashed water at Greenie. "That seems fair. Permission granted!"

"Witnessed and approved," Chiron said.

After ostentatiously turning her back on the pool of water, Greenie licked her lips. "Do tell them the rest, honored Chiron."

His tail flicked rapidly, though his expression did not change. "The Council recognizes your ignorance, and thus you have not been awarded additional quests, only bidden to complete three quests, as before. In their wisdom, they have decided it was my failure to draw the lines clearly enough for you. In my stead, they have awarded the position to the next eldest councilor." Here, his countenance flickered as he glanced toward the slumbering silenoi.

Silenus scratched his butt and flopped over, never pausing in the steady rumbling snores.

Wyn eyed him. "Should we wake him?"

"No need." Greenie flourished the spear. Her malicious smile spread. "Although I am only a humble dryad, the wise Silenus appointed me to speak in his stead."

A particularly large snore interrupted her gleeful pronouncement.

Chiron's voice was quiet. "It is as the daughter of the oaks has said."

Zita kept her voice low and slipped into English. "Well, now we know why Greenie's so smug. Are you certain that punching isn't an option? I don't usually hit trees, but I'll make an exception. This quest stuff sucks."

When Greenie and Chiron's words were translated for him, Andy shook his head. "I wish I could argue with them, but in the tales of both my mother's and my stepfather's people, breaking the rules was punishable by the offended parties. Normally out of proportion of the original offense, even if the breach was inadvertent. By those standards, replacing the original tasks with new ones is almost lenient."

"Agreed. That makes it two votes to one, then. We shall continue with the quests," Wyn said.

Good leg jiggling with impatience, Zita shook her head. "If this is an endless stream of quests, would you at least think about ways to get home without continuing to run every dangerous errand they dream up?"

Her friends both nodded.

"I've been alternating finding a cure for the basilisk with finding a way home. I don't want to go, however, until we've resolved... the stone issue," Wyn said softly.

Zita huffed. "I'd rather be partially stone at home than have your aunt suffer because I was too slow. Don't wait to go home because of me. Thanks. I'll settle for that."

Andy squeezed her shoulder.

With a toothy smile and her expression otherwise serene, Wyn folded her hands in her lap and turned back to the nymph. "So, Chiron is no longer the Voice of the Council, correct?"

Greenie smirked. "Yes."

Glee dancing in her voice, Wyn said, "Then we, as grateful guests, may now give him a gift and honor the laws of xenia. After all, he has housed us, fed us, and given us baths. That seems fair, yes? We will do so in front of all the Council so there can be no doubt that we received permission and ask nothing in return."

Chiron's brow furrowed.

Pursing her lips, Greenie began to speak, but before she could do so, one of the giants interrupted.

He grunted. "Fairly spoken. We should allow it."

"We concur. What gifts these godlings would give him make us curious. Centaurine weakness may stop us from bacchanalian bliss, but anything that makes these proceedings more festive would gladden me," a fish-man said, propping his head on his hand, elbow on the edge of the pool.

A faun perked up. "Is it alcohol? Wine brings joy to all."

With a scowl, Greenie closed her eyes a moment. After a breath, she reopened them and tapped her spear on the ground. "Very well. Though this grants you no favors from him."

"Aiding others for no reason other than to help is a joy in and of itself, perhaps one you will experience one day. Chiron, would you allow me to cast magic upon you?" Wyn fluttered her eyelashes and moved slowly to the old centaur.

Feel the burn, tree girl! Zita sent and then interpreted the conversation for Andy. As xenia's translation would've required an explanation, she simply used the Greek word to hurry things.

Wyn's amusement sang down party line.

The centaur nodded.

Andy asked, "Xenia?"

"It's like extreme hospitality, like the kind of stuff you'd do for a mother-in-law who hates you, but you want to impress," Zita whispered back.

"You know about it?"

She narrowed her eyes at him. "I know things! And I maybe asked earlier when she mentioned it in the bath."

He glanced at her sidelong. "I see." Over party line, he laughed. *Not going to let the dryad stop you from fixing his injury, are you, Wyn?*

Bless her heart, I wouldn't have been able to do anything without Greenie's coup. I may not have solutions to traveling home or the petrification yet, but this I can and will do, Wyn replied on the same channel. She moved closer to the centaur. "Please give me a moment. This injury has three parts to resolve: the physical poison, the magic that amplifies its impact, and the curse that ensures it persists."

After a few minutes, Wyn made a few gestures, murmuring, and the gentle glow of silver and green magic wreathed the centaur's afflicted haunch. *My previous experience healing those injured by the Key of Hades means I already had spells that countered the magic and the curse, so the only new part is handling the actual venom.*

Chiron gasped, and his hooves clattered on the fine tiles. He whirled in a circle.

"Father?" Melanippe rushed to him, followed by the other centaurs.

The light of the spell died, and Wyn folded her hands in her lap. If serenity could be both smug and fierce, she was the epitome of it.

Shock on her face, Greenie lowered the spear, pointing it at the witch. "What have you done? If you have broken xenia..."

For once, the old centaur made no pretense of being stoic. Jubilation filled his smile as he twisted to view his hindquarters. The raised, ugly lump of a scar was gone, replaced by a starburst of white hair. "It's gone? The pain? I had forgotten how it was to be without it. The old gods said the venom of the hydra had no cure."

Melanippe squealed and bounded over to her father.

Chiron swept her up and whirled the sturdy mountain nymph around as if she were weightless. A moment later, he set her back down and straightened his toga, his usual composure returning. "Thank you! I'll be able to visit my wife and other daughters much more often! It is a journey too far and time-consuming for a cripple to make often, and they cannot leave their mountains long. As soon as this Council concludes, I will go see her."

Zita paused in her interpretation for Andy a moment. *Ay, that's sweet. He's going to be one of those old dudes holding his woman's hand on a bench... maybe next to it given the horse half.*

Her smile radiant, Wyn glided back to stand beside Zita and Andy. "You're welcome. It's not right that you suffered any longer than necessary when it could be mended, politics or no. The old gods must not have known enough to heal it."

Greenie's shock gave way to annoyance. "You assume they tried. Enough of this. We will give you the next quest now."

"Hold it," Zita said in Greek. "Since I clearly don't know the rules here, I want to ask a question. We were given a bag of food to have for lunch. Can we eat that without losing another quest, or is that against the rules too? I'll hunt us some lunch if I have to... unless that's forbidden?"

The nymph took a step toward her, nearly growling. Tension showed in the lines of her body. "Show me this food. If this is one of your tricks, centaur, you will lose more than your office..."

The lone minotaur did not glance up from his knitting, but his deep voice filled the hall. "It is cruel to make another miss the midday meal. What would be the harm of it?" He got no answer.

Wyn withdrew the bag and set it on a nearby table. She pulled at the knot, letting the fabric fall open to show the contents.

Storming through the crowd, Greenie set down her spear and shoved the food around, spreading it out on the cloth. Salted fish, olives, bread, cheese, and figs tumbled out onto the coarse fabric. She even seized the waterskin and opened it, sniffing.

"Hey now! Don't touch. It's unsanitary if we're going to eat that later," Zita said. *Rude.*

One giant tilted his head. "It is as she said, a simple repast. I see no harm in it."

From his pool of water, one of the fish-men called out, "If you suspect foul play with the food, my brother and I will test the fish. They smell delicious." His companion hooted.

The nymph checked every fold, surveyed the food, and her shoulders relaxed. "Very well. The Council is in agreement? They may have this with no penalties?"

At the chorus of agreement, she retrieved her staff and banged it on the ground. Her earlier smirk returned. "Done. You may have all of the food upon this cloth and the fabric itself. Now, for your quest..."

Wyn interrupted, her voice syrupy and sweet. "One moment. We must prepare our food for the journey ahead."

Greenie blinked. "You expect us, the representatives of the Council, to wait so you can perform a petty domestic task?"

"While the Council undoubtedly did not mean to question our integrity or that of our gracious hosts, we would be remiss if we did not reclaim our food and package it in front of so many noble witnesses. It would be better to avoid future unpleasantness, wouldn't it?" Wyn batted her eyelashes.

No burn like a polite one, Wyn-style. Zita fought the urge to laugh and instead bent her attention to repacking the abused food and whispering an interpretation to Andy. A fig might've found its way into her mouth as well.

He covered his mouth with his hand, eyes dancing.

Chapter Eleven

A few minutes later, Zita finished tying the cloth. She scanned the table in case she'd missed something and then eyed the room. Around them, most of the Council had commandeered snacks of their own from the assorted platters in the room, and some had even been delivered to the fish men in their pool. Melanippe was a blur of motion as she played hostess, and Silenus still snored on his table. Greenie and Chiron stood nearby, the dryad fuming.

Zita handed the wrapped food to Wyn, who stood nearby with Andy. "Would you mind?"

"Of course not," her friend said, squeezing it into her purse.

"Have you quite finished dawdling over your petty task?" Greenie asked for the third or fourth time.

Zita narrowed her eyes at the nymph and switched to Greek. "Listen, tree-girl, not all of us survive on sunshine and bitterness."

Wyn grabbed Zita's arm and gave her a pointed look.

She rolled her eyes and returned to English. "Fine, yes, you handle it."

Her friend folded her hands in her lap and smiled at the nymph. Her sweet voice and sugared tones rose over the low murmur of conversations, drawing attention from the Council. "Yes, I believe we are done. We thank the members of the Council for their gracious patience. What problem may we aid you in solving now?"

"Finally." The nymph huffed. She banged her spear for no apparent reason. "For your next quest, you must capture Cerberus."

Chiron stiffened and bit back an exclamation. Melanippe jerked to a stop beside him, her eyes widening.

Wyn cautioned Andy and Zita with a gesture, then folded her hands over her stomach. "One moment. According to legend, the dog suffered when Hercules took him from his home before. We won't torture anyone, especially an animal."

Triumph flashed across Greenie's face. "If you refuse—"

One of the giants interrupted. "She speaks truly. While I would've expected the sentiment from the virgin huntress, we should not punish the dog unduly, for he is true and faithful in his service. We are not unkind human kings to so abuse our power."

"Virgin, what now?" Zita could feel her eyebrows rising.

Wyn nudged her. *Let it go. Now is not the time to argue your virtue or lack thereof.*

Me? I thought they meant you and was going to object to the huntress part. It's none of their business that you've probably got the most active love life of the three of us. Zita slanted a sideways glance at her friend.

His face red under his bronze skin, Andy interrupted before Wyn could reply. *Can we pay attention to whatever they're saying that doesn't involve sex lives?*

His face pale, Chiron trotted forward. Despite his white knuckles and tense posture, his sonorous voice was even and calm. "Cerberus serves a purpose where he is, and it is best the exits of the Underworld are kept fast shut. Would your trees take over guardianship if Hades' great dog is gone?"

Greenie pursed her lips. "No, but..."

Another male in the crowd raised his voice but did not come forward. "Rather than tormenting the Cerberus, mayhap they could steal a pinch of fur? That way, he may keep to his post, and the godlings may prove the cleverness with the apple is not merely a fortunate fluke nor collusion with a teacher overeager for new students. All know the hellhound's heart is not easily won nor does the beast fear to bite even the great Zeus Pheletes."

Zita eyed the crowd. Her mind whirled as she tried to find the speaker. The scaly men were throwing small fish into each other's mouths and paying little attention to the proceedings. The satyr's voice was too high to have been the speaker, and the giants seemed to speak only in stentorian bellows. *One of the other centaurs must have made the comment.*

Stroking his beard, Chiron scanned the crowd. His head tilted, and his body relaxed. "An excellent idea. Since the honored Council claims previous quests were too simple, have them retrieve a vial of the dog's hair... without broaching the Underworld at all. That will make it much more difficult."

A hum of agreement came from the assembly.

Acid rose in Zita's mouth. *I thought at least the old guy was on our side, but I guess when even your own people are throwing shade at you...*

The nymph scowled. "Fine. Cerberus' hair, but without entering the domain of Hades." She banged the spear of office, but the action seemed more petulant than officious.

"Done. We'll bring it back here once we have it, then." Wyn inclined her head and withdrew to the doorway. *Politics. He's already lost his position to Greenie. Perhaps his Council seat is at risk. As Machiavelli says, a ruler who wants to stay in power is often forced not to be good.*

Andy grunted and followed.

Zita stared at the assembled creatures and joined her friends. Mindful of the need for diplomacy, she switched to English. "Do we have to bathe the dog too, or do something special to get his hair? I'm going to guess that Car Brush—"

"Cerberus," Wyn corrected absently.

With a wave of her hand, Zita dismissed the correction. "Whatever. I'm assuming he's not a normal, friendly German Shepherd who drops enough hair over the course ten minutes to make a second dog?"

Andy snorted. "You guessed right."

Wyn reached to her shoulder as if to toy with her hair, and her fingers stopped when she touched the edge of the wimple hiding her chestnut locks. "Technically, he's the Greek version of Garm. He guards the underworld and is notoriously dedicated to his job. Dependent on the myth, he may be poisonous, in addition to being a giant monstrous dog with up to one hundred dog heads. He might also have a mane of snake heads and at least one serpent tail."

The words slipped out. "How can anything stay upright with that many heads? How do they decide who controls the body? What kind of internal organs do you need to do that? Biologically, it shouldn't exist. To be honest, a lot of the stuff we're seeing here can't exist." Zita glanced at the myriad half-human creatures around them and then back at her friends.

"Magic. They're real enough here." Andy cut off whatever Wyn would've said.

Zita huffed. "Right. My favorite explanation."

Brows raised, Wyn put her hands on her narrow hips and tapped her fingers. "Is that so?"

Everything other than the two women seemed to require Andy's undivided attention.

"Unless you're the one casting the magic, por supuesto," Zita added hastily. She forced a smile.

Mollified, Wyn nodded and began to stride away.

As soon as the witch's back was turned, Zita made a face at Andy.

He made one back. Raising his voice, he called out, "If I'm flying, we should be outside the outer ring of walls so I can take my other shape without knocking anything over... given the state of many of the buildings."

Without acknowledging his statement aloud, Wyn left.

"Guess we're going, then," Zita said in Greek.

Andy glanced at her. "She's under a lot of pressure with the time constraints and... things."

"My leg? You can say it. Whether we talk about it or not, is not going to change it. Ándale, we got to go before she gets lost in the woods."

He grimaced, and they hurried to catch up.

They had made it through the inner gate and were approaching the second one when Melanippe melted out of the ground. The shadow of the great eagle-embossed gate hid her face as she stood half out of the ground, half in. "Wait!" she hissed in a low voice.

Wyn halted, and Zita and Andy stopped by her side.

Flicking her gaze to the left and right, the nymph rose until only her feet remained in the ground. "My father cannot speak with you due to politics, but we must warn you, so I am here. I dare not stay in case the trees bear witness. Abide strictly by the limitations. Do not set even one toe into the Underworld now. If you do so, you'll be unable to leave. Chase Cerberus, but draw him out."

"What if you're caught speaking to us?" Wyn frowned.

Melanippe waved her hand. "Unlike my father, I am only a lowly nymph and sometime oracle, not a member of the Council. It would be ill for me, but it would bode worse for you were we seen speaking. So, remember. It's not time. Stay out of the gates, or you'll never return home. I must go before we are seen."

"If we cannot enter the Underworld, how can we lure out Cerberus?" Wyn asked.

"He is the guardian of all the portals to the Underworld. If any entry is breached, he knows about it and can be there. Find one, and you may lure him hence with a honeyed call. Remember, do not enter the caves." After another check over her shoulders, the nymph sunk back into the ground.

Zita and her friends blinked where she'd been.

"Thank you?" Wyn said to the ground. "Oracles in Greek myth tended to be accurate, so let's make sure we stay out of the Land of the Dead. If nothing else, Cerberus definitely attacked people trying to leave the Underworld. Most of the entrances are either in the Peloponnesian region of southern Greece or in Turkey."

"Let's go for the closest first and move outward from there," Andy suggested.

Zita nodded.

They continued on their way and had just exited the outer gate when a shout came from behind them.

"Godlings!" Despite the mellifluous nature of her voice, Greenie's call was an angry squawk. The dryad stormed toward them with Chiron and a satyr cantering behind. Two cyclops brought up the rear with slow, ponderous steps.

"Now what?" Wyn asked. *I hope Melanippe wasn't overheard.*

Even if they heard her, she didn't tell us much. They already made staying out of the Underworld a condition. Zita crossed her arms. "Probably wants us to do it blindfolded or something."

"Sounds about right," Andy muttered. *Melanippe gave us a hint of how to handle it, though.*

Greenie gestured behind herself with her spear. "Now that you go, take this with you."

The cyclops plodded up, carrying a long pole between them.

"Let me out, you idiots!" Garm howled, struggling from the confines of a golden net that hung from a pole carried by the giants.

"¿Qué? What did that chingado wolfman do now?" Zita tilted her head, puzzled. "And why would we take him with us?"

Without seeming to need an interpretation of the Spanish that crept into her reply, Greenie narrowed her eyes. Her cheeks were warm with color, and her posture suggested she was contemplating using her symbol of office to stab Zita. "Are you refusing the Council?"

The old centaur's hooves pawed the ground. "Are reports mistaken? Did the wolf come to our lands with you or not?" Despite having handed over his spear of office, the others around quieted at his outburst, even the irate nymph.

"Well, he did come with us, but he's not a friend," Wyn said.

Chiron bowed his head. "Then, his offenses are yours to mend."

Zita slashed the air with her hands. Without conscious intent, her body fell into a defensive stance, ready to wrest away the spear if necessary. "Wait, Garm's been pissing people off, but we're the ones being held responsible? How is that even fair?"

The dryad stomped her bare foot and nearly screamed back. "He is yours! Your responsibility! Your pet desecrated a sacred tree! Attacked multiple people! Scattered the herds of the silenoi yesterday so they still seek their own. He profaned trees!"

"He's not a friend, and people can't be pets... and is one of those complaints he peed on a tree? Are there seriously no dogs in this world? I mean, I know he's a man who uses the form of a wolf, but have you heard yourselves talk lately?" Zita's eyebrows rose. In an aside, she let Andy know what was going on.

He shook his head and dropped it into his hands.

From the way his ears pricked up when she spoke, Garm listened as well but subsided into a sullen, low growl.

"Of course, there are—" Greenie shook her head and glared. "Do not attempt to distract me. What is he then?"

"The local guy who would set a bag of poop on fire and then blames you for it? Biting people I'd expect, but to get mad because a wolf peed on a tree and chased a few goats or whatever... Aren't you all supposed to be in tune with nature or hugging trees or something? You do realize that trees are just trees in our world, not houses?" Zita said in Greek and then repeated herself in English.

Garm growled and went limp in the nets. "I am surrounded by idiots."

Wyn pinched her own forehead. "Please let me handle the conversation, Arca. I believe you've made your opinions clear enough, and we don't need more complications," she murmured in English.

The satyr stroked his goatee and cleared his throat. "Perhaps the charges about the tree should be dropped. Verily, the attraction of canines to trees is known to all."

The two one-eyed giants exchanged glances. "Even we recognize the truth of that statement."

Greenie crossed her arms over her chest, her spear of office nearly hitting the satyr who'd spoken.

He retreated from the weapon, hands lifted. "The truth of Nature demands her due, noble Speaker for the Voice."

The nymph sniffed. "The Fates long ago declared that the presence of deities calls to others of their ilk simply by existing in a place. Distance only lengthens the time before they meet and clash. Heroes and monsters like the wolf are the flotsam drawn into their wake for which the gods must take account. So it was before and is again, now that they have been reborn to the worlds. Not even gods can escape the grasp and scissors of the Three Sisters."

Wyn's eyes grew distant. When she spoke again, she used English. "Where have I heard something similar before—ah, right, Dr. Mwangi mentioned it when he was encouraging us to leave his clinic. He said, 'Those of power attract others of ability, like a gathering of lions and just as dangerous. The closer together they are, the more often they clash.'"

"Well, he and Greenie can bond over how much they want us to stay away. You should probably get them to let Garm at least stand up. Hanging upside down too long could scramble what little brains he has." Zita grumbled, keeping to English.

Spreading her hands wide, Wyn appealed to the nymph and the other creatures present in Greek. "We can explain to him what he did wrong. He doesn't understand your language and is unfamiliar with your ways. Surely he will do better once everything is clearer."

Greenie banged her spear on the ground. "No matter what ignorance is involved, the wolf came with you from your land, which means his actions are seeds you sowed. Even if you still cling to the claim that you are merely heroes, he is yours. Take him away, so he walks no more near Olympos. Kill him. Keep him with you. Abandon him in the northern lands. We care not, but he may not remain here. If you refuse this most basic of responsibilities, I do not see how the Council can choose but to exile you."

Chiron frowned. "The Voice and their Speaker do not make that decision, daughter of the oak trees. The duty is merely to communicate the will of the Council."

The nymph whirled toward the centaur. "Had that been true of your tenure, instead of doing as you wished and then wheedling the Council to an agreement, you might still wield this office. If they comply, we will loose him here, and they may be off with him. The Council agreed to that. If they will not be with us, they must be gone. Even you must grant that logic."

The old centaur seemed as if he were struggling to hold back a retort, and then his face smoothed out. "It would at least require discussion."

"That debate would be over before it began. We will free him here, and you will take him with you. He ate a mule that was serving as a companion, and who knows what other wrongs are laid at his paws? What other trees have been outraged?" Greenie warmed to her topic and started ranting about possible crimes with a focus on those against vegetation.

After tuning her out, Zita said in English, "Has anyone else here noticed how out of proportion they blow everything we do? This is ridiculous."

"Please don't tell them that. Whatever she's saying doesn't sound like a recitation of compliments," Andy said.

Garm growled. "I can't believe the idiotic little shapeshifter is the most sensible one here right now."

Wyn said, "Hush your mouths. We don't have any alternatives. They know how to get us home, and they're willing to play rough."

Rubbing a hand over the top of her head, back and forth, Zita sighed. "Let's go take Garm for a playdate then."

***

After dismissing the map she'd been consulting, Wyn hesitantly walked over to where Zita stood and craned her neck to see below. "We should be near Lake Lerna."

Zita padded a few steps closer to the edge and checked below.

Rather than the varied microclimates and relative lushness of Olympus, this area seemed similar to the Greece of home. Mountains covered with brush dropped off abruptly into the sea with limestone shorelines where nothing other than cliffs or stony beaches were visible. Separated from the Aegean by a series of dunes, a lagoon glimmered blue below, with green and brown marsh encroaching upon its edges. Boulders dotted the area; two of the largest shadowed a cave mouth at the western end of the lagoon where the mountains resumed. A single large white rock tilted crazily at the high tide mark, as if someone had started to build a monument and then abandoned the beginnings of it. The only tree was an old salt-twisted oak at the top of the cliff above the lake.

Good area for bouldering and climbing, she thought with a pang, remembering similar thoughts about the terrain near where they'd tried to stop Tiffany. She moved her stone leg uncomfortably, promising herself internally she'd learn to climb with it. "So, this is a big dog with an extra head or two?"

Wyn clucked her tongue. "Three heads, most likely. Most of what we've seen follows the common ideas of creatures rather than conforming to all of the original myths, which is a good thing. At least one of the older myths claimed he had a hundred heads and dripped poison so vile that deadly flowers sprang up anywhere his drool landed."

"That makes no sense. If it was really that nasty, wouldn't it kill plants instead of making them?" Zita said.

Her friend had an odd expression. "I mentioned it could have a hundred heads, and you're focused on the flowers?"

"We already talked about the too many heads thing. Repeating stuff doesn't make it any more logical," Zita said simply.

"Wingspan, this should be the right area. Would you land, please?" Wyn didn't bother to raise her voice.

A chorus of wordless assent came through the party line from Andy's massive bird form.

"Should we wake Garm now or after we land?" Zita glanced down, even though she couldn't see where Wingspan's talons caged the unconscious wolf. When he'd refused to come with them and acted as if he planned to attack, Wyn had used her sleep spell on him.

Wyn's gaze followed hers. "He can wait until we've landed and are ready to handle his inevitable hissy fit. If I can verify the area is clear of anyone he can harm or any trees of note, we can leave him here, so he's not a risk while we're running quests."

"I do only see the one tree, but it's an oak. Everything else is a bush with delusions of grandeur."

Proving she'd paid attention to Greenie's earlier rant, Wyn smiled demurely. "It would be a terrible shame if an oversized irascible canine were to deface it, wouldn't it?"

Zita snickered. "We should be so lucky."

Chapter Twelve

Once they'd landed, Wyn took Zita's arm and gestured toward the empty cave mouth. "I had been concerned that it would be hard to identify the crossover to the Underworld, but it's clearly delineated, almost glowing. I can only assume it is some form of portal. Can you see it?"

After staring at the spot her friend had indicated for a minute, Zita slowly spun in a circle, scanning the area. "No, sorry."

In the only spot big enough, Andy's avian form shimmered, lightning racing over it. When that faded, Andy stood there. He glanced at the nearby sleeping wolf shifter and then walked over to the women.

Wyn asked him the same question once he arrived, absently handing him his cape.

As he fastened on the clothing, he replied in the negative.

The witch she sighed. "If I create an illusion of a boundary, would you draw a line in the ground? Perhaps we could find a stick or something? I'll make sure it's far enough from the actual portal entrance so you can't accidentally step inside. None of us want to delay our return home through another disqualification. Their handling of the honey quest shows their interpretations err on the side of strictness."

Andy offered them both a tight smile. "I'll draw it."

Wyn gestured, and white light ignited on the ground between a triangular rock and a lumpy, lichen-spotted one on either side of the cave mouth. She glanced at the wolf shapeshifter. "He is easier to handle while he's asleep. Should we leave him like that while we search for Cerberus?"

Zita pursed her lips. "He'll awaken if something hits him, right?"

Her friend nodded. "Or after about an hour."

"Normally, I'd be all for waking him sooner, but he'd probably insist on fighting Cerberus for piddle rights or something. It'd probably be easier to keep him over there, away from the entrance, so he should be safe while we do our thing with the dog. We'll get him after."

"Agreed." Andy jogged back down to the lake, scooped up a flat rock the size of a chair, and returned. He dragged it along the illusory line, leaving a trench several inches deep in the soil.

An enormous dog, the size of an elephant, raced from the cave, multiple heads barking and snarling as if he were in a murderous, rabid rage. His body had a barrel chest, thin midriff, and thick, muscular legs. A double coat of fur covered his body with a shorter, woolly layer peeking out through a longer, wiry, green-tinged outer layer.

Everyone froze for a second.

"Line's done. Found Cerberus," Andy said weakly, dropping his rock and backing away slowly.

One head, which resembled a demented German Shepherd, slavered, growled, and snapped at the air. Another head, that of a pit bull, barked around a bone in its mouth, but seemed a little confused. The third, a hound, just seemed happy to be making noise, a forked tongue slipping out the side of its mouth. Fire burned in all of their eyes.

Wyn gasped. She gestured, calling up a bubble around herself and Zita.

The dog jerked to a stop when it reached Andy's shallow trench. With a wary glance at them, he dropped his bone and lowered all three heads to sniff the line. He paced along it, quieting to a combination of a low, constant growl and a multi-octave whine.

Zita frowned, noting the coiling, twitching snake that coiled and hissed where a normal dog tail would be. "Seriously? Can't anything just be one thing here?"

"It's Cerberus, Arca. Guardian of the Underworld. That's how he's supposed to be." Wyn watched the animal warily.

Zita snorted. "The dog's too extra for my tastes. So, what's our plan?"

Both of her friends fiddled with their clothing and stared in different directions, neither meeting her eyes.

Zita smacked her forehead. "We don't have a plan, do we?"

"We kept getting interrupted on our way here?" Wyn offered.

"And this dog is super extra." Andy snapped his fingers and laughed. "That's it. I've got a plan. Muse, do you have scissors? Or a sharp little knife?"

Her expression puzzled, Wyn reached into her bag and retrieved a small, metal object where a thin strip of bronze connected two blades. "So much for the cute little scissors in my adorable manicure kit. They're now these things," she mourned.

"That'll work. Can you get the satchel of lunch out and give that and the shears to Arca? I'll get you a new pair once we get home. Arca, you hungry?" Andy grinned.

As she accepted the items from Wyn, Zita's stomach rumbled. "Duh. Why?"

A sly smile teased at his lips. "Don't take this the wrong way, but would you make a sandwich the way you like them?"

Wyn arched an eyebrow. "That's going to help?"

"Definitely. Who doesn't think better on a full stomach? Even if Greenie pawed through it, we've still got a nice haul for lunch."

Saliva filled Zita's mouth as she opened the cloth satchel and surveyed the contents. She stacked layers of food on the bread, mashing it down ruthlessly to get more on. Soft cheese and a piece of fish oozed out one side.

Cerberus whimpered and crept forward but did not cross the borderline.

Zita licked her lips and sniffed appreciatively. "Sandwich done."

Andy whisked the sandwich from her hands. "That's so enormous you'd have to unhinge your jaws to eat it. Perfect. Be ready to snip the hair off the dog when we get a chance—you're the fastest and the best with animals, so hopefully, you can do it while he's distracted."

Wyn laughed. "I get it now."

"Me too. Clever. I can make myself one of those sandwiches when we're done, right? We are going to eat at some point?" Zita eyed the food longingly as she flexed her hand, accustoming herself to the operation of the archaic shears.

Andy giggled. "The sandwich is not a lie," he promised as he set it down on a flat rock ten feet away from the boundary line.

Zita padded close by the food, careful to stay out of the direct path to the sandwich and to not stare at Cerberus.

The enormous dog quivered but did not cross the boundary. Long strings of drool came from two of the three mouths, and the hound head gave a querulous cry.

Wyn snapped her fingers. "Some sources claim sunlight hurts Cerberus, so you'll have to do better to lure him out. I know how, too. Arca, do you have any cakes packed in any of those butter containers you have me hauling around?"

"No, closest I have is protein bars and trail mix, and most of those have chocolate and raisins in them, so they're a no go," she said absently.

Wyn nodded and pulled the jar of honey from her bag. She poured the honey over the sandwich until the golden liquid dripped from it, and then she backed away.

"Why did you do that? I wouldn't even eat... actually, no, I would still eat it. Might dust it off first, though."

"More importantly, where's the dog?" Wyn whispered, retreating to a spot behind Andy and putting away the remains of the honey.

In her peripheral vision, Zita saw Cerberus hovering at the edge of the shadow, his gazes fixed on the food. She turned away more.

Cerberus ran the last couple feet, and the three heads dove into the food, snarling as they pushed each other out of the way trying to eat.

Zita pounced, seizing a handful of cool, coarse fur along the dog's haunches and slicing it off with the shears.

The snake head-tail lunged at her.

She jumped back.

Jowls bulging with food, the dog whirled and ran back to the safety of the shadows, honey, figs, and fish smeared all over his faces.

A fistful of green and black hair in her hand, Zita retreated to her friends.

The dog wagged and then backed farther into the cave, so only the crimson glow of its eyes showed.

Zita whooped and danced over to her friends. "We did it! Good thinking, guys!"

After wrapping the fur in a scarf and putting it safely in her purse, Wyn allowed herself a relieved smile.

Andy grinned.

"Now what? Should we wake Garm? I don't like to haul him around unconscious. It's too much like kidnapping," Andy said.

"Agreed. Perhaps he will agree to remain in this area while we perform our quests? If no others live nearby, it limits the havoc he can cause, and he has been adamant in his desire to avoid us."

Zita eyed the area, clomping down to the lake to peer at the water. "Plenty of prey here for him to eat, and the lake is okay for a wolf. It's rocky, but there's enough overhangs and such he could shelter in if the weather turns. This could work for him, given his refusal to use his natural form."

"I'll check for sentient life." Party line disappeared. Wyn's eyes grew glassy and distant.

"If you don't mind swamps, it's nice enough, I suppose." Andy stood protectively by the distracted witch.

A moment later, animation returned to Wyn's face, and she blinked. Her voice was barely above a whisper as she spoke. "The area seems safe enough. I sense no sentient minds, save ours, for miles, with two possible exceptions. The first is that I can't sense Cerberus, so more creatures could be on the other side of the Underworld line."

They glanced over to the big dog, whose eyes glowed in the dark cave.

Smoothing her toga, Wyn continued, "Second, I'm not certain I can sense nymphs when they're merged with their element and not paying attention to the outside world. Greenie is in the oak tree, watching us, but she's not fully melded with the tree. She's paying more attention than the tree would, so I can detect her."

"Safe enough then," Andy said, glancing at the tree.

After she unrolled her toga, so it hung to her ankles to disguise her problematic leg, Zita rubbed her hands together. "I'm in. Wake him and see if he wants to hang out here while we finish our quests. Why don't we take a few steps back? Anyone want to place a bet on if Garm wakes up cranky, extra cranky, or so-extra-drama-overload cranky? Loser buys me lunch when we get home."

Wyn sniffed. "As if any of us would be foolish enough to take a wager with such odds." Warmth blossomed in Zita's mind as the party line returned.

Andy snorted. "No interest in the sucker bet, thanks."

"Had to try. Ready to let sleeping dogs wake?" Zita rocked on her feet, ignoring the stiffness of the one.

Andy eased between the sleeping shifter and Wyn. "Ready."

After Wyn made a quick gesture, Garm woke with a snort. He leapt to his feet, teeth bared. "I'll kill you all! Where are we?"

"Lake Lerna. We had to gather the hair of Cerberus for a quest and had a proposition for you," Wyn said.

"I hope you die horribly." The wolf shifter snatched up a branch as thick as Zita's leg and bit down, gnawing until it snapped in half.

"Dramatic. You can tell he missed us," Zita said to her friends, not bothering to lower her voice.

Garm snorted and let his chew toy drop. His eyes slid almost shut. "Why am I here, losers?"

"I'll translate for you guys." Using a deliberately silly voice, Zita said, "Why, how lovely of you to visit. You all seem awesome today, especially my hero, Arca. She's looking particularly jacked lately."

Wyn touched her shoulder. *Stop antagonizing him. Let me handle this.* Aloud, she said, "We couldn't leave you there. You've angered the locals to the point that they considered your death a suitable outcome," she said softly, folding her hands in front of herself.

The great wolf glared at them.

Cerberus barked, a querulous howl among the cacophony.

"What is that?" Garm leapt to his feet, stiffening.

Zita nodded toward the cave where the dog was now visible again, all three heads focused on them. "Cerb over there? Is he your kid, Garm? Normally, I'd say no, but he's got your eyes and the way things work around here..." The words slipped out without a conscious decision.

The wolf shapeshifter glared at her. "How stupid are you? No."

Wyn seized Zita's arm. *Stop it. You're not helping.*

He's a dick. Zita scowled but kept her complaint silent.

Wyn's reply came over their link. *Perhaps, but this will be a great deal easier with his compliance. Give me a moment. Perhaps I can smooth matters.*

Garm spoke first. The enormous wolf shook his body as he stood, sending dust flying in a cloud. He sauntered a step toward them, the hackles on his back raised. "No. Get lost. I'm not here to help you with your quest, make friends, hold hands, or sing songs. You can tell the locals to stay out of my way, and they won't get hurt. I have no interest in them and will utterly destroy anyone who comes after me."

Zita rolled her eyes. "Again, drama."

I love how you're letting me handle it. Truly, you are an inspiration. Wyn folded her arms. "Garm—"

"Silence, witch! I'm done listening to you all babble about your petty concerns. Die. Go find your way back home. I care not, and I have no interest in our old world, especially if this one is free of the scourge of humanity. You all did me no favors when you saved my life, and I owe you no debt. For not destroying you for that, you owe me." With an exaggerated turn, Garm put his back to them and began to run away.

Cerberus whined, growled, and uttered a puppyish howl.

Wyn's hands flashed in a rapid pattern, and a bubble appeared around the wolf shifter.

He jerked to a stop, then snarled. After a few experimental steps forward, he started to move, pushing the bubble with him.

Shifting to a bear, Zita sprinted in front of him, easily outpacing the wolf. She halted in front of the bubble and hit it with a paw. It rebounded off her belly. She staggered back.

With the sudden reversal of direction, Garm hit the wall of the bubble and crumpled.

Guilt ran through her. *I didn't mean to hurt him.*

Sheepishness flavored Wyn's apology. *Sorry, I used the physical shield, not the magic one, and didn't have a chance to allow us to get through.*

Before Zita could do anything, Garm groaned and pulled himself to his feet, shaking his ruff. He growled.

She shifted back to Arca. Relief mingled with frustration as she realized her one leg was now stone to her thigh. A horrible suspicion sprang to mind, and she squashed it before it leaked to her friends. Her next words were harsher than she intended. "Don't make me switch back and roll you around like a goth hamster. Chill."

Wyn strolled over. "Perhaps we could come to an agreement before you go? You don't wish to be with us. We would rather not hold you prisoner. If you don't hunt anything that talks or go after herds, we'll leave you here alone for a while. We have to finish several quests to find the way home."

"I hope you choke on them and die," he snarled. "You will regret doing this to me!"

"The area seems pretty deserted. A canine could run a long way here without having to talk to anyone, especially if you avoid the trees. If they hunt you down, one or more people will die," Andy tried.

Zita ran a hand over her long hair. "You'll definitely be one of the corpses. Dude, take the deal. Muse will talk at you until you agree if you don't."

Garm snapped at the air, and his tail lashed. "Fine. Free me."

Wyn eyed him for a long moment. "Do not forget our bargain. I will remove the bubble." She made a curt gesture.

"It's about time. Did you forget how to do it?" Garm's lip curled.

"Whine, whine," Zita murmured.

"Show some respect! I am king of the monsters, and none have beaten me," Garm said, glaring.

Andy seemed very interested in the ground. He rubbed his hands on his thighs. *I want to make a Godzilla reference so bad right now, and if I could work in Mothra, I'd be so happy.*

Zita snorted. "Oye, we're sorry your heart got broken, but you need to use some reality brakes in that runaway car of delusion. I've beaten you a couple times, and the bear-guy won the stare-down at the museum. I also doubt you could take Wingspan here or Dragon."

Garm puffed up his fur, spine stiffening, ears and tail erect. He took a step forward. "Vile trickery, not true challenges in all those cases. You will bow before me."

"He does seem enraptured of his illusions, doesn't he?" Wyn arched an eyebrow.

Andy snorted in agreement and folded his arms across his chest.

Garm snarled, his ears going flat against his skull. "You talk too much, little shifter. You and Wingspan are lower shifters. He turns into a weak bird, and you cannot even commit to a single form. I will accept your accolades, but you will stay out of this. Your lesser witch is beneath notice."

"And yet he's talking about her," Zita muttered to Andy.

From behind her, Wyn's soft voice said, "Lesser witch? Compared to?"

Unlike the wolf, Zita recognized the steel beneath the sweet tones. He'd chosen the wrong approach to use.

"Halja, of course. My former queen might be a treacherous, cold-hearted bitch, but she is so far above you that you should pray for the chance to kiss her feet," Garm replied.

Wyn examined her fingernails as if bored. "She's a lazy dilettante who relies on her blood-magic potions and other people's enchantments. As of yet, I have not seen a single one of her castings where she's written actual symbols instead of poorly drawn scribbles mixed with the occasionally correctly drawn letter that's wrong for her purpose."

Zita nodded, determined to stay on Wyn's good side. It didn't hurt that everything her friend had said was true. "Muse totally won the witch-off every time she and Tiffers have tangled, and I've beaten you a few times. By your standards, she and I should battle it out for top dog or witch position, but we just don't care."

"Empty talk from petty, puny fools." Garm sniffed disdainfully.

Breaking his silence, Andy laughed, a mirthless sound. "You really don't know me," he said. "Trust me, I'm the biggest monster in the room, ah, meadow, at the moment, but like the girls, I just don't care."

Garm laughed, a nasty, patronizing sound. "Go ahead and shift. I'll feast upon chicken for dinner."

"Monster is the wrong word for you, mano. You're pretty. We've got the space, and it'd end this silly conversation. Shift and show him," Zita said, giving Andy a light punch on the shoulder. *I thought we were past that, and you were happy with your bird form these days?*

He sighed. *Pretty? Seriously? Thanks for the support, Z. And, happier with it. Still not thrilled that I ate a dinosaur.*

Better an animal than a person. And yeah, you're pretty. Golden eagles are sweet to start with, and the lightning aura jacks up the style. Way better than being a marabou stork.

A what?

They're like long-legged turkey vultures, but balder and with crazy eyes. Oh, they poop on their own legs and feet.

Andy rubbed the back of his neck. *I bow before the expert. I am, indeed, a pretty bird.*

I told you I'd make you say it someday. You owe me one of those home-cooked dinners your stepmom freezes for you in case of random starvation. I'm not picky, so you choose which one. Zita smirked.

After he handed over his cape, since it wouldn't shift with him, Wyn said, "We'll get out from underfoot, Wingspan. You can toss him in the ocean, and we can return to Olympus for the next quest." She tugged on Zita's arm, and both of them walked backward to avoid allowing the irate wolf shifter to come at them from behind.

Tension vibrated through Garm's body as if he had just realized what she'd implied.

Andy eyed the werewolf, moved to the largest clear area, and shifted. Lightning crackled over his body. The light spilled out and surrounded him until it was so bright that afterimages danced on the backs of Zita's eyelids. His giant eagle shape, the length of or longer than a commercial jet, replaced his human form. Shimmers of electricity ran over his enormous body and glowed in his eyes. Despite his size, he shuffled his feet delicately, avoiding people, wolf, and most of the local foliage.

The wolf fell back, his tail diving between his legs and his shoulders hunching. Garm licked his lips before he bared his teeth, ears lying flat against his head. He snarled at the massive bird and backed away.

While Andy did not deign to turn his head, his multitude of voices rang out, seeming to reverberate in Zita's bones. "Speak. What happened with the herds near Olympus?"

Garm retreated from the huge bird. He gnashed his teeth. "I culled them by eating an old mule. The rest scattered, with one colt even sprouting wings on his ankles." As if afraid answering had been too helpful, he appended another threat.

It would be much more intimidating if his tail weren't tucked so far between his legs and if his threat were physically possible, Zita thought with amusement.

Garm continued retreating, pausing by one massive talon. He glanced at the nearby brush, and then at the leg beside him, far thicker than any of the nearby shrubs. Quickly, he lifted a leg and let fly a stream of liquid.

Andy's avian form stepped aside, wings flaring in surprise. One knocked over the big white rock by the shore, shattering it with a loud crack.

Wyn gasped.

"Dude, not cool! At least don't fight like you're a toddler," Zita said. Picking up a rock the size of a strawberry, she hurled it at him.

It bounced off his heavy forehead, and he sneered.

Something slithered into the water nearby, but Zita didn't catch what it was. It didn't sound exactly like the basilisk, but her heart sped up at the sound.

Wingspan's massive head turned toward them at her words, and he flexed his claws, stepping away from the werewolf. "Disrespectful," he rumbled in his unique chorus of men's voices.

Garm ran off toward the trees.

This time, Wyn barred Zita from going after him. "Let him leave. This is what we wanted, right? Let's finish this as soon as possible."

Zita grunted. "Verdad. Not to mention, Wingspan's going to want to bathe for hours after he changes back."

Chapter Thirteen

Once they returned to the gates of Olympus, a young centaur escorted them into the city and back to the megaron. The same assortment of Council members was there, though Silenus had awakened and was in an animated discussion with someone his body prevented her from seeing. The rest of the room was unchanged, other than the food being suitable for lunch rather than breakfast. Even Greenie's scowl seemed unchanged.

Stepping forward, Wyn offered the dog fur to the dryad. "We have completed the quest for Cerberus' fur. None of us set foot in the Underworld, and the dog is unharmed."

To their surprise, the long-haired Harpy shoved her way past Silenus and through the crowd to snatch it from the witch's hand. The bird-woman sniffed and then licked it. She spat a clump of fur and spittle at Zita's feet. "It's real. I'm done with all your foolish blather now."

The Council accepted the quest as complete and withdrew to deliberate on the next task. The Harpy hopped toward the exit, glaring at Zita and muttering about vengeance as she exited. Only Silenus waved as she left. "Farewell, fierce Podarge!"

"Bath time! I can't wait!" Andy crowed, once they'd interpreted for him.

As the Council members drifted away, Wyn took a deep breath and stared at her hands, spreading her fingers wide. "Before we go bathe and eat, we need to stop by Arges. My previous spells, though failures, were educational. This new one should work." She bit her lip. "I hope."

"Excellent! Which chicken gets it first?" Zita said. She rocked back and forth on her stone leg, impatient to have full use of her body back.

"If it works on the first one, I will free all the birds and then Arges. It seems to be a stasis effect, so he should come out of it in whatever state he went in," Wyn said.

"Minus the toe. I think the basilisk ate it." Zita grimaced, remembering the missing digit.

Wyn's nose wrinkled. "Yes, minus the toe."

"I hate to bring up something so horrible, but what if it isn't stasis? What if he's gone insane? Do you think that's what wrong with the stone goose? Last time I saw it, it was chasing a faun away from the tower." Andy asked. He smoothed the edges of his cape.

Zita laughed. "No, he probably started out that way, and on the bright side, his territoriality keeping people away from Arges is what Chiron wanted. We're just lucky it wasn't a swan. Those are nasty, mean birds."

"One of the reasons that we shall test it on a chicken first, though, how do you know if one has gone mad?" Wyn grimaced and rubbed her forehead.

For some reason, her friends looked at Zita.

Following their gazes, Chiron's forehead crinkled, and he cantered closer. He peered at her as if he could determine why she held all their attention. "Was there something you needed? What has the trickster done?"

She spread her hands wide and protested, first in Greek, and then repeated herself in English. "What? Why does everyone assume I've done something?"

"I learn quickly," the centaur said.

"You're the only one here with experience being a chicken," Andy said.

"Doesn't make me the chicken whisperer. Average animal temperament doesn't apply when I'm shifted. From taking care of my tía's chickens, though, I can tell you they've got their own minds and personalities. Pues, if I have to choose, a hen might be less aggressive." Zita harrumphed for good measure.

Andy nodded sagely. "But, you have practiced the form."

She cleared her throat. "Yes, of course. What if I needed to use it someday? They see ultraviolet, you know."

Wyn giggled and echoed her. "Of course." She gave Chiron a quick summary of the discussion.

The centaur stared at Zita. "In truth? The ancient gods had little interest in such a domestic creature. Perhaps your gentle and womanly nature influenced your choice."

Wyn snickered. A second later, when she interpreted for Andy, he laughed outright.

Hating haters. Zita flexed her shoulders. Gruffly, she said, "Being female had nothing to do with it."

Chiron tore his attention away from her, and his hooves stamped a couple times. "While I cast no aspersions on your magic, Lady Muse, should he be mad, it were best that he be outside the walls of the city. The wards that protect Olympos would prevent his entry, had he ill intent, but if he remains inside, my home and what is left have little defense."

Her expression sobering, Wyn inclined her head. "No offense taken. If I am successful with the poultry, we will take him outside the city, and have you and yours stay within it... in case it becomes an issue."

Zita added, "We'll use the clearing outside the gates. It doesn't have any nymph trees, right? Last thing we need is to piss them off more than we already have." She interpreted over party line for Andy.

That's... surprisingly diplomatic of you. Did you know some dryads die when their tree does? Aloud, Wyn commented, "Yes, should he be mad, we would wish no harm to any locals."

Zita blinked. *They do? This place is so messed up.*

Oblivious to their silent conversation, Chiron tugged at the edges of his chiton. "Agreed. Did you wish to tend him now while the Council deliberates? I'll send someone to allow you in and out of the walls."

Greenie hurried back into view and scowled when she saw him with them. "Chiron! We await you!"

"Yes, before we have more of an audience to protect," Wyn replied. *Or to condemn us for any mistakes, imagined or otherwise.*

The centaur nodded and hastened toward the dryad.

Andy rubbed his hands together. "Well, if it works on the first one, I guess I'll be carting around statues. Arca, are those guns just for show, or are you going to help? Let's get started. I have a long, long bath to take once we're done."

***

Following Wyn's success at curing a chicken's petrification, it took a few trips, but less than an hour, for them to move all of the remaining stone menagerie and Arges to the clearing outside Olympus. The centaur who allowed them in and out of the city elected to stay safely behind the gates. Local wildlife was silent, possibly due to the loud and abrasive nagging of the stone goose, who had been stalking them since they began moving the stone birds.

Wyn fussed with her wimple, alternately smoothing and fluffing it. Her breathing was too fast. "My aunt needs me. My cats need me. I can do this. Undo the petrification and figure out a spell to get home."

Zita gave her a thumbs-up, elated that her own condition would soon be fixed. "Why are you so worried? You can. We think you can. You just did with a chicken."

"Now I'm the Little Witch Who Could? I appreciate the vote of confidence. I know you both have things to do as well." Despite the concern in her voice, Wyn restlessly straightened imaginary wrinkles in her toga and lined up an assortment of herbs and other items she claimed would help with the spell.

Andy nodded. "We do, assuming we haven't missed them. And Arca's right. We have faith in you."

Lifting her chin a notch higher, Wyn assured him, "I'll get it right this time. After that, we just have to finish our quests, then I'll cast the transport spell, and we'll go home. You'll get to your interview and job. Arca will have dinner with her family and tell the mercenary to leave her alone."

Something in Zita's heart twisted at her friend's words. She frowned and ran a hand over her hair.

Before she could say anything, Andy cleared his throat. "Thanks. And honestly, I think Arca should go for it with him."

Wyn whirled, dropping the honey candy she'd been fingering last. "What? Why would you say something like that? He's a murderer! He might not even be interested in her. A cold robot like that could be using her to collect the bounties on us."

Weird that they're blathering about this right now. Is Wyn delaying on purpose? What bounties? Maybe I should listen better to her current status recaps. Zita clapped her hands together loudly. "Wingspan, don't you have a no-comment policy on romance stuff? I really, really like that policy. We should all follow it! In any case, guys, shouldn't we be concentrating on the whole getting rid of stoning thing?"

Wyn ignored her, too focused on the argument. "Please. As if Arca would give any real romance a chance. It's a farce! She'll never change." Wyn scowled.

Andy rubbed the back of his neck and gazed skyward as if he wanted to fly away as much as Zita did. "She's been drooling over him since they met. He's actually made it through several dates with her, even if she didn't know that's what they were."

"What he thought they were, the creep," Wyn muttered.

Zita tried to slip in a few words. "He apologized about that."

His face solemn, Andy leaned forward. "Can you think of many people who will accept 'I have to vigilante now' without taking it personally when she suddenly leaves or cancels? Not to bring up bad memories, but wasn't that part of why Rani felt the need to end things?"

"You're just saying that because you're—" Wyn cut herself off. "And Rani left in part to concentrate on her dream career. Fine. Arca's going to do what she's going to do, but we can all hope it'll be the right thing. The one that doesn't end with bullets in all our heads."

Zita clumped over to the closest bird statue. "Great! Not that I don't value your unasked opinions and all, but none of that's going to matter if I'm a lawn ornament or we can't get home. Can we get on with making the chickens cluck again?"

Wyn stared at her a second. "Right. I was getting distracted. Here goes." She picked up a handful of components, walked over to the first stone bird, and began working her magic.

***

Four stone chickens and a pigeon later, Wyn cast her spell on the cyclops. As it had with the poultry, gray drained away from Arges, retreating up his massive body as his skin warmed to olive. His eye blinked once, and he squinted downward. He rubbed his eye, brow furrowing. "What?"

The stone goose ran to him aggressively and hissed, battering at his lower legs. That set off the chickens in a cacophony of clucking. Startled, the pigeon screeched and flew up, almost into the cyclops' face, and then away.

Arges made a choking sound, the pupil in his single eye dilated, and his body stiffened. His massive frame trembled, and sweat sprang onto his forehead. "Basilisks!" he bellowed, hurling his mug at the birds.

The mug hit a tree and shattered.

Chickens panicked, squawking at a volume loud enough to bring involuntary tears to Zita's eyes. They fluttered and ran around, with two taking refuge at her feet. The goose shrieked and hissed.

Even though she could understand why the combination of sounds reminded him of the basilisk, Zita called out in Greek. "Dude, calm down! There's no basilisk here!"

Wyn started chanting, her hands moving in intricate patterns.

The birds seemed to madden the cyclops even more, as he roared and pulled a long, polished cudgel from his belt. When his gaze fixated on the two hens cowering behind her, he howled and charged, sweeping his weapon in a wide arc at them.

As the cudgel descended, Zita grabbed Wyn and yanked her friend back and away from the cyclops. She stumbled but kept upright as she dragged the witch several feet backward.

Wyn cried out in surprise. *Lost my spell!*

The birds escaped in an explosion of noise and feathers, apparently unharmed.

Andy ran to the cyclops, hands open in a pleading position. Apparently forgetting the other man didn't speak English, he called out, "Arges! Stop before you hurt someone!"

Wyn shook her head and began casting again.

The stone goose shrieked and ran up to peck at the cyclops, treading on his injured foot.

Arges shrieked and kicked at the bird and then at Andy.

Dodging to the side, Andy grabbed the cyclops' calf and shoved upward in a slow, strong movement.

Arges toppled, dropping his cudgel.

Still gripping the leg, Andy flew up, exerting pressure in a move that should have forced the one-eyed giant onto his stomach to better control him... if Arges had not been too big.

Still prone, the cyclops reached out, grabbed Andy, and tossed him aside.

Like a rock skimming on a pond, Andy flew across the open ground, hitting occasionally and bouncing farther away. His startled shriek had a weird ululation every time he hit the ground, and it ended in a thud as he rolled to a stop by a sapling.

Unable to even do a ginga, the most basic of capoeira moves, Zita held herself in as much of a defensive position as possible with a leg that wouldn't bend. *I don't think I can hurt Arges without shifting, and my condition will throw my balance off too much to fight as I normally would.*

A pink mist began swirling around Arges.

Please go to sleep. If this doesn't work, what next? Zita tried to shoo away a chicken hiding behind her without actually kicking it.

"Witch!" Eye wide at the smoke, Arges scrambled away from it, grabbing his cudgel. He hurled it at Wyn.

Reacting without thinking, Zita grabbed Wyn and teleported several feet away, well out of range of the weapon. She ignored the fact that she'd lost all feeling in her other foot, though she had an ugly suspicion that using her powers sped up the petrification process. *I need a solution where I don't use my powers. If Wyn were freaking out, I'd remove the triggers.*

"Hey! I was casting! The spell's less effective on someone hysterical already, you know!" Wyn complained.

Andy ran back toward the women. Dirt and leaves decorated his toga, and his cape was askew and showing rips. "You guys all right?"

Arges stood and stomped toward them.

Hissing, the goose dashed toward Arges and then away, flapping its heavy wings.

The cyclops screamed and tried to smash it.

"Weasels!" Zita shouted. "Wingspan, hold off Arges. Muse, make with the weasels! Lots of big ones!" She limped as fast as she could toward the goose.

Andy was already in motion to intercept Arges.

Where are you going? Wyn whispered a few words and threw out her hands with a flourish as if she were a stage magician at the big reveal. Four long-tailed weasels, easily two feet in length, appeared. Each illusory animal ran after a different bird.

Taking her attention from them, Zita chased after the obnoxious goose.

It made her task much simpler when it saw her running for it and charged at her, fluttering in the air to bite at her face. At the last second, it veered away.

"Yes! More weasels, witch! Kill all the basilisks!" shouted Arges.

A chicken and the weasel chasing it crossed her path.

She lunged for the goose, managing to catch it and to barely keep her balance.

Chased by two weasels, another chicken raced by her feet and disappeared into the forest underbrush.

Zita tripped. Out of habit, she twisted to avoid landing on the smaller creature, a move she regretted as her body was crunched between the stone goose body and the ground at the same time. "At least I've still got it," she muttered.

Granite wings battered her face and chest, but she struggled to her feet, one hand controlling the head and neck to stop the beast from biting her again. She hobbled as fast as she could toward the outer gate of Olympus, concentrating to keep hold of her squirming burden.

From her peripheral vision, she saw Arges standing unmoving in the center of the clearing, surrounded by a furry, writhing mass of patrolling weasels, big tears running down his face. He wiped his eyes and then his nose on a long piece of purple cloth.

Andy stood nearby, watching. Wyn stood not far off behind him, her face deep in concentration.

The goose bit her in her moment of distraction, and she concentrated on moving faster to reach the town. She shoved the goose inside Olympus and slammed the gate closed.

From the other side of the gate came a startled shout and an indignant honk.

With a deep breath, Zita turned and hurried to rejoin her friends.

"All the birds are gone, and Arges seems calmer. Should I drop the illusion?" Wyn murmured quietly in English.

After a moment assessing the cyclops, Zita nodded. "Body language's not aggressive anymore, and his cudgel's back on his belt again. That said, let's not get too close in case the chickens return."

"I'm good with that," Andy said.

After a few more moments, Arges blew his nose loudly on the cloth, the sound reverberating. Meekly, he offered it to Andy.

"No, that's yours now. Use it in good health." A cape-less Andy backed away, lifting his hands in the air.

Wyn interpreted for the cyclops.

Arges shuddered and squared his shoulders, hanging the handkerchief from his belt. "I thank you. If my brothers discovered how I... loathe... those birds now, I would spend eternity being mocked."

Her voice sympathetic, Wyn said, "We won't mention it to anyone."

"Speak not of me at all. Do not appraise them of my freedom nor my whereabouts. Only time can calm my mind and mend my broken courage. The shame of this..." He hung his head.

Holding out her hands, Wyn said, "You were a victim of the basilisk. There is no shame in that. It would help us with the Council if you would come forward and let them know that we aided you."

He replied with a bitter laugh. "Not yet. Not until I have regained... not until I can cope..." The cyclops glanced at Zita's leg. "You should concentrate on your own problems."

Zita interpreted for Andy in a low voice.

"Tell him we can take him home, but the basilisk is still there. We could try to figure out how to kill it," Andy offered.

When she'd repeated the offer, Arges shuddered. "No, thank you, all of you, but especially the goddess of the weasels. I will walk and think, but never will I will return to that island. It was my haven, a place where only my animals and I lived, but it was too quiet. Even sirens came not too close to the shore. Also, even if you destroyed it, what if the basilisk laid eggs first? No."

Wyn lifted her hands, her voice a melodious, soothing murmur. "We won't make you return if that is not your wish. Speaking of homes, we're trying to return to our realm. Would you know anything of how the ancient gods traveled between worlds? Perhaps part or all of a spell to do so?"

"By power. Before they reached the fullness of their might, Hephaestus had a clever trinket that helped train them to walk between worlds, but only the gods knew its secrets." Arges shrugged.

Wyn's shoulders slumped. "Thank you for your answer."

The big cyclops paused, harsh lines of his face softening. "Twice now, I've lost my home with no hope of return, so your pain is one I know. In return for the service you have done, my island is yours now, and all of my belongings... save my clothing.

Keep it, give it away, burn it. I care not. Farming is a pleasant enough chore to keep my mind occupied, but how could I face a barnyard?"

The answer slipped out before Zita could stop herself. "Why don't you farm weasels? They'd dogpile on any basilisks that come along, and you'd buy time to deal with your problem. You might have to rebuild some though." She flushed. "Sorry, I'm trying to help?"

"Wherever I go, it will not be back to the island. I'll have nothing of it. It is yours. Remember, speak of this to no one." The cyclops turned and began plodding away from the gates.

"Arges, buey, you got family. Can't you at least speak to them? It's wrong to leave them not knowing your fate like that!" Zita said.

He hesitated but continued on his way.

"Well, we tried. I assume so anyway. Arca didn't piss him off, did she?" Andy said philosophically in English.

Wyn gnawed on her lower lip and smoothed imaginary wrinkles from her toga. "No, she was fine."

Zita's skin prickled. She slapped her friend gently on the back. "You did great! You calmed him and figured out how to reverse the petrification! And he's alive and not mad or living rock or exploded! Plus, that cooking pot is pretty awesome."

Wyn's shoulders slumped. "We're now the proud owners of unlivable real estate in a land we can't wait to leave where everyone hates us. And we still haven't managed to get home. My poor aunt... and..." She sniffled.

Desperate to avoid her friend's tears, Zita tried to find something positive. "The island's got a nice view. If we want, we could drop off the stone goose there as a security guard. Maybe it will kill the basilisk since it's already stone. Not many homeowners can claim an anti-basilisk guard goose, right? And it's not everyone who hates us, just a majority."

Oddly, Wyn did not seem comforted.

Andy cut off anything else Zita would've said. "What she meant was that we only have a couple more things to do, and then we can go home."

Zita slung an arm around the other woman's shoulders and tugged her into a quick hug. "Sure. What he said. Do me now."

Andy tried to turn a snicker into a cough. "Sorry, that just sounded wrong."

"Perv." Zita grinned, releasing Wyn.

Slowly, Wyn cast her spell again.

When her friend fell silent, Zita glanced down. Nothing had changed. Her throat went dry, and she forced herself to breathe evenly and smile. "You need more ingredients? Anything you want, I'll fetch it for you."

"I knew it!" Wyn broke into full-blown sobs.

"Don't cry. Why are you crying? Are those happy tears? Please let those be happy tears. I'm supportively listening and not offering solutions." Zita reached out to her friend before pulling back, hands balling into fists. Her stomach roiled.

His face lined with concern, Andy wrapped his arm around Wyn. "What's wrong? We're here."

Wyn hid her face against his chest for a moment, and then pulled away, dabbing at her eyes with her wimple. "The method I used to free them won't work on Arca. They're all magical creatures, despite being animals, so I used their innate magic to separate the basilisk's effect and dispel it."

She thought about it. "So you peeled off the layer of basilisk magic?"

"Yes. It won't work on you, though. I tried. Wingspan has a little magic in human form, and he's fully magic as a bird. But you? Nothing. You're the least magical person I know. Perhaps because of your shapeshifting, your body has incorporated the petrification as if it were natural to you. I can't cure it."

Zita fought to swallow the lump in her throat. It tasted like fear. "Maybe you just need a second try? Like an extra round of medicine?"

Wyn sniffled and repeated the ritual.

If Zita could've tapped her feet, they would've been vibrating with her need to move. As it was, she settled for flexing her shoulders as she shoved her disappointment down into the furthest recesses of her mind. It wouldn't help Wyn. "Oh, well, then. That's a problem. You'll keep working on it, though, right?"

Wyn's head shot up. "Of course I will!"

"Well, then. I got faith in you. You'll get it. If I go all the way to stone, how about you use the same spell on me as you did on the evil goose? I'd rather be an awesome walking stone than in a granite coma."

Her friend's mouth was hidden, but her head lifted. "That might work. I could try."

"There we go. If I end up a rock, you'll make me a walking, talking rock. Just think of all the money I'll save on food. That could be a major benefit. You know how I love a firm, tight budget." Zita paused, her mind drifting other places. "Or a man's nice—"

Andy interrupted. "We get the idea! Now we have a plan for when that happens, why don't we focus on the next task? Arges is free, so we don't need to worry about leaving him trapped in stone forever."

After a long moment, Wyn nodded and straightened to her usual perfect posture. She smoothed her hands over her face, straightening the fabric strips of her mask. "Yes, of course. Let's return to the city and see if we can bathe or if the Council has decided our next task."

As her adrenaline wore off, the pain set in. Every part of her felt bruised, save for the stone ones. Her toga was sticky with blood on one throbbing shoulder where the goose had managed to bite during the struggle. Zita winced. "Mind healing some bruises before they send us somewhere I'll collect new ones?"

Unharmed, but considerably muddied, Andy plucked a feather from her hair. "I'm not the only one in dire need of a bath, too."

Chapter Fourteen

Andy and Zita had plenty of time to bathe. The Council did not summon them again until the next morning.

"Not that the javelin practice wasn't enthralling, and I'm certain Muse appreciated the time to work on her spells, but this better not be another silly fetch quest. I'm more than ready to be done with all this." Andy voiced all their impatience while they waited in the megaron for the dryad to speak.

Zita nodded. "That's what I been saying!"

Wyn shushed them.

Greenie seemed to be enjoying herself as she waved a hand and pounded the ceremonial spear on the ground. "The next task is that you must pass the trials at the sacred Temple of the Gods. When you have won your awards, take the Sword of Heracles so your victory may be proven to our Council. Take only that and nothing more." She eyed Zita.

Folding her arms over her chest, Zita said, "Still not a thief."

The nymph sniffed and raised her eyebrows at them. "So you claim.

"Oh, it's on, algae-breath," Zita muttered.

Wyn poked her. "Hush your mouth. Don't insult them."

"She probably doesn't speak English."

"Are you certain of that?" Wyn quirked an eyebrow at her.

Zita closed her mouth. *For someone who's part tree, girl is bloodthirsty. Just saying.*

Chiron sighed, and his tail flicked rapidly.

Her eyes distant, Wyn gestured for attention. "Forgive us, but we are new to your land and unfamiliar with this temple. Where might we find it?"

Chiron nodded. "It is far to the west and south on Mount Strongúlē. None have lived on the island since the hero Aeolus died. The mountain boils and seethes constantly. It is close by Arges' hermitage."

Before he could finish speaking, the mean dryad stepped in front of him. "Help them no more. Part of the task is the learning of it, and even the teacher of the gods must honor that. This warning will I grant you, though. None may tread there save the gods and those deemed worthy. Those you name Clockwork and Dragon never returned from the temple. Your blood may be the next to water the dark fields of Mount Strongúlē unless you flee to the northern lands."

The old centaur scowled. "Every journey must begin somewhere."

"Theirs begins here. We'll be watching." Greenie narrowed her eyes at them.

The words slipped out in Greek, despite Zita's best intentions to keep her mouth shut. "Good. Maybe you'll learn something other than how to be a total b—"

Slapping a hand over Zita's mouth, Wyn grabbed and yanked on her arm, mouthing platitudes.

Zita growled and switched to English. "Let go. I'll be quiet, even if I'm totally right about her."

Her friend released her.

Once he had a translation, Andy said, "Sounds like an Italian island. You think they could mean Mount Stromboli?"

Wyn hummed, her eyes unfocused for a moment, and then nodded. "It seems likely given what Chiron was able to tell us."

"I suppose it's too much to hope that it's a mountain of delicious flavor." Zita grumped.

"If we ever need to beat such a mountain, you're the first person I'd summon," Wyn replied.

She had to smile. "Works for me."

***

Zita frowned as she hobbled up the side of the desolate mountain to the barely visible ruins. Sweat dripped down her neck, where the long hair of her Arca form lay in a sweltering, itchy line down her back. Beneath her, the earth shivered as the volcano belched. The air was thin from the elevation, forcing the trio to move slowly as they picked their way to the ruins. Ash clouded the air and piled in a silty layer on everything. Between that and the reek of sulfur, her mouth had an unpleasant, gritty taste.

"Chiron made it clear it was an active volcano, but he didn't mention it was on the verge of an eruption," she grumbled. Since she couldn't feel her feet, she kept her eyes trained on the ground.

Wyn coughed and nodded, wiping her face with a cloth already smudged with gray spots. As the only one of them with feet that could be injured by the sharp-edged chunks of dark rock littering the ground, she picked a slow, careful path between the others. "Be happy we found it at all. Let's not get our feathers ruffled, literally or figuratively. We'll search the temple, accomplish our goals, and depart as quickly as possible."

The protective courtyard had long ago succumbed to time and the harsh environs. The walls were barely more than the suggestion of a symmetrical rectangle surrounding a collection of rock piles. A solitary, dilapidated building still stood in the exact center. Most of the pillars of the colonnade were cracked or broken. Friezes above the pillars held incised scenes, though only a few figures and objects were identifiable. The best of the images held a centaur, a one-eyed giant, and a woman bowing before another figure, who was only represented by a bearded head, the body missing in a wide swath of destroyed stonework.

As they hiked toward it, Andy eyed it dubiously. He seemed not to notice the difference in elevation, but the purple of his clothing was dulled with a layer of the ever-present ash. "Are you certain this is the right location? It honestly seems like the kind of place that even tomb robbers couldn't find anything of value in."

Wyn minced after him, lifting the hem of her dress to watch her steps. "I cannot be certain, but it's my best guess. With the assumption that it mirrors the Grecian temples in our world, the interior of the building should be one big room with an idol. If Clockwork visited this temple before he disappeared, we might find his remains."

Zita shrugged. "Chiron mentioned Dragon was here too. It's possible she snapped and ate him. If it's like you said, it'll at least be a fast search." With a cautious eye on the destroyed pillars, she skirted a broken column and approached the front.

The entrance was two metal doors, closed tight. A small gap, about the size of a hand, was carved chest high where the edges met. Three deep gashes marred one side.

"Wonder what did that?" Zita said, waving her hand at the marks on the metal. She was careful to keep her hands from touching them for fear the edges were sharper than they seemed. *I may be up-to-date on my tetanus shots, but no need to test it more than necessary.*

Wyn stayed at the base of the steps leading to the porch area. "It could've been Dragon, but who knows? Greco-Roman mythos borrowed heavily from its neighbors, so any amalgam of monster or being is possible. What if we can't get the door open?"

Andy bounded up the steps to Zita's side. "I can do it. They probably just need oil or someone strong enough to move the metal, though I'll have to be careful not to break it. Maybe the air will stink less inside." He thrust one hand into the gap. Rock groaned, and he stepped backward.

Zita had already rejoined Wyn and had one hand resting on her friend's shoulder. Despite her caution, she couldn't resist rocking on her heels.

The doors squealed in high-pitched protest as they dragged on the ground and opened.

"Buey, how hard did you pull?" Zita asked.

His long braid flew in the air when he shook his head. "I didn't pull. I just put my hand in the hole, and it opened. I'm officially creeped out. Just wanted to be the first to say it," Andy said.

"Loco, but we knew these quests would be full of suck. It shouldn't need to air out with the hole in the door, so let's see what's left. With any luck, it'll be more complete than the smashed outside." Zita adjusted her toga, rolled her shoulders, and marched to the doorway as best she could. Gritty with the fine ash, the ancient stone was pocked but cool beneath her bare hand when she touched it, despite the oppressive heat in the air.

After making a raspberry, Andy muttered something about bad ideas and horror movies. More loudly, he said, "I'll guard the rear. Muse, stay in the center so we can protect you."

Straightening so her posture was painfully erect, Wyn lifted her chin and daintily followed Zita up the stairs. "Or perhaps I shall stay in the center so you may both be included in any protective shields I cast."

"Either way, I'm leading." Zita snickered and entered.

Dusty, but lacking the omnipresent, unpleasant ash outside, the large circular room in front of them seemed larger than the exterior had suggested. Along the boundaries of the room, five doors, green and brown with age, gaped open. One room was filled with rubble. Chunks of stone, sliced into pieces almost identical in size and shape, sat near the destroyed room, suggesting where the door had gone.

"I don't remember seeing any rooms off the main one from the outside. The proportions are off," Andy said from behind her.

Zita inhaled, the action oddly easy after trying to breathe the nasty, thin air outside. Normally, she would've shifted to gain better senses, but she had no desire to risk losing more of herself to the encroaching stone. She suppressed the flare of worry at the thought. "I don't sense any corpses. It smells old and dusty and a bit metallic."

When she spoke, a few tiles fell from the ceiling, bouncing into their path.

"And unstable. I really don't like this." Light glowed in a magical diamond that floated above Wyn's head.

Andy set a hand on the witch's arm. "If you need to, I can drop you off somewhere safer. Either of you."

"We've come this far. If we can nail this one, we're that much closer to home," Zita pointed out.

Wyn pressed her lips together and shook her head. Her back straightened. "We're here and need to do this. The center of this room has a sacred circle incised in it, and the walls seem to provide instructions of some sort. Arca, help me read them."

The women studied the symbols.

Wyn ran a hand along in the air as she read. "Lots of invocations to gods, death to the uninvited unless they've got... I'm not certain." She blushed.

"That's a dick joke," Zita said, examining the spot where her friend had stopped.

"Seriously?" Andy said. His expression was torn. "Is it funny? No, don't answer that. I don't need to hear ancient humor like that."

She shrugged. "If that's what it is, it's not funny. Basically, you've got to measure up, and the gates will open. If you don't got an invite, you need to earn it in one of the trials, whatever that means." An evil idea occurred to her, and she grinned at Andy. "So, whip it out, and hope Zeus wasn't all these walls claim he was. Muse and I aren't equipped for the task... if you know what I mean."

He stared at her in horror, his mouth falling open. One hand started to lower toward his waist protectively.

Zita snickered, then laughed. "Just kidding, mano. I'm certain you're not actually supposed to do that." *Mostly.*

Wyn tsked. "Play nice, children. We have to figure out the trials. Perhaps the adjoining rooms will have more clues? Can you check them out and see if there's more information? Once we've done that, I'll sit down and see if I can determine our next move."

The witch broke off and eyed the area, her nose wrinkling and hands curling. "Or not. I'll stand here and see if they have any clues to the exact ritual we need. Perhaps we'll need to offer a sacrifice to the major deities, which we should be able to do with no bloodshed if we're clever. Grain for Demeter, poetry for Apollo, and so on."

After exchanging a glance with Andy, Zita shrugged. "You're the expert. If this does go to poetry, it's all you. Where do you want me to start?"

Her countenance thoughtful, Wyn waved at the closest doorway. "The friezes above the doors have words woven into the scene. See if you can decipher those while I work on the floor mosaic."

"You got it." Zita paused as she translated, flitting from entry to entry. She pointed to each door as she spoke, "Fire, water, earth, air, and ... aether, whatever that is."

Andy knelt by the doorway filled with rubble. "Which is this?"

Zita glanced at it. "Aether."

He thrust a hand into the pile of rocks and pulled out something. Metal gleamed in his palm. "Recognize this?"

The two women gathered close.

"It's like a metal ant head. The pincers are all banged up, though," Zita said.

Wyn nodded. "Far too new to belong here. It must've been one of Clockwork's inventions."

His expression grim, Andy said. "These resemble the insect robots we fought in Vegas that were attacking tourists for no reason."

Pinching her forehead, Wyn grimaced. "Of course they are. And since the ones we destroyed in Vegas were in top shape, he either made it out of here or someone's inherited all his deadly toys. As we know Dragon is in our world, my assumption would be that they escaped together, and whatever they did destroyed the aether room. Which should we pick?"

Zita contemplated their choices. "You couldn't pay me to go in the fire door. I'll try water. Any liquid probably evaporated long ago with the whole dry active volcano air and all."

"Don't!" Wyn said.

"We've got to go forward, and I don't see another way. If nothing else, I'll just translate whatever's in there. Andy can do the heavy lifting to solve it. He'll have my back, right, mano? He probably can't drown."

He nodded, his lips pressed together. "Most likely, though I'd rather not test it. With your condition, though, I should be the one to go in."

"I'm not helpless." Annoyance had Zita stepping through before he could follow through on his words. Her lips pressed together as she examined the room. A small rectangle, it had none of the decoration of the main area outside, other than a curious pattern in the floor, like a wave curling in on itself. "See? Nothing here. Pan comido." She stepped forward to examine it.

Andy threw his hands in the air. "Doomed, I tell you."

The door slid shut behind her.

She whirled toward it, but it had already closed. A rising thrum of sound, stone grinding reluctantly against stone, vibrated through the floor and up her body despite her condition. A hole opened in the floor, filled with a glittered, frothing mass stinking of brine and fish. Seawater. It lapped at her feet.

Caramba.

Chapter Fifteen

Warm water swirled around Zita. Despite the short time the door had been closed, the briny liquid was already thigh-high and still rising. She stifled a disbelieving laugh. *Well, drowning in seawater is not a common hazard in an active volcano.*

Panic pervaded Wyn's mental voice. *Zita! Are you okay? We're coming. Andy's going to break down the door.*

Don't! The room's filling with water. I can shift to something that can breathe water and find the sword. You can't, and if it fills the temple, you won't be able to do any other magic necessary for this stupid quest.

If you're certain. Wyn and Andy's concern vibrated over party line, so much so that she couldn't tell which of them had spoken.

The flow showed no sign of abating and had almost reached her chin.

After running through a quick mental catalog of fish, Zita took a deep breath. With concentration, she tried to keep her thoughts from leaking to her friends. *Here's hoping I'm wrong about my powers making me turn to stone faster. I'll pick something other creatures will hesitate to eat just in case all this water brought in a predator or two.* She shifted to a lionfish.

The rushing waters threw her small body around, but she fought to keep herself from hitting the walls, until finally the water reached the ceiling and stilled. Not only did she have to work hard to swim with most of her tail fin as dead weight, but she took far longer to regain control of herself than she'd hoped. The currents died.

Zita let herself drift through the room, exploring it while keeping alert for an attack. The simple stone room was bare, except for the hole in the center, presumably the origin of the saltwater. She tried to inject confidence into her mental voice to soothe her friends, squashing her own doubts. *I can do this. Swim around, find the sword, come back. Let's wait to destroy the door until I'm done.*

I don't like this, Andy sent.

None of us have been real thrilled about anything since we ended up here. Except the food. That's pretty good. Zita continued her search. As no more water surged out to push her away, she swam close to the hole, hoping to catch a detail she'd missed. Her eyes weren't sufficient to make out the patterns, and her nose bumped a tile.

A shockwave rushed through the water, and the hole gurgled and sucked her down.

Under other circumstances, Zita might have enjoyed rocketing through the water, but she'd chosen the wrong form. Rough currents spun her through a tunnel, banging her against the walls and slicing her long fins.

Party line disappeared.

Pressure rose as the temperature dropped, and utter darkness surrounded her. Pain and cold ripped through her, and she was blind. Even in her fish form, she struggled to draw a breath. *Need a deep-sea animal!*

She switched to a cusk eel and spent a moment gasping and regaining her equilibrium. With the horrible squeeze of the unexpected depth gone and the temperature more comfortable for her current form, she centered herself in the tunnel. Her streamlined body avoided further injury from the walls, though her sides ached from the initial headlong descent, and she suspected she'd find several scrapes later on parts that remained flesh. She couldn't feel her tail at all and used the remainder of her body and pectoral fins to control her movement.

So not happy to be right about my powers and the petrification.

A few minutes later, her body slammed into an invisible barrier, almost rebounding off it before it gave way with a disorienting pop, and she was thrust into a wide, open area.

Calm, motionless water surrounded her on all sides, except below, where the largely bare ocean floor stretched. Marine snow, detritus from the upper layers of the sea, sprinkled the water in a constant bath of tiny particles. An occasional rock and a few starfish with long, scraggly arms broke up the coarse, large-grained sand and clay ooze below her.

She took a moment to accustom herself to the eel's shape, now that she wasn't focused on surviving. At a foot long from stubby snout to the tip of her tapering tail, she suspected she was one of the larger predators in the area. While her eyesight was terrible, other senses, some of which she had no names for, contributed enough information for her to get an idea of where she was. *I'm lucky the descent wasn't any faster, or I wouldn't have survived. This is deeper than I've ever dived... maybe somewhere in the midnight or abyssal zone? At least seeing the ocean floor lets me know which direction is up, and it's not the hadal zone. Wherever I am, I'll have to be careful shifting, as the pressure will kill animals not adapted to it extremely quickly. I wish I'd spent time practicing in this form and a few others that survive at these depths, rather than relying on my memory of a few deep-sea creature specials.*

A rapid humming vibration whispered in the distance, where she could only make out some kind of pale light. *Given the lack of anything else, the glowing, vibrating object is probably what I'm here to snag. Wyn's magic glows, Tiffany's magic sometimes does too, so that must be the enchanted sword I'm here for. I can't quite make it out well enough to teleport there, though. So, I guess I'll snag it, then go back through the tunnel.*

When Zita twisted to see what she'd emerged from, she only saw more of the same scenery with minor variations. *It's gone? Dumbass chingado magic. I better not be stranded under here.*

Uneasy in her new form, she descended until she hovered immediately above the ocean floor. To conserve her energy, she propelled herself slowly toward the strange white blur in the distance. After a near-miss with a cute little dumbo octopus, she reoriented herself over a seemingly endless herd of almost translucent creatures with stubby appendages—sea pigs, she guessed—and caught the sneaky scuttle of a small king crab hiding beneath one of them.

She had to push down the instincts that urged her to hunt it. *I'm hungry, but I'll save eating for human form. Still, a snack would be super awesome.* Zita laughed inwardly at herself.

Several more minutes of labored swimming brought her close enough that even a cusk eel's poor eyesight could make out the marble statues of a man and a woman, poised with a coconut-sized gold coin joining their hands. Myriad raised shapes decorated gleaming golden bracers on their wrists. Something white tangled in the tines of a trident held by the male.

She swam closer to determine what the strange shape was. After a second, however, she gasped. *A plastic bag? I must be back in the normal world. I could teleport home!*

For a second, temptation teased her. *I could be there for my brother at his class thing and not disappoint my family, not be the irresponsible one for once... But I can't abandon Wyn and Andy, or even that loser Garm in the Greece of half-human everythings.*

Steeling herself, she swam toward the disc on the statue. *This must be what I'm here for, since I don't see any swords.*

She studied the statues, working to understand them despite the difference in vision. The female figure wore a toga with armor over it, a helmet, and an irritable expression. A tiny owl perched on the shield in one hand, and a scroll dangled from her waist. She shared the medallion with a muscular bearded guy in a toga. His other hand was raised as if to strike with his trident. Both wore golden bracers with words set in gemstones on them, and golden stripes covered their hands.

She tried to seize the disc in her mouth. It wouldn't budge. Backing off, she glared at it.

As she watched, the light flared, and more Greek words appeared along the coin's edges.

The medallion read: *There is a house. One enters it blind and comes out seeing. What is it?*

A puzzle? Underwater? Even if I solve it, how do I say the answer? Zita frowned, or tried to, but her shape did not allow for the expression.

Maybe the fancy bracers are a clue, like that show Andy made me watch with the hungry dog. If I push on the right word, they'll drop the coin, or a secret passageway back will open, or a cookie will fall out, or something. What are my options?

She frowned, eyeing the possible choices. *Anything I can't read is out, since magic would hopefully keep the answer from rubbing off. So, that limits my choices to dawn, womb, school, temple, government, or conversation.*

Easy. I know the lyrics to "Sublime Gracia" and what makes the blind see. Lacking any appendages, she nosed "temple."

Electricity jolted through her, and she crashed to the ground.

Carajo. Guess people pretending to be gods aren't real religious. Well, that leaves five choices. Laboriously, Zita swam back to hover beside the coin.

Flashing light, like the disorienting strobe of an undersea disco ball, caught her attention, and she glanced up to see a giant squid, or what seemed like one given her current proportions, rapidly jetting toward the statue, feeding tentacles outstretched.

Caramba. Her eel instincts urged her to hide in the sand, but she put her mouth on the medallion and tugged, in case the shock had loosened it.

The squid paused a few feet away, seeming confused, before it lashed out. A tentacle seized the bag and ripped it from the statue, passing it along the suckers and shredding it as it went, until the powerful beak tore through it.

Zita tugged at the coin harder, but it refused to budge. *Come on, you stupid...*

Fragments of plastic drifted away as the squid abruptly spat out the bag and threw it aside. A tentacle grabbed her. As she was manhandled and thrown away, thankfully before reaching the beak, tiny teeth and hooks tore at Zita.

The animal wound both feeding tentacles around the coin with no more luck dislodging it than she'd had.

Zita forced herself upright again, feeling herself tiring at the effort of keeping her partially stone form moving. *I need to get it off the coin. Fighting is out. I've never been a cusk eel before, let alone one who can't use part of its body. It's never been anything other than a giant squid. In a straight-out fight, it's got all the advantages. I hate to shift again, but maybe I can go smaller—octopi are pretty strong—and slip a few tentacles in there. Once I wrap a few limbs around it, I can slip out and go through the portal before it catches me. Or... perhaps the squid will help me with the riddle.*

If she could've, she would've grinned as she shifted to a dumbo octopi. She tried to ignore the multiple limbs floating limp and gray in the water.

Zita had to take a moment to accustom herself to the untried shape. Normally, she could rely on her animal instincts to control basic movement while she focused on other things, but locomotion and sensory information was different from most of the forms she'd practiced. *It's closest to being an insect, though instead of having to understand the world at a much smaller scale and interpret hundreds of images, I have to swim using these ear-like flaps and control tons of suckers.*

After a minute, she realized she was swimming upside down and did a slow roll to right herself, studying the squid. Its body had not yet enveloped the coin, only a tentacle, so her plan might work.

She drew in water and teleported to one of the bracers, hovering over the "government" characters.

The squid lashed out at her.

Expelling the water, she jetted away from it.

It hit the word, and its body stiffened as current ran through it. Tentacles fell away from the medallion.

While the squid jittered from the electrical shock, Zita slipped in and wrapped herself around the coin.

The squid recovered enough to try to pry her off the still-glowing medallion.

While her stone limbs took the brunt of the attack, teeth still broke her delicate skin. She clung with her whole body, pulling.

Got to go for it. Let's hope the scroll means the cranky lady is a fan of books. She squeezed out one of her tentacles, blood trailing from the limb, and slapped "school" on the bracers.

The coin came loose.

Light blinded her.

Agony roared through her as if every inch of flesh were exploding.

Instinct took over, and her body reshaped itself into a familiar, pain-free form even as she felt herself flop onto dry stone. *Hard, dry stone.*

More pain, localized to her face, had her wincing and curling into a ball. *Chingado quests.*

Chapter Sixteen

While her friends were happy to see the coin, they were less thrilled that the petrification had spread, and she now had only one working arm and her head left unaffected. She'd provided an abbreviated account of her underwater adventure, and her guess as to why the petrification had advanced. Her description did not include the hard, burning lump of panic in her throat every time she ran up against new limitations.

Her magic glowed as Wyn healed the injuries to Zita's remaining flesh. "No powers. You're not going to use them again."

"Maybe I should use them more. If I go all the way stone, you can use whatever spell you used on the goose on me." Zita craned her neck to see around her one arm, which blocked part of her line of sight, as it had frozen bent at the elbow, her hand upward, fingers spread, as if she were preparing to catch a ball or roll for impact. *At least my legs are stuck in a standing position, not mid-kick or something, and they don't appear damaged by any of my recent actions.*

Finishing the spell, her friend wrung her hands. "The whole reason I've been so cautious about trying new cures is to avoid hurting living creatures. I'm not certain that'll work on you, and I don't want to risk exploding you."

Her mind shied away from picturing herself like that, and Zita slapped on a smile. "That would suck. I've got faith in you though. You'll fix me up soon."

"What was that?" Wyn's voice was pitched higher than usual.

Zita tilted her head. "What was what? I was just saying you'd find a cure soon."

Her friend shivered. "No pressure, right? Zita... I might not be able to."

"You will. It's only a matter of time." She shoved any doubt down, so it wouldn't leak over the party line.

Wyn tilted her head skyward and pinched the spot between her eyebrows. "But what if I can't do it? I can't solve my aunt's Alzheimer's. This could be like that. You can't risk using your powers again until we know for certain that I have a solution for your problem. I have to get us home, too. All the pressure you keep putting on me to work on it isn't helping either."

Zita twitched her good shoulder. "Sorry, I didn't mean to pressure you. I was trying to keep you from getting so upset that..." She managed to stop herself from finishing the sentence. Frantically, she tried to think of a way to say what she meant without insulting her friend.

"That I what?" Wyn said.

Help. Zita mouthed the word at Andy.

He nodded, almost imperceptibly, and stepped forward, sliding an arm around Wyn's shoulders in a quick hug. "Zita's just... trying to build your confidence."

Wyn still seemed dubious but leaned into the hug for a moment.

After pulling away, Andy smoothed his hands on his toga. "You're an amazing, accomplished woman, but you tend to doubt yourself, especially when the stakes are high. She was trying to affirm your magical abilities, and it backfired."

"It is Zita," Wyn said slowly.

"Sí, that! I'm hopeless." Zita blinked. "Wait..."

Andy clapped his hands together. "And there we go, all in agreement again. Yay! Now, we have things to do, right?"

"Yes, let's get to it. I'll try not to use my powers unless I have to. Pinky swear. So, what'd you figure out while I was underwater?" Zita said.

Wyn's expression lightened.

"Can I carry you to the main room?" Andy held out his arms.

"Sure." She gritted her teeth.

He carried her, setting her down beside one of the columns and turning her so she could see most of the room. Thanks to the water still dripping from her long, hopelessly tangled hair, a briny, fishy odor mingled with the stone, dust, and metal of before, but little else had changed. It was still an empty room with a crumbling ceiling and ornate mosaics on the floor and walls. Soaring columns framed the only entry and exit.

Zita flexed her fingers, willing herself to ignore the strange numbness of most of her body, and the fabric drying itchy with salt on her good shoulder. *I could really go for a shower and some fried calamari right now,* she thought. A pang ran through her when her stomach didn't rumble.

Wyn walked over to the center of the room and gestured to the wall opposite the entryway. "While *someone* went swimming without us, I noticed that the mosaic on that wall has seams of gold, which implies sections of it will open. It's probably a doorway to another level of the temple, like the one hidden behind the altar in Brazil. See the gold hands in the center? They're just big enough to fit that medallion."

Andy held up a warning hand. "I should be the one to put the medallion into place since I'm the hardest to hurt. While we can't be certain how this temple works, I've played role-playing games before. It's probably an opening, and if we don't have to fight our way through a dungeon stuffed with creatures that want to eat us, something awful will come out of that hole."

Philosophically, Zita said, "At least on land, I can kick giant squid culo." She remembered her current limits. "Or bite it, anyway, if it lines up with my head."

Her friends shot her curious looks.

"Is that what put those nasty circle cuts all over your face? Or was that from the fall, like the broken nose?" Andy asked.

Zita grimaced and eyed the barren temple. "I'll tell you guys all about it later."

"Arca, do you see any warnings in the floor or wall mosaics? It seems innocuous enough to me, a celebration of Hephaestus." Wyn gestured to their surroundings.

Zita craned her neck to check. "No monsters, just some gold chicks having a dance party. However, it's magic stuff. You do whatever you think will work. Muse, you should get back to the doorway in case your moving floor theory is right since he's the only one of us who can fly in human form."

Oddly, Wyn turned a delicate rose color for a second. Her eyes glinted, and she cocked her head, the blush fading. "Are you actually doing what we ask without arguing? I'm impressed, though it breaks my heart to know things had to be so dire to get you to listen. Go ahead and put the medallion in, Wingspan. I'll be back here with a counterspell ready, so I can stop any nasty magic. The circle has a long-dormant spell on it, but because it's complex and inactive, I couldn't say what it does yet."

After wiping his hands on his thighs, Andy took a deep breath and collected the medallion from Wyn.

Zita harrumphed. "For the record, I'm perfectly willing to listen to experts who know more about stuff than I do, but I got to say something when things seem whack. The problem with magic is that it doesn't usually make sense."

"It does once you catch on to the system. However, we have more important things to do than to debate the pros and cons of the arcane arts." Wyn sniffed and hurried to the doorway. She positioned herself behind a column near Zita.

"Here goes nothing," Andy muttered. He walked forward and slid the medallion into the hands, and then backpedaled rapidly.

Nothing happened. "It's not doing anything. Can you make it do something?" Zita whispered.

"Give it a minute," Wyn replied.

Andy retreated a few more steps, his body falling into a ready position.

In her normal voice, Zita commented, "Pues, that was worth almost getting eaten by a squid for and losing control of half my body. Maybe there's a giant gumball machine we can use it in later."

With a horrendous grating sound that had bits of mosaic falling from the ceiling, the wall opened around the hands, which belonged to a seven-foot-tall golden robot. While her face held an eerie resemblance to the woman's statue under the water, the automaton had the muscular form of a female bodybuilder in a very short toga. A sword belt with a very long, wide sheath hung at her waist. The handle of the weapon was gold. She pressed the medallion against her chest. It dissolved into her. As the statue's eyes snapped open, yellow light poured from them and suffused the metal frame.

"Sheath." Andy nodded toward the weapon. *Think that's the sword we want?*

It's gold. Hephaestus was renowned for his fondness for the material, so likely, Wyn replied.

In a voice that resembled both a squeaky door and gears grinding against each other, she spoke in ancient Greek. "Greetings, godlings, you have passed the first test. If you wish to walk the halls of Olympus, you must face true danger."

"Already been there. Not impressed, thanks." Zita tried to slip into a defensive pose, forgetting for a moment. When her body didn't move, she frowned.

Wyn shushed her, interpreting for Andy.

The statue took three steps forward and withdrew an enormous gold sword from her sheath.

"Yep. Giant statue fight. Never doubt the wisdom of gaming tropes. Do we get dramatic battle music or a save point?" Andy said.

"Mano? You feeling okay?" Zita said.

As he edged closer to the statue, Andy sighed. "No one understands my pain right now or my need to wield a sword bigger than my body. I'm fine. Don't worry about me, even if I don't have cool spiky hair."

"Mano. There are so many problems with that sword comment and your sudden hair obsession. All we have to do is disarm her and go, right? That's got to be the sword. We got this." Zita remembered, and bitterness filled her mouth. "You got this. You can take her."

Andy gestured in resignation as another wall opened, and another golden woman stepped out. She carried two small golden spears. "And there's her backup. I'm guessing it's a fight to the death. Or destruction in her case."

"At least there aren't twelve of them." Zita attempted to cheer her friends up.

Wyn winced. "Refrain from jinxing us further. These must be Hephaestus' golden maidens who helped him in his Forge. The metal is magic and said to be far stronger than iron and nearly unbreakable."

Some of Zita's enthusiasm abated. "Caramba. And here I was hoping for a quick fight and done. I really need a snack, a shower, and a snack."

Andy pointed out the obvious as he put himself between the statues and the women. "You said snack twice."

"I need at least two. It's been a busy day." Zita tried to keep her tone light, even though her mouth was dry.

Tucking an errant curl under her wimple, Wyn frowned at her. "Your stomach is stone. How can you be hungry?"

If Zita could've moved her shoulders, she would've shrugged. "I don't know. Maybe it's a habit? Do you think they'd give us the sword if we ask nicely?"

Both of her friends scoffed.

The golden woman leveled the sword at Andy and advanced on him.

Her companion hefted a javelin and hurried a few steps to the side. The robot threw it at Wyn and Zita.

Golden sparks sprayed from Wyn's shield as the spear skittered off, and the bubble disappeared.

The sword-wielder swiped at Andy.

He dodged and squared his shoulders. "Maybe if I can get the weapon away, the battle will end. Probably not with our luck, but a guy can hope." He ran toward the sword-wielder and hit at her wrist.

A dent appeared.

Wyn squeaked and hid behind her pillar more. Her hands trailed silvery magic as she wove a complicated pattern in the air, and another bubble rose around her and Zita.

The second robot withdrew the other spear and threw it at Wyn and Zita as she strode over to pick up the first javelin she'd thrown.

Zita jerked as her attempt to move failed. She swore under her breath.

A nonplussed expression appeared on Andy's face as he tried to avoid being hit by the continuing, relentless advance of the swordswoman. "My hit should've sheared off the robot's wrist. I've punched through softer concrete." He kicked out at the robot.

She stumbled but scored a hit to his side.

"It was supposed to trip," Andy said weakly, a hand rising to cover his injury. Blood leaked through his fingers. Lowering his head, he charged the sword wielder, pushing her back and against the wall. *Ow. Weapons are definitely magic.*

The wall cracked, and rocks fell from the ceiling.

Oops, Andy sent. He swung the sword robot to the side and got behind her, trying to pin her weapon arm and keep her still.

The sword robot stabbed ineffectually at him.

After the javelin robot threw again, it walked over to retrieve the second spear. With a golden shower of sparks, the javelin popped the bubble and bounced off the column, landing near Zita.

Sweat beaded on Zita's forehead, and she felt like screaming. *Carajo. If I could just move, I'd be able to keep them off balance. They're slow, powerful, and capable of breaking magic shields, but they don't seem fast enough to keep up with me in fighting shape.*

Wyn gnawed her lip as her hands flew in elegant patterns, and she gabbled something. Another shield appeared around them. The witch panted. *Every hit destroys my shields.*

From where he held the sword-wielder, Andy grunted. "If I tighten my grip to crush the metal, my hands slip off. I'm actually exerting myself to hold this one back. Not much, it's like lifting a fifty-pound bag before we got our powers, but still..."

"Can you unmagic them?" Zita tried again.

Wyn winced as the spear wielder destroyed another bubble. "Not without study, and I doubt they'll peaceably let me examine them. The old Greek gods were handsy. It's possible part of the magic animating her includes a compulsion effect to prevent anyone from manhandling her." Her hands flew, and she mumbled her spell again.

An idea hit Zita with the force of a blow. "Muse, grab the next spear off the ground and bubble the robot before it gets the other javelin."

Her tone dry, Wyn said, "I hope you know what I'm doing."

A shield sprang up around the weaponless robot.

Andy swore, struggling to keep a grip on the swordswoman.

Wyn darted out to retrieve the closest javelin. While she seemed to strain to grasp it, she staggered backward as the weapon abruptly shifted shape to be much smaller. "Now what?"

The spear-throwing robot punched the walls of her prison in a methodical series of strikes but seemed unable to pierce the shield without her weapons.

Dios, please let this work. Zita licked her lips. "Give it to Wingspan. Don't get in sword range. Mano, use the javelin!"

With the golden weapon clutched to her chest, Wyn scurried over to stand just out of reach of the trapped swordswoman, who still fought to break free.

Andy spun the sword wielder and shoved her away. He turned back to Wyn and held out his hands.

"Catch!" Wyn tossed him the weapon and retreated.

The sword wielder rotated to face Andy again and charged him.

Andy grabbed the javelin and whirled, throwing it at his attacker.

The spear pierced through the robot.

With a smooth move, Andy rushed forward, yanked it out, and then stabbed again.

The swordswoman collapsed, golden weapon clattering to the ground.

Andy tossed aside the javelin and snatched the sword.

Inside the shield, the robot abandoned its pugilistic stance, lowered her arms, and walked over to the closest javelin. It scrabbled at it, unable to penetrate Wyn's magic enough with its fingers to reach the weapon.

The spear wielder's alcove in the wall lit.

"Drop the bubble, but stay out of her range," Zita said, hoping she was right. She gestured with her free hand for her friends to hurry.

Her expression dubious, Wyn frowned but made a gesture.

Interposing himself between the witch and the robot, Andy held the sword at ready, if awkwardly.

The shield disappeared.

The remaining robot collected both javelins. She walked back to her original alcove and backed into it. Crossing her arms over the spears, the light disappeared from her eyes. The wall closed around her.

Her eyes on where the javelin-thrower had disappeared, Wyn retreated to the room entrance. "Are you okay, Andy?"

He peeled the toga away from his side and studied his injury. "Shallow and messy, but I'm guessing not serious. Heal me once we're in the courtyard?"

The witch flexed her hands. "Definitely. We have what we came for. Why don't we depart before we meet any more obstacles?"

Andy hefted the weapon. "You have my sword."

"I would've been happy with a gumball. Can I get a lift, mano?" Zita said.

Chapter Seventeen

Twenty minutes later, conversation in the megaron stopped as Andy set Zita down in slow, careful movements. Chiron, Greenie, and a scattering of Council members conversed in clusters around the room. Silenus still slept, though now he snored from atop one of the tables, his cup cradled close like a teddy bear and the purple fleece now a pillow.

"They have returned." Greenie had the expression of someone who'd bitten into a rotten lemon. Surprise and pity crossed it when she reached Zita.

She stared at everyone, silently daring them to say something.

Chiron's face was polite, but his body was taut, and his tail flicked in a steady stream. "So they have. Do you have something to give to the honored surrogate for the Voice of the Council?"

Wyn withdrew the sword from her bag and dropped it on the table closest to the nymph.

Greenie stared at the golden weapon. "Can someone confirm this is the Sword of Heracles?"

After a moment, thunderous steps sounded, and a cyclops plodded over to the weapon. He had similar features to Arges, without the terror or dirty clothing. His sole eye was red-rimmed and angry as he surveyed Zita and her friends. When he touched the blade with a finger, a note rumbled, so deep that it was a bone-jarring vibration rather than a sound. "Aye. They have the true-forged sword, given by Athena, created by my brothers and Hephaestus."

The dryad stared at him for a moment, and finally, smiled. "And yet nothing has changed, has it, Chiron? Perhaps the esteemed Council should heed my advice—"

With an edged smile, Chiron cut her off. "The Speaker for the Voice may only communicate what the Council wishes, and at this time, the Council has declared they must complete their quests."

Greenie nearly snarled. "Odd how few times that has stopped you in the past, Chiron. Very well, then. Brontes, the Council thanks you for your service. You may go. Little gods, you may bathe if you can and eat of our midday repast if you wish. Would you have the next quest now, or after you dine?"

The cyclops strode out.

"Now," Zita said in Greek, not even waiting for Wyn to finish interpreting for Andy.

Greenie tapped her spear on the tile. "Very well. Does the Council concur that they have completed the task?"

A variety of assents followed.

The nymph nodded. "Done. Now, your next task is—"

Silenus did not allow her to finish before sitting up and cutting in. "Finally! When your wolf disturbed the herds of my people, my son was frightened and ran off. He's too far for us to find him, and he has not come home of his own. Bring him back to me. He is too young and foolish a colt to live on his own yet."

The words burst out of Zita in a roaring torrent of Greek. "Some poor kid has been missing for days, and you're just now getting to it? You ranked a sword and some hair from an overgrown mutt over returning a child to his parents? What's wrong with you people?"

Andy touched Zita's good shoulder. His body was tense and ready to fight. "What's going on?"

"Silenus' kid is missing, and they want us to find him. He's been gone since before they dumped Garm on us."

He scowled. "Why'd they wait that long?"

"Because they're all pendejos?" It was the only answer Zita could give him.

Wyn pinched the skin between her eyebrows and blew out a puff of air. Turning to the Council, she said in Greek, "We accept the quest, though we continue to maintain that we are not responsible for Garm's actions."

"We had hoped he had not gone far and would return by himself. You're going to go find him?" Greenie asked.

Her expression puzzled, Wyn nodded. "Of course. We're not monsters. This shouldn't have waited. In good conscience, we can't allow a child to wander lost somewhere longer than necessary. Can you give me his full name and something of his, any personal item?"

Zita interpreted for Andy.

Silenus took a long drink from his cup. The scent of wine drifted around him as he staggered closer. "Bring him here. His name is Xanthus, son of Silenus. Someone fetch the blanket from his stall." He waved his cup.

Her mouth a tight line, Greenie propped her fists on her hips. "We thought you'd refuse the task. One of my sisters will bring his blanket here within the hour."

Wyn stared down her nose at the dryad. "We'll depart as soon as we have the blanket. While we wait, we'll take quick baths and grab some food. Arca..."

She grunted. "I can wait here while you get washed off. Dump some water over my head before we leave to wash off the worst of the salt, and I'm good."

Her friend chewed her lip and glanced at Andy. "We'll be back as soon as possible." They scurried away.

Zita did bicep curls with her good arm until it ached with effort. She managed to wait a few minutes more before she broke the silence on party line, which had been very quiet, presumably as the others had been bathing. *Guys? You done washing yet? They don't have the blanket here. Did they bring it to you?*

Yes, I have it, Wyn replied after a few seconds.

Zita perked up. *Good. When will you be here so we can go?*

A wave of discomfort preceded Wyn's reply. *This is an easy one. I cast the spell, we go to where he is and pick him up. You sit back and relax. You'll be safest there, and you'd be no help if you came. We'll see you soon.*

That is a chingado load of steaming—

His tone apologetic, Andy interrupted. *Sorry, Z, you'd slow us down. We all want to go home as soon as possible.*

The truth in his words stung Zita into silence for a moment.

The witch's voice was stern. *We made our decision. We'll see you soon. Try to relax.*

Party line cut off before she could say more.

She found her voice too late. "You could've at least asked me."

***

Zita fumed as she gazed at the room full of Council members eating, drinking, and enjoying themselves. After her friends had gone, a herd of cooing nymphs descended on her, led by the purple-haired one. Against her loud complaints, they had a giant carry her to the baths, where they sponged her clean and washed her hair. They'd even taken the time to play with her hair, weaving blossoms and ribbons into it. Only the fear of being fully petrified had stopped her from teleporting away.

Eventually, they'd had the giant return her to the megaron, where she now alternated between trying to move limbs she couldn't feel (and failing) and simmering in frustration. Perhaps sensitive to her anger, most of the Councilors kept away and at least attempted to keep their stares discreet.

To her surprise, Greenie sidled up to interrupt her solitude, a cup of kykeon in her hand. "Thirsty?"

So you can poison me? Zita managed to keep from saying it out loud. "Thank you, no. Don't touch me."

The green-haired nymph gave a harsh laugh. "You need not fear that from me."

"I'm surprised you don't seem happier. This is what you wanted all along, isn't it? To kill us?"

Greenie sipped the barley drink. "No. I would have you gone. Though you be young, you are gods. I had hoped you would show wisdom and flee, and yet... you did not."

Zita eyed her. "Why are you really here? It's not to offer me a drink."

"You speak the truth. Of your fledgling pantheon, you are the least likely to take aught I offer, especially now. However, I wished to tell you that I will grant you a boon, so you need never come to the darkest end. Your friends have abandoned you already, so someone must care for you."

Her ear itched where a stem irritated her skin. "I'd rather not have my hair done again, thanks."

"Nay, I would not bother you with such petty things. The fawning flowers seek your patronage, as who would want to be seen as you are? You will most likely remain behind here when your friends return home. I make you a promise, by the bark and leaf. Should you remain like this or turn to stone fully, I will hide you away until you are forgotten. None will abuse you nor take that which is yours for their own."

"First off, my friends will be back. They're just fetching the missing kid," Zita said.

"The Council has not told you all of the dangers around the son of Silenus. Nor of additional information we have received of late."

"No surprise there. We expect that at this point." *Or at least I do. I hope my friends do.* Giving herself a mental shake, Zita continued, "Second, Muse will cure me. And third, what are you talking about abusing or taking things? I'm mostly rock. There's nothing to take."

Greenie swirled the drink in her cup. "Were you simply a pretty, innocent statue, that might be true, but the puissance of a god beats within you. Many covet that, even locked within stone. And until you open to new powers and free yourself, you can do naught to stop them from siphoning it off to enrich themselves. They would use you to harm others."

Oye, talk about being creepy. I guess I don't take the prize for worst people skills in the room. Whatever her reasons, she's not offering out of the goodness of her heart. Zita raised her eyebrows. "Spent a lot of time thinking about this, have you?"

Eyes hooded, the nymph brandished a half-smile. "When one is prey, one must either avoid or outsmart predators. My bond has been given, no matter how the last quest concludes."

"I don't think of myself as either. If trouble's coming my way, just say it instead of all this dancing around it. While I don't object to being prepared for future threats, your methods suck."

"Perhaps, but my leaves still dance in the wind, while you are granite." The dryad raised her cup to Zita, took a delicate sip, and sauntered away.

✶✶✶

Exhausted from frustration, worry, and the strain of not thinking about her future, Zita was dozing when warmth flooded her mind, and party line returned.

Still angry with us? Wyn's voice was quiet.

Zita didn't even have to think about it. *Yes. Pretty steamed at both of you. Are you guys okay? You've been gone all day.*

We're fine, but as usual, the Council left out important details. Xanthus is a pony. He was on a peninsula with the mares of Diomedes...

A teenage stallion ran to a herd of mares? Doesn't sound bad if you can get him away from his harem. And seriously, genetics here are messed up if Silenus is fathering ponies. Zita snickered.

The mares seemed to be more motherly toward him than not, but the problem was that those horses are carnivores. Voracious ones who tried to snack upon us.

She shook her head at the absurdity of it. *Meat-eating horses? This place! So, you had to be more careful.*

Andy broke his silence and took up the thread of the tale. *I caught some rabbits, and we fed them to the mares to calm them, but the colt spooked and took off again when I tried to pick him up. And I do mean took off—he flies. Repeat that a couple times. When we caught up to him again, he'd found a village of fauns. Of course, before we reached them, most of the village and the colt got themselves petrified.*

Zita shivered. *More basilisks?*

A pair of very unhappy gorgons, snake-headed ladies that do the same thing as a basilisk. We're staying with one of the remaining villagers overnight. The bright side is that the fauns are loaning us a bridle and rope so we can stop him from running off again next time something spooks him. The bad news is that Wyn's going to need time to release everyone and the animals, plus we have to figure out an answer to stop it from happening again.

Zita had to stop herself from swearing. *So, what's your plan?*

Wyn's mental voice was unhappy. *We can't kill the gorgons— they're definitely sentient creatures, after all. However, the village and the gorgons' cave share a single water source, so conflict is inevitable unless we find a viable alternative.*

His tone thoughtful, Andy sent, *Perhaps we could relocate them. If we use your scarves, they might not be able to petrify us.*

I can verify turning to stone sucks. Zita tried not to let her bitterness seep through.

It must've leaked, given Wyn's next few words. *I'm sorry, Zita. I haven't figured out a solution for you yet, but I'm thinking about it as much as possible.*

Whatever. Zita considered it. *How about we give them Arges' hermitage? Nobody else lives on that island. We don't want it anyway, and we could throw in that stone goose if they want a pet or some entertainment. The only thing they'd have to do is deal with the basilisk, and they might be immune or at least resistant, like snakes and their own venom.*

That's... not a bad thought, Andy mused.

Wyn sent a pulse of agreement. *We'll have to try that. I need to concentrate on casting the spells to help the villagers, so we're going to go. We just didn't want you to worry. Take care!*

Before she could protest, the link was gone.

Like I can do anything dangerous? Zita closed her eyes and took a deep breath.

***

Her friends were gone for another half-day blur of naps and interminable boredom broken only by the occasional conversation, attacks of panic-laced frustration at her situation, and nymphic makeover-assaults. While Zita did not seem to need food, a sip of liquid helped moisten her throat and mouth, so she tolerated them assisting her to drink. They learned not to coo at her as if she were a baby after she bit the first one foolish enough to do so. Nothing she did could deter them from playing with her hair, descending upon her to redo it before each meal, keeping their fingers away from her face. True to Greenie's earlier dismissal of them, they smelled of flowers and warm meadows rather than trees.

Andy and Wyn arrived, using a rope and harness to lead a pretty pony with a pale yellow coat and the lanky legs of youth. His mane and boots were striking, inky hair and feathers mingled together and fluttering with each movement. His dark eyes were wide, head tossing as they entered.

"My son!" Silenus cried out and sat bolt upright.

The colt stilled at the elderly silenoi's voice, his ears twitching. Then he exploded into a flurry of rapid movement, hooves clattering on the tile, only to be stopped by the lead rope.

Silenus set his cup down and ran to the colt. As he stripped off the harness, he stroked his son and whispered to the pony. The elder turned to Melanippe. "Have your sisters carry word to Podarge that our son has returned."

She nodded and sank into the ground.

"Podarge? A harpy is his mother? That would explain the flight and feathers." Wyn tilted her head.

Zita gaped. "A harpy and a mostly man made a pony? How does that even work? I mean, biologically..." She blinked. "Wait. On second thought, I don't need to know. In fact, I don't want to know."

Silenus smiled, his expression dreamy and lascivious. He raised his cup, saluting her. "My Xanthus is worth every bit of frostbite his engendering caused."

Wyn started to interpret.

Andy put his hands over his own ears. "I don't need to know whatever he just said. Only interpret the bits that don't involve sex."

"For once, I'm with the prude. Let's just move on," Zita mumbled.

The colt preened, tossing his head and prancing. Tiny feathers at his ankles fluttered. He batted his eyelashes, and his tail swished.

His father beamed. "Isn't he exceptional?"

Her face softening, Wyn cooed in English, "He is so adorable."

"Given how many times he shied, and we had to chase him down, it's a good thing he's so cute. Escort quests are the worst," Andy muttered.

Zita sniffed. "He held his own among meat-eating horses. Don't discount the cute, little ones."

Andy chuckled. "You would know."

She narrowed her eyes at him. "Come over here and run yourself into my elbow. Home is calling."

Wyn drifted closer to the reunited family. "Silenus? We're happy to have reunited you with your son. So, have we officially finished our third quest?"

From behind them, Chiron coughed. "He cannot make that decision. The Council must meet to officially determine that, as they did when I was the Voice. If it would not be too great an imposition, would you remain here so we might confer over there?" He gestured toward the other end of the great hall.

"What's to determine? You said bring Xanthus back. We brought him. Done." Zita frowned. She tossed Andy a quick interpretation.

Wyn touched her arm. *Zita, please.*

The old centaur did not answer her.

Greenie rolled her eyes. "Teacher, it is no longer your place to ask such things."

"Silenus was busy and you silent, so I thought I would aid you. My apologies if I have overstepped my bounds." Chiron gave an exaggerated bow.

If we go now, perhaps they'll stop squabbling and get to business. Wyn pinched the skin between her eyes and spoke in Greek. "Fine. We will wait."

Zita snorted. *It's politics. They're going to fight no matter what we do.*

Let's hope you're wrong. Andy pulled a pair of benches over and invited Wyn to sit on one in a gesture. He slumped onto the other and nodded to Zita. "By the way, nice hair."

"I have a bad feeling about this. They accepted the sword right off." Foreboding filled Zita.

Andy's expression was grim. "You're not the only one."

Party line disappeared.

Wyn did not answer, her gaze distant. Finally, she nodded, her fingers curling into fists. Her breathing quickened, and words poured out of her in an angry torrent. "My aunt is possibly dying. We're all missing out on our lives, and you know what they're talking about? That hesitation and the rush meeting? I skimmed Chiron. They're going to disqualify our last quest and send us on another because they're waiting for something that hasn't happened yet. Even if the mythic cycle demands quests as a cost for the achievement of a goal, I have no desire to live like Odysseus, perpetually running from one thing to another in a torturous attempt to go home!"

"Isn't that what I've been saying all along?" Zita said.

His brows drawn together, Andy said, "This isn't a time for I told you so."

Zita made a face at him. "Then when is? I get you said the quests are important, but why are we just going along with whatever they come up with? They can't even agree among themselves. I got no problems bringing the kid back home, but they basically had us sorting out their supplies and risking our lives pointlessly in the temple. Not to mention Greenie setting us up to run into the basilisk. We all know how well that went."

"They're coming back." Wyn hid her face in her hands for a second, exhaled deeply, and then lowered them, her usual serene mask in place. Party line returned.

Chiron, Melanippe, Greenie, a giant, and a faun rejoined them. The fish-men lazed in their pool, and the other Council members returned to eating and conversing. During the discussion, both Silenus and Xanthus had fallen asleep, with the father snoring on his son's haunches.

The dryad spoke, her tone sulky. "The Council finds issue with your last quest. First, only two of you went, while the last bided here."

"I didn't have a choice!" Zita protested.

Greenie continued talking as if she'd remained silent. "Second, while you were in Lerna, you freed the hydra from the rock that held it captive since Heracles conquered it. It now destroys all that it is near. For these, we disqualify your next quest and bid you kill it for your last quest. Since you have struggled so with your previous tasks, the Council will loan you the Sword of Heracles. Do try not to fail at this as well."

Zita summarized for Andy. "Because I didn't go on the last quest and breaking some rock let a hydra loose when we got the dog hair, they're disqualifying the quest to find Xanthus. They're saying we have to kill the hydra for our last job."

"No. Not happening. Translate for me," Andy said, stepping forward.

Wyn stepped forward and opened her mouth.

He stopped her with a gesture. "No, Arca should do it. She won't sugarcoat it."

"That's what I'm afraid of. I'm not entirely certain I could be genteel at this point either, though," Wyn murmured, but she subsided.

Let me know if you disagree, but we're finished running around at their whims. Andy stepped forward and spoke, his hands on his hips. "We're done with your quests. In the interests of cooperation, we went along with all of them, even when you decided to saddle us with additional errands for weak reasons."

Zita interpreted.

Before her friend could finish speaking, Greenie stepped forward, eyes blazing. "When we first met, you said you'd protect me. You said similar to others, and yet you will do naught when your actions will bring death upon many of us. Know this. The hydra poisons the land and water everywhere it goes. The lake spirit hovers near death. Creatures that have not been killed have fled. The plants sicken and wither, and it will only spread as the creature ranges farther in search of prey. If it returns to the lake, eventually its poison will spread to the nearby sea as well."

After a pause to receive an interpretation, Andy said, "We didn't say we wouldn't handle the hydra. We said we wouldn't accept any more quests. Since we created the hydra problem, we're going to solve it, but you're going to keep the Council's end of our bargain when we come back."

She repeated his words in Greek. *Mano, count me in.*

"Finally. I thought you would never show the pride of your power. A god should not run errands, beg approval, nor ask to assist in household chores," a fish-man said. He waved a webbed hand at Chiron. "Our opposition is removed."

"Is the hydra sentient?" Wyn asked in Greek.

"It's animal, and not known for cunning. They know only the need to destroy and devour. They do not think or reason," Greenie said.

Wyn nodded. "Good." *I agree, as well.*

With a glance at the giant and faun, Chiron said, "We agree. No more quests. We will give you our aid to return to your homes once the hydra is gone."

Melanippe's eyebrows shot up, and she tilted her head at her father.

"We will not break our promises, and if this does not accomplish the task, well, then, it were better they were on their way," Chiron told her.

Greenie threw her hands in the air. "Stubborn. Had you listened to me, they would be gone already."

"Ever feel like we're missing something?" Wyn said sotto voce to her friends.

"All the time. Grab the sword, and let's go kick some hydra culo! Or whatever they have instead of one." Zita waved her arm at the sword.

Wyn smiled at the Council. "We need a moment."

Chiron bobbed in a bow and backed away, followed by the others, except for Greenie, who stared at them for a long moment and walked out the door.

Once the others had left, Andy held out a hand. "Whoa, Arca. You're not coming."

"Why not?" Zita said.

Wyn gestured to her body. "You're mostly stone. Killing the hydra was a labor of Hercules, a mammoth task. You wouldn't be able to do anything, and you're safer here."

"You know we love you, right? We're not going to take you along just because you're bored and have a death wish." Andy backed Wyn up.

Zita took a deep breath. "It's not just boredom. Yes, that's part of it. It's torture enough not being able to move without adding in the terror of my two best friends fighting a walking environmental disaster without me. I don't have a death wish. Pues, you should understand better than most. We were all terminally ill together. Who knows better than us that our bodies will someday betray us and steal away our strength again, be it through illness, old age, or basilisk petrification? All that aside, I can actually help."

"How?" Wyn's question came out like a challenge, but Andy seemed to be listening.

Zita took a deep breath. "I'm mostly stone. So as much as I hate to say it, I can't fight."

"Exactly," said Wyn.

"I'm not done. We've been to Lerna. There are no good hiding places for Muse that aren't in the Underworld. She can hide behind me since the poison doesn't eat rock. If it does, I don't feel anything in my petrified parts anyway."

"I have my shields," Wyn said.

"Which you can't use if you're healing or casting. Additionally, my advice was useful with the gorgons and the robot ladies, wasn't it? I can help here. I've got experience fighting and being all sorts of reptiles. And let's not forget that I can keep watch if something thinks to attack while you're fighting."

Andy touched Wyn's arm. "You've made your point. I think she should come with us."

"But if she uses her power..." Wyn protested.

Zita broke in. "Are you going to make my decisions for me again like when you left without even asking me what I wanted? Of all people, I'd hope you two would understand the concept of allowing people free will."

A hand flew up to cover Wyn's mouth. "I didn't mean to—"

Clumsily, Zita lifted her stone hand and tapped her friend's arm with it tentatively. "I know you didn't, which is why I'm pointing it out now. This is *my* life. This condition doesn't choose for me. It just limits my options. If I have to use my powers to save yours, I will. If I turn completely to stone, turn me to walking stone like the goose. You're worried about it, but I have faith in you. And apparently, I won't even notice time passing if you fail."

Wyn seemed to waver.

She snorted. "If nothing else, the Hercules dude dropped a rock on the hydra-head to keep it pinned, right? You could use me until you found a better rock. Well, maybe not better. I am pretty awesome, even as a rock. We can do this together." Zita smiled at her friends.

Her eyes teary, Wyn nodded. "Together, then."

Andy rubbed the sides of his toga. "Together. When did I end up in an anime?"

Chapter Eighteen

Zita clucked her tongue, one of the few actions left to her as Andy set her down in a sheltered alcove beside the cliff. Far overhead, the old oak oversaw everything as before, but that was one of the only things that had not changed. Before, the area had been a vibrant marshland. Since their last visit, however, the thriving lake was quiet and still, the waters an unhealthy dark shade. No birdsong or insect calls broke the silence, and the overriding scent was that of putrefaction. All of the visible flora had withered. The cave that led to the Underworld gaped wordlessly above the dying lake, and threatening gray clouds hid the sun. The rock that Andy had accidentally broken stood out in a heap of brilliant white against the dark soil.

Even if she only voiced the obvious, Zita spoke. "Oye, that's not good."

Andy hurried back to where he'd landed, grabbing the firewood and kindling they'd brought with them to ensure they had dry wood. He carried armfuls of it to a spot near the lake and started constructing a fire. Around his waist, a belt held the sheathed Sword of Heracles.

Beside her, Wyn shuddered and rubbed her own arms as if cold. She plucked a scarf out of her bag and tied it over the mask that already hid her mouth and nose. "The Lernean hydra was said to be extremely poisonous. We should cover our noses and mouths to avoid any dangerous fumes while we're close to it."

"Well, then, that's why you're going to be ready to un-poison Wingspan whenever he needs you to, right? I'll just be... standing around," Zita scowled, hating her inability to move. As if in agreement with her frustration, a low rumble of thunder came from the clouds gathered over the lake.

Wyn tied a scarf over the lower portion of Zita's face, fussing with it until it satisfied some inner need. "You agreed to our plan. Wingspan will fight the hydra, cutting off the heads and cauterizing the stumps, one by one. I'll shield the two of us and heal him if necessary. You're going to tell him if you see a weakness he can exploit and provide a screen so I don't draw its attention. We wanted you to stay on Olympus to keep you safe."

She snorted and waved her good arm, her motionless gray fingers like a claw. "As if I'd stand around being fed grapes and having my hair done while you two risk yourselves. Mano, are the clouds your doing, or is it going to rain?"

Andy sat back on his heels and gazed skyward. Lightning flashed in his eyes. "It's not me, I think. It's going to storm soon."

Wyn nodded and gestured toward the mouth of the cave. "Then we should hurry so it doesn't put out our fire. Our boundary mark has been partially erased, though I can't tell if it was purposeful or merely environmental. We should set that up again to ensure we keep out of the Underworld. The last thing we need is to have Cerberus attacking while we fight the hydra. Would you mind, Wingspan?"

He nodded. Withdrawing the sword, he clomped over and stabbed the ground, dragging it to create the trench again.

"I can't believe you're using the fancy sword to draw a line in the sand. What if you're dulling the tip or breaking it or something?" Frustration freed the words before Zita could bite her tongue.

Andy lifted it from the dirt and examined the edge. "Doesn't appear to be damaged. Super-hard gold, remember?" As he reached the end of the line, he blew on it. Dirt flew. The sword glinted. "See? It's fine."

"Guess we're lucky then. Since the rock's already broken, why don't you use the white kind to make the boundary with the Underworld stand out more?" Zita said.

Andy grunted and filled the bucket, tromping over to pour it into the renewed trench. "Good idea. Easier to see."

"That's the idea. I'm guessing a hydra is pretty distracting and not in an ay, papi way. Then again, this place is nuts." Zita rolled her eyes.

He shot her a smile. "Anything's possible here."

"Be careful. We can't set even a toe over that line," Wyn fretted.

She couldn't move enough to see her own toes. If she could've, Zita would've been vibrating with impatience. As it was, emotion filled her and sharpened her tongue instead. "Thanks, Mom, I'm sure he's forgotten that in the last five minutes."

Wyn flinched. "I was trying to help."

Inwardly, Zita swore at herself. "Sorry. I didn't mean... I'm an idiot. Sorry, guys."

Her friend set a (presumably) gentle hand on Zita's gray shoulder for a second before she went back to feeding the fire. "Understood. We're still good."

"Yeah, thanks. Try putting a little bigger piece of wood on now. The kindling's going good." Hair prickled on the back of Zita's neck... or at least her instincts told her someone was watching, as she couldn't actually feel her neck. She wanted to move so badly that her eyes watered. *Stupid allergies.*

Scanning the landscape, her eyes met a pair of horrified red ones. The wolf shifter's canine face held an expression that resembled pity.

She lifted her chin. With a sniff and a wrinkle of her nose, she announced, "Furball's here. Did you guys get the whiff of that wet dog stench on top of the rotten swamp odor?"

I guess he didn't get eaten, Wyn murmured over party line. She handed a scarf to Andy.

As he tied it over his nose and mouth, Andy wondered, *Are we happy or sad about that?*

Any sympathy fled Garm's face. He sauntered out of his hiding spot and plopped his body down at the top of a small hill, curling his tail around his haunches. "I see Arca's found her true calling as mouthy statuary. Going swimming?"

Happy-ish? It'd be wrong to wish another person dead, even if they're an evil pain in our asses. It's possible he could turn it around and start a soup kitchen or cure cancer or something. He'd probably still be a jerk though. Zita wanted to move so badly, but she couldn't even twitch. Restlessness poured over into her words. "We're going to kill the hydra. That's a multi-headed lizard thing that lives in the lake."

Scorn practically dripped from Garm. "I know that. What kind of idiot doesn't know what a hydra is, let alone the Lernean one? Not to mention, I've seen it eating the local wildlife."

Zita bristled. "Different places focus on different things. Some schools teach more useful stuff than lists of obscure mythological creatures."

"Yes, we also learn about white man's victories and how utterly depressing life can be." Andy's tone was deadpan, though his mental voice laughed as he added, *Good thing we had physics to cheer us up!*

His lips curled as the wolf scoffed. "Cretins."

Wyn cleared her throat. "Shall we focus on the task at hand rather than analyzing curricula deficiencies?"

Modification to our plan. Zita, you watch Garm and ensure he doesn't attack us while we're busy with the hydra. Andy hefted the sword in his hand, wrapping both hands around it and trying different grips. "Yeah. We'll need to lure it out."

"Garm, you might want to move along. Since you're an expert on the hydra and all, you know it's going to get dangerous around here." Zita made a face.

The werewolf rested his head on his crossed paws. "And miss this farce? Not a chance. If I'm fortunate, you'll wipe each other out."

Crazed barking started from the cave, and Cerberus ran to the edge of the entrance, stopping well before the line. All three heads barked independently, with the hound head emitting a high-pitched howl that made Zita's ears throb.

Zita snorted. "Calm down, puppy."

Garm's ears flicked, and he rose from his hill. He paced closer to the cave. "Go away. Shoo, stupid thing. The hydra's going to eat them in a minute, and I don't have any meat," he growled at the dog.

Cerberus pranced back and forth, and the barking took on a whiny edge.

A massive roar overshadowed the three-headed dog's cacophony as a huge form rose improbably out of the shallow water at the end of the lake. Multiple heads that resembled Gila monsters rose on snaky necks, writhing in a tangled mess that made it impossible to count how many were there. They joined a massive, low-slung body like that of an alligator from a horror movie. Inky black liquid oozed from between yellow fangs and dripped to the ground, where it hissed on contact with the dirt. Step by slow step, it emerged from the water, its attention on Andy and the sword. Multiple heads shot toward her friend.

"That water should not be deep enough to hold a body that big," Zita said, eyes widening. "You got him though, mano."

Andy gulped and squared his shoulders. Lifting the sword, he glanced toward Wyn and Zita and then charged toward the monster.

Three heads struck at him. Others spat poison at Zita and Wyn, but the nasty, viscous fluid hit the shield and slid off.

Andy dodged them, but a second set of heads sent him flying thirty feet to crash into a cliff with a high-pitched wail. His sword flew another direction.

If Zita could've winced, she would've.

Rock shivered and crumbled, raining down pebbles on his head.

Garm laughed.

Wyn bit her lip. "Goddess," she breathed.

"I'm sure he's fine." The bravado of her statement might've been lessened by the tremor in her voice.

The hydra came farther onto the shore, hissing, its eyes fixed on the fire.

Andy got to his feet, hair white with limestone, and flew back toward the lake. He detoured to retrieve the sword and ripped off the tattered remains of his now-smoking cape. Gripping the sword in both hands, he swung at a head and missed.

When the hydra snapped at him again, one head bit down and threw him again against a different spot in the cliff.

A low, malicious chuckle came from where Garm watched. One glance showed he'd settled down again, not far from where Cerberus watched the fight with an intent expression on his faces.

This time, at least, Andy kept his grip on the sword. When he clambered out and attacked again, he missed, but he dodged the follow-up attacks.

Zita watched, counting seconds mentally. *It's too big to fight you with all its heads at once, mano. It can't attack with more than three at a time, so hit it between attacks. That's your opportunity. Go for the necks. If you cut off the head, it can't bite you with it.*

Got it. Andy darted in, dropping his sword.

The creature attacked.

In the interval between attacks, he grabbed two of the necks, and whirled, yanking the massive body out of the water. He hurled it against the cliff opposite the shore.

Hissing, it hit the rock with a thud and a squishy sound and slid to the ground.

"How do you like it? Not fun being tossed around, is it!" Andy shouted, picking up his weapon again. Gripping it in both hands, he stood in a ready pose.

The hydra charged at him, making the ground vibrate beneath its bulk. More rock cascaded down from the cliff face.

Andy ran forward and hacked off a head, sending black blood flying, and then seizing a torch. He waved it at the creature.

Two heads sprouted from the stump before the fire could hit it.

Thunder rumbled overhead, and the clouds dumped torrents of water on everything.

Spitting out a dripping strand of hair, Zita bit her cheek to avoid calling out and distracting her friend.

Andy tried again and ended up creating two more heads. He dodged another attack. *This isn't working. I'm trying to use a weapon I'm unfamiliar with to do attacks that require the kind of timing I don't have. And I have to sear it with a rapid, precise second hit? I'm just making it bigger and more dangerous. I should be playing to my strengths, not yours.*

She couldn't help it. The thought slipped onto party line. *Do you really think solving physics equations will kill it?*

His mirthless chuckle came over party line. *Not that one. Stay under the shield. Wyn, get behind Zita if you can.*

Wyn glanced over at the fire guttering out in the downpour. *What about your torches?*

Forget them. Andy stabbed the sword into the ground between two rocks.

Zita didn't bother to hide her dubiousness as she answered. "Not like I have a choice."

Very well, we're ready, Wyn sent.

His eyes shone white, and Andy rose straight up.

The hydra stretched its many necks out, biting and hissing.

Andy shifted into his massive bird form and zipped into the clouds. A second later, he dove from the sky, lightning coruscating over his body and snatched the entire hydra from the water with his talons. Flapping his wings and sending deafening thunder vibrating through the ground, he rose higher and used his sharp beak to sever multiple heads.

One of them bounced off the shield protecting Wyn and Zita.

A second later, a lightning bolt arced out of the clouds and hit him and his captive.

The hydra shrieked and went stiff.

Andy shook the hydra like a snaky set of maracas and bit off more heads, spitting out black fluid.

Lightning struck his form again, racing over Andy and sinking into the hydra.

He did it again until he'd severed the last head and hit the stump with lightning.

The last hydra head glinted evilly as it tumbled to the rocks below. Instead of glazing over like the others scattered on the beach, the dark eyes seemed to promise retribution.

Wyn shouted, "The last head is supposed to be immortal. Hercules pinned it under a giant rock to keep it from regenerating."

Shifting from Wingspan back to Andy, he landed on the shore and stumbled over to Wyn. His face was pale beneath the warm bronze of his skin, and his toga was visibly worse for wear, muddy, ripped, and dripping wet. He coughed, spitting up blood. "Guess the poison's magic. Burns inside…"

On the sand by the lake, the last hydra head righted itself on tiny legs that would've been comical under other circumstances.

Cerberus stood and began barking, his gaze on the head.

"What now?" Garm rose, cocking the head at the canine.

Silver and green embraced Andy's body in a magical filigree design as Wyn worked. A curl slid out of her wimple and into her eyes, but she did not seem to notice. Her bubble was gone.

Evil eyes fixed on the three-headed dog. The hydra opened its mouth.

"No! Stupid dog!" Garm darted between the dog and the head.

Zita teleported in front of the hydra, between it and Garm.

It spat.

Most of the inky liquid splashed her stone body, but her cheek burned where the poison had splashed it. Remnants of her scarf fell away.

The head wobbled and skittered toward the water's edge.

Can't let it get away. They're both busy. Silenus did say something about needing a change when fighting a multi-headed beast. This qualifies. Zita exhaled. *My shifting is limited to real things, but they're real enough here.* "Stay back!" she called out.

"What?" Wyn said from somewhere behind her.

Andy coughed, the sound somehow cleaner than before.

Zita shifted to a basilisk and glared at the remaining hydra head. As her vision grayed out, she saw Garm overhead.

He blinked. "What's all the fuss? It's just a—"

***

Something was tickling her nose, and everything was purple. Dogs howled and cried mournfully nearby.

Zita brought a clawed foot toward her face but couldn't reach. *Oye, being a statue is weirder than I thought, but at least I don't hurt. Wait. My hand?* Her body tensed, and she wiggled her toes, then her tail. She could feel every inch of her body. Exultation spread through her, and then she remembered. *The hydra!*

"Don't try to take it off, just shift back to Arca." Wyn's voice trembled and choked.

Zita obeyed. "No crying. Did it work?"

Wyn plucked the scarf from Zita's face, her eyes teary through her mask. "Yes, you petrified it! More importantly, you figured it out a way to cure you! That was brilliant of you to take a magical form! Once you did that, I could use it to remove the petrification. I don't know why it didn't occur to me with all the time I spent working on it! We should've had you try that earlier."

"I had time to think about it?" Zita lied and tried to hide her surprise.

Either she didn't bury the thought deep enough, or Wyn wasn't fooled. "You didn't plan it? You did that expecting—I swear, there are tree stumps with higher IQs. What were you thinking?"

"Isn't most of the plant life around here infested with chicks or something?" she tried.

"You know perfectly well what I meant! What were you thinking?" Wyn scolded.

Zita levered herself onto her elbows and glanced around. "That you guys were busy, and Wingspan wouldn't want to fight that thing again? Where is he? I didn't get him, did I?"

"He's fine. He took the petrified hydra's head to drop into the Stromboli volcano before the petrification wore off, and it could regenerate. The volcano is still active in our world, so it should keep the hydra from regenerating anytime soon. Even if it does, nothing lives there, not even plants. You didn't get either of us, but..." Wyn said.

Zita got to her feet. "But what?"

Wyn stepped aside, letting Zita see what her body had blocked.

Right beside Zita, his forehead wrinkled and confusion on his face, Garm stared sightlessly at her.

"He didn't keep away," Wyn said.

Guilt lanced through Zita. "Of course not. Why would he listen to me? Is he dead?"

Wyn walked over and examined the statue. "Your petrification effect is weaker than the gorgon and basilisk ones. I think it'll wear off on its own soon. Maybe in an hour? His company is much more tolerable in his current condition."

Remembering her own brush with becoming statuary, Zita shuddered. "It's not right to leave him like that if we don't have to."

After a long, silent appraisal of the wolf, Wyn nodded. She smoothed her hands on the front of her toga, having managed somehow to come through the battle spotless. Her lips curved upward, and she cast a spell, sprinkling something on the werewolf. As the gray disappeared and his body relaxed into a limp position, she backed away to stand by Zita.

"Now I die... at long last. Done in by an idiot lizard." Garm coughed.

Zita eyed him. Other than the white whorl of fur where he'd been stabbed, his midnight fur was unmarred. "Muse fixed you. You're not a garden statue anymore."

The big wolf shifter closed his red eyes and shivered. "No, life departs my body. I would rather be dead than endure your presence any longer."

"Dude, seriously, you're uninjured," she said.

"This was the last thing we needed to do before we left, so as soon as Wingspan gets back," Wyn soothed, "We'll head to Olympus to get the spell and go home."

With a wordless yowl and a fluid twist, Garm got to his feet.

Zita yanked Wyn, shoving her friend behind her.

Nimbly, Garm darted toward the partially scattered line of white rocks in front of Cerberus' cave.

Wyn shouted, her tone despairing. "Don't cross the line! You can't—"

Garm glanced back, sneered, and deliberately stepped over the line.

Cerberus pounced on him, tail a scaly blur. Three huge pink tongues slathered the werewolf so hard that even Garm's massive form was driven to the side and farther into the cave. The big dog rolled onto his back and wiggled, legs kicking in the air.

A laugh escaped Zita. "Made a buddy while we were gone, huh?"

Garm emerged from the darkness, nose lifted high as he stepped around the other dog. "No. I hunted. I killed. I ate."

The three-headed dog stretched into a bow, and then bounced to his feet.

Wyn giggled.

Landing near the witch, Andy grinned. "Aww. Garm made a friend?"

"No!" White teeth flashed bright as Garm stepped toward the line, his fur ruffling and posture threatening.

Cerberus bounced around the werewolf, so full of glee that he almost knocked him over.

"Back away, you foolish puppy!" He growled.

"Well, caramba. You're in the Hotel Cauliflower now, Garm." Zita shook her head.

Garm's head tilted. "What?"

Andy coughed. "California. Hotel California. Nice try, Arca."

"Whatever. Once you go into the Underworld cave, you can't go home again. I don't know why." Zita stretched, luxuriating in the ability to move freely again. She flexed and threw herself into an impromptu cartwheel. When her long skirt almost tripped her, she took a moment to roll it up to her knees.

"Traditionally, Cerberus barred the passage from the Underworld to anywhere else to the dead. Living creatures could leave without issue, but we were warned we would be stuck here forever if we entered." Wyn tapped her fingers on her lips.

Andy frowned at the line. "We'll have to ask Chiron when we get back if that was just a quest requirement or something more."

"At this point, I don't consider Chiron and his Council real reliable, but it's probably better to be safe. Would it have killed you to listen to us for once, Garm?" Zita demanded.

The shaggy black wolf shifter huffed, and his mouth opened in a wide canine smile. "I am Garm. I go where I please, and I have no interest in returning home. Your limitations are not mine, but if that means you won't follow me, I'm exactly where I need to be. Come, Cerberus." He turned and disappeared into the black cave.

With a whuff, Cerberus bounced after him.

Avoiding a hydra head, Zita did a quick flip for the joy of the motion, then did a series of rapid shifts in under a minute. She returned to her Arca form, grinning. "You want to grab the sword and go back? Once Wyn gets the spell, we can ask Chiron about it."

"Sounds like a plan." Andy scooped up the sword.

Wyn's tone was dry. "Do we do those?"

Chapter Nineteen

After a few minutes of calling to Garm, who did not respond, they returned to Olympus. Unlike their previous trips, no one met them outside the town. Despite that, the ornate gates swung open as they approached.

"That's new," Andy craned his neck, checking around them.

"Perhaps they didn't expect us back so quickly?" Wyn picked her way daintily along the well-trodden path.

Zita pushed a mass of snarled hair out of her face. Her fancy hairstyle had not survived the fight or her shifts. "Or at all. Let's get this done."

They trudged through both gates and went to the megaron.

Inside, the same assortment of creatures milled around, most in more relaxed poses. The fish-men appeared to be tossing a ball back and forth with each other and some of the fauns. Still on the same bench, the minotaur knitted with a different ball of yarn.

A faun turned, almost dropping a honey cake. "They have returned!"

Andy's eyes went wide. "Hey! I understood that!"

Greenie bit off an exclamation. "Yes, and we understand your primary language now. You would have done better to run to the northern lands as I'd advised, but you have lost all hope of escaping your fates now."

Gee, I thought all the negativity was just Zita's translation. Andy rubbed his hands on his toga, where pants pockets would have been.

Zita snorted. *Nope. It's all her. Mostly. They were eating cakes without us? Rude.*

Chiron's face held only a hint of triumph in the upward curl of his lips, but his tail was raised high, and his gait held the hint of a bounce.

Melanippe was less subtle. She had a smirk that gave her features a fierce cast, quickly masked as the mountain nymph sank into a deep curtsey. "Hail to the new gods of Olympos, Keepers of the Land, bound by deed and blood, chosen by the fabric of the Olympos itself, and acknowledged by the Council."

All those assembled sank into variations of bows and curtsies, even Greenie, who offered a grudging head nod to them.

"Please don't do that," Wyn said.

"Bound? Still not gods." A shiver ran through Zita, and she twitched. *This doesn't sound like a crowd that's planning on sending us home any time soon. We been played.*

Andy frowned. "Keepers? Was this all a trick to have us tied somehow to this place? I can feel it now like I can the Southwest and Pacific regions of our home."

The old centaur cantered closer. "Come. I will explain. That is if the Council would permit now? Speaker? Are we agreed?"

Wyn folded her arms over her chest. "That would be for the best. We performed your quests in expectation of aid returning to our own realm."

"Aye, we will help you leave and return again. Council, what say you? Are we agreed?" Chiron turned to the others.

Each word slow and grudging, Greenie stared at her feet. "The old gods would never have sacrificed themselves for anyone else, let alone saved a monster like the wolf."

They were spying on us. That's not adding to the creepy at all. Zita bristled. "Whatever. Garm's still a person, not a monster. He just forgets it sometimes. That's totally not an endorsement of any sheepherding or babysitting or other services he might offer, by the way. I wouldn't leave your animals or your babies with him. Or your good sandals."

To her surprise, Silenus was not only still present, but upright, perhaps because he leaned on his son. He staggered a little but waved his hand. "For a deity willing to do that, we will grant you that which is sought. Chiron, with the return of my son, I withdraw my opposition and grant you your office again."

Chiron held out his hand, and Greenie placed the spear in it without otherwise acknowledging him.

His body tight with tension, Andy said, "Not to interrupt Council politics, but how do we get home?"

"Do you all truly wish to go? I understand you may have legions to lead..." one of the centaurs nodded at him.

He coughed. "What? No, I'm not military."

"Perhaps the little huntress?" A satyr stared at Zita.

She laughed. "Nope."

"The lady goddess can't be the general among you. She is the epitome of noble," one of the fish-men said.

Wyn covered a smile with a hand. "None of us is any kind of a soldier. I'm a scholar, he's a scientist, and she's a... ah... tax counter and artisan and athlete?"

Greenie laughed, a harsh sound that seemed to slice the air. "Not a warrior among them! This is what you've pushed to bind us to? I need not watch any more of this travesty."

"Still you protest, daughter of the oaks. Had they failed, you might not long be able to complain. I, for one, would welcome a different dryad to my mountain," Melanippe said.

"Such still might be the case, but had your precious little godlings listened, they would not be corpses in the path of whatever other gods seek us. Perhaps we would have been forgotten enough that they'd find nothing and no one to conquer. At least fading into obscurity was painless."

That sounds bad. Zita nudged Andy.

He elbowed her back, almost imperceptibly. *It does.*

Melanippe stepped close to Greenie and whispered something.

The dryad's eyes widened, and her face darkened.

Andy eyed the quarreling nymphs and stepped closer to Chiron. "Do we have to be here for this argument? What did you do to us, and what does she mean?"

With a sidelong glance at Zita and her friends, the old centaur said, "Nymphs. Please resolve your issues outside."

Wyn hugged herself. "Wingspan asked a question that we'd all like to hear the answer to, Chiron."

Settling into a comfortable position, the centaur spoke, his tones those of a professional lecturer. "Of course, Lady. The old gods fell to old age, as mortals do, when their time was done. When they passed on, we were free, molded only by the beliefs of humanity, much as gods are formed by the ideals of humanity."

"You call us gods, but we are only human, much as we were prior to receiving our powers," Wyn said.

Chiron chuckled. "Of course. However, the amount of power you have and the forms it takes are dependent on your will, and also on humanity as a whole. In our time, those with power became gods, because that is what the people wished. Worship strengthened them, and they granted boons or curses as their whims took them. In yours? I do not know."

"Superheroes. That explains so much, especially the villain monologues!" Andy said.

Zita frowned at him. "The endless babbling when the bad guys tell us their plans and gloat actually has a reason? While it's handy, it does seem counterproductive to the whole crime rampage thing."

The old centaur bestowed a smile on them, but his tail flicked rapidly. "We can speak at length of such things as you wish, whenever you are here and wish to. You have but to summon me and I will attend. But to answer your original question about what she meant, you must understand what that means for us. With no gods ruling over us, the cost was that our lands shrank as we wasted away, adrift from your realm. In time, nothing would have remained. But now, that has ended. You are tied now to Olympos and us to you. No other may claim these lands or us, nor even set foot here without your permission. You'll know if any try, and we shall be shaped by your will more than any other, so long as you all live."

"That last bit is what I'm getting a little worried about," Zita said.

Andy nodded.

Wyn's face shone with avid curiosity. She began to speak but cut herself off. A moment later, when she did, her hands were clenched so tightly in her lap that the knuckles were white. "That's all fascinating, but what about the spell to get home? We can go home, right? Are you going to teach us the spell?"

The centaur's tail swished, and he studied something on the wall. "All of you may come and go as you please, though the manner will reflect your powers. You must carve your own path, as we do not have one you may follow, since none of us are gods."

Wyn drew herself up very straight, and her voice dripped ice. "After all that, there is no spell?"

Perhaps sensing her anger, Chiron paused and studied the witch. "None, but we can offer a magical object. Many of the gods used a portal while they trained their powers to allow them transit at their will. It is yours. Once you attune it to yourself, you may use it to return to your home. When you wish to journey here again, you may use summat of your own devising. The portal will be your entry point to Olympos until such time as you learn how to choose another destination, such as your homes here."

Zita snorted. "Why would we want to return? You haven't exactly been welcoming."

The centaur studied their faces. "We're yours. If someone attacks, you will know they seek that which is yours. They cannot enter or conquer without your approval or defeating you."

"While I share your reticence to return, Arca, we'll need to come back for Garm at some point. He went into the Underworld alive. Can he come out again?" Wyn's voice thawed only slightly.

"He what?" The centaur paled, and he glanced at his daughter.

Worry on her face, Melanippe shrugged. "I see only one or two paths possible, not all of them. It's likely that because he's not a god, he will do no harm and simply die when his thread is cut."

"If we came back to get him, could we go to the Underworld and back again? Or would we be trapped?" Wyn asked.

Chiron stroked his beard. "You must not walk the paths of the Underworld yet. You've not enough allies and are too new to your powers. It would be the end of you. We have some congress with those who live in the realms of the dead. I will ask them to watch for your... companion?"

"Great, we're not high enough level," Andy muttered.

"Mano?" Zita frowned at him.

He waved his hand. "Don't worry about it."

Focus. Wyn kept her attention on the centaur. "You don't know a spell. What did you mean that we had to devise something with our powers?"

"As the Witch, Lady Muse, you should be able to create a spell. For noble Wingspan, it will be some form of flight. For Arca... I do not know, but you will gain the ability with time if you have no ability now. Perhaps you may walk here, following some trail only you can see? I believe that is how Pan did it, but he preferred to leave everyone questioning his methods."

"And motives," a faun added.

Another snickered. "Oh, those were pretty obvious when a lovely nymph or goddess was near."

"Give us a minute." Zita's feet beat a rapid staccato of her annoyance against the floor as she paced. *Just saying, if they'd mentioned this at the beginning instead of all those quests...*

Wyn's lips pressed tightly together, and her fists curled. *The entire hydra and basilisk debacles could've been avoided. I would've spent our time working out spells to return home instead of all the quests, though, of course, I would've helped with Chiron's wound, Arges, or Silenus' son.*

One of the fauns waved a hand at Zita and her friends. "Why do they gaze at each other, making faces?"

Her mind whirled as Zita tried to think of routes home. *We could return to the temple and go through one of those challenges together, but I don't think we want to. The water one was rough, and I don't see Wyn or myself surviving fire. Earth probably means being buried alive, which is out. Maybe air?*

Wyn's negation was swift and firm. *No temple.*

Well, all we need now are some ruby slippers to click together, Andy sent.

Andy, you may be a genius. That gives me an idea of where to start. Wyn's hands uncurled, and her usual mask of serenity settled over her. She smiled at the assembled creatures. If it was grimmer than her usual one, it still had half of them grinning back foolishly. "We're merely processing our disappointment that y'all felt the need to trick us rather than simply telling us at the beginning."

The room went silent. Even the fish-men stopped their game.

Melanippe stepped forward, her chin lifting. She set down a wrapped bundle on the table near Zita. Although her movements were graceful, her muscles were tensed as if expecting a blow. "It was my oracle they followed. If you seek vengeance, spend all your wrath upon me and spare them."

"Daughter, no! Not again," Chiron gripped her shoulder, fear on his face.

Zita wondered, *Vengeance? What are they talking about? As much fun as it'd be to slap sense into Greenie, I wouldn't actually do it.*

The nymph gave his hand a squeeze and stepped forward. A shiver ran through her strong frame. "My prophecy swayed them. I will accept whatever retribution you decide to give."

Chiron's head bent, and he pursed his lips. "Please do not read ill intent in our withholding of information, for we merely meant the best for all. We intended no true deception or ill to you. Had we not done so, you and we would be ill-equipped to face the future together. I beg you show us mercy." For a moment, he seemed very old and fragile.

The ancient Greek gods were known to torture and kill those who offended them, Wyn finally answered.

Zita wrinkled her nose in disgust and horror. Her friends wore similar expressions. "So not happening. You can stop groveling. We don't play that."

His head bobbing in agreement, Andy said, "No torture. No killing."

"While we'd prefer you were more honest and open with us, we don't do that sort of thing," Wyn said.

"You're not going to...?" Melanippe closed her eyes, and her body sagged for a moment as her muscles relaxed.

As color returned to his face, Chiron straightened. "If no other god invades, we will make no demands upon you. Should you wish to return, we would be pleased to tend to you and yours. We will prepare palaces for you. It is the least we can do for your august protection and our continued existence."

"We don't need palaces or servants." Curious, Zita unwrapped the bag Melanippe had set near her and discovered honey cakes. She licked her lips.

The nymph caught the movement. "Those were for you. Please, take them."

A giant rumbled, "We enjoy building. We will build. You may choose what you want."

Wyn said, "Thank you. You assume we're coming back, though. If Garm cannot be returned to our realm…"

The old centaur shot a glance at Melanippe, who nodded. "We believe you will. If naught else, most of the time, our realm is quiet and safe, a place you could rest. Should your realm grow too perilous, you and all you love can be kept safe here, if you allow no others entry."

If they're not invaded, Andy sent.

Wyn studied the centaur and his daughter. *Indeed. They must know some danger is coming based on the hints they've dropped.*

Zita had to agree. *Verdad. If our identities hit the fan, it would be nice to have somewhere to hide our loved ones. Assuming they'd agree to come and whatever invasion isn't going on. This lot wouldn't have a clue what hit them if Mamá were here—she'd have them whipped into shape in no time. None of this tricking people into running dumbass quests.*

Andy covered a laugh with a cough. *I can see that.*

Tapping a finger against her chin, Wyn nodded. *I will admit, should it become necessary to hide her, it would be good to have a safe place for my aunt, though I doubt the medical care is up-to-par with what she receives in her nursing home.*

You'll figure out a cure someday. That or there's some super out there who can fix that sort of thing. Zita snagged a honey cake and offered one to her friends.

Wyn smiled and hugged her. *You may be right.*

Don't seem so surprised. Zita patted her friend's back and then slipped from her grasp.

Andy snickered as he made his contribution. *It happens occasionally.*

Zita harrumphed and bit into the cake. *Oh, sí. This is the stuff.*

"We'll think about returning. Right now, we all badly need to return to our homes. Now, where is this portal, and what can you tell me of the magic used to activate it?" Wyn hid a smile behind her hand as she addressed Chiron.

"Please, follow me." The old centaur gestured toward the entrance and cantered that way. The golden Sword of Heracles hung at his side, and his staff of office was sheathed across his back, angled to avoid his withers.

As her friends followed him, Zita grabbed the cloth and hastily tied it shut around the cakes, jogging to catch up.

They left the enormous building and traipsed through the inner city.

Chiron and Wyn chatted about magic, a discussion Zita ignored entirely in favor of finishing her snack. The minotaur from the Council trailed behind, his knitting gone or stowed in the leather bag hanging from his belt.

The centaur stopped at an open courtyard, waving to it before he entered. Zita and her friends followed him. It had a simple stone floor with pillars, one in each of the four cardinal directions, and no roof, instead opening to a clear and sunny sky. In the center, vines had pushed through the mosaic of the floor and reached up, nearly strangling a marble arch. Through gaps in the foliage, fine golden runes glowed in the smoothed and polished rock as if natural inclusions had happened to form the shapes of Greek words. Deep gouges marred sections where it seemed as if chunks of rock had been chiseled off—the only remaining words in that section were Athena and Poseidon.

Spreading his arms wide, Chiron stopped under the arch. "This is what you have sought. It is the portal of the gods, what they used when they first began to travel here. Later, they needed it not, and it became the way that the favored heroes might win their way here. To grant it the power to traverse our worlds, each of the gods gifted a drop of their own ichor. You will doubtless need to do the same."

"Donating what?" Zita's forehead furrowed.

Wyn replied absently, "Blood."

The old centaur reached out and yanked off a piece of the vine strangling the arch, tossing it aside. He smiled.

Zita wrinkled her nose. "Is all magic obsessed with blood?"

Wyn cleared her throat, her posture too-perfect and face serene. Despite that, her hands fluttered restlessly, as if that small movement were her only way to release tension. "No, it is not, though it is a powerful symbol as well as a mystical link. Obviously, we won't create a new custom arch to serve as a doorway so much as modifying this one to serve our purposes. In addition to the blood, I'll temporarily enchant items to represent each of us for the spell and paint our names on the arch as Arca is too short to reach the open section."

Zita perked up at the thought of doing something rather than waiting for the spell to work. "Height discrimination. I could do it as a monkey. Climb on up, hang there, and paint. Might be fun!"

Her friend shook her head. "Let's not risk introducing any shapeshifting variables into the magic. The last thing we need is to end up stuck in unfamiliar forms."

Andy rubbed his thighs and held out his hands. "I don't object, but I don't think a pin is going to work to draw blood."

Chiron tapped the sword at his side gleefully. "That's why I brought the Sword of Heracles. It has power and may be able to aid you."

With a frown, Andy eyed the sword. "This is only a pinprick, right? Not a full-on stabbing?"

"Yes, of course," the old centaur replied.

Wyn took control of the conversational thread before Andy could say more. "Moving right along. Once we have the tokens for each of us..."

While the witch continued talking, Andy leaned over to Zita. Sotto voice, he said, "No monkey business for you."

She chuckled, smothering the laugh when Wyn frowned at them. "We're totally paying attention and are all focused. And serious. Tokens and symbolism and all. You got this. We're along for the magic ride."

Her friend did not seem convinced but retrieved her purse. She paused, one hand hovering above the opening. "I'll get out the items I've selected as tokens for each of us. I apologize, Arca, but your boots will likely no longer work for sports once they've normalized to this plane. However, they are not only linked to you, but they're also the article of clothing we own closest to a pair of ruby or silver slippers."

"Someone made shoes of gemstones?" Chiron asked. "Fascinating. Please continue." For once, he seemed more interested in observing them than talking, even though he was with them ostensibly to answer any questions.

Wyn reached into her bag and pulled out Zita's bright red snowboarding boots. Snow dripped from the toes. She gaped. "They didn't change. They're exactly as they were when I put them in?"

A touch of smugness colored Chiron's answer. "Our world is tied to yours now. Your belongings will no longer conform to the expectations here because you link the realms now. Your home must be very different. I have never seen such shoes or materials!"

"I can have pants again?" Andy perked up. At their gazes, he shrugged. "Togas aren't the best choice for flying. Not to mention, I miss everyone else being dressed. Especially the men."

Zita grinned. "Bit drafty for the boys, huh? I'm just happy I don't have to go find new snowboarding boots in my size."

Reaching into her purse again, Wyn withdrew a feather followed by a small hand broom.

"Why a broom? I mean, you're a witch, but you never flew on one." Zita stared at the cleaning utensil. By virtue of biting her tongue, she managed not to comment on Wyn's housekeeping, which erred on the side of reading amid vast herds of dust bunnies.

Her statement met with silence as her friend's face flooded with pink.

Zita gasped. "You did? And you didn't tell us? I thought we were friends! When can I try one? How do they handle?"

"I thought you'd mention dating a killer for hire, but that didn't happen either." Wyn twitched.

"Seriously, give the dude a chance. It was a misunderstanding on his part, and he apologized as soon as he realized."

Andy cleared his throat. "As much as I hate to derail any pointless bickering, perhaps we should let her focus on the spell, Arca? You might want to bathe. Or get snacks for the road. I'm certain she'll tell us the story if she wants us to know, later."

Choking down the urge to defend Freelance further, Zita let it go. "Yeah, yeah, I do, and I should, in case we end up somewhere else weird."

Hurt filled Wyn's face.

"Not that we will, because we're traveling with the best witch ever, so I'll fetch some cakes and be right back. And if you ever want to talk about broom flight, I'm here for you," Zita added hastily.

"Smooth move, Ex-Lax," Andy murmured.

"Shut it, birdbrain."

Wyn got to work.

Epilogue

Compared to explosions that crossed dimensions, portals were anticlimactic. Once Wyn had finished casting her spell, the three had joined hands and walked through a marble arch. Instead of finding themselves in the same courtyard, they now stood in the middle of the ruins of an enormous building. A low fence surrounded the rubble beside a dirt road.

Several people gasped. All of them seemed human, wearing modern summer clothing and a variety of accessories.

"They live!" Someone exclaimed.

Another said, "What are they wearing?"

"We made it!" Zita said, smoothing her toga.

Her face perfectly serene, Wyn smiled and waved to the tourists, angling her head so her wimple hid her face. She murmured, "Wingspan, would you get us out of sight? Arca, would you take us home after that?"

Phones lifted, pointed their direction.

Andy nodded uncomfortably to the crowd, grabbed Wyn and Zita, and sailed upward. Once they were hidden by the clouds, he put on speed. After a minute of that, he came to a stop, still hidden.

"Basement?" Zita asked.

Her friends nodded.

She teleported.

***

In the blink of an eye, they stood in the dimness of Wyn's basement. Boxes surrounded them and almost hid the HVAC equipment in the corner. The scent of old incense and herbs hung heavy in the air, almost hiding the odors of cardboard and must. The only sounds came from her friends breathing and the yowling displeasure of angry cats upstairs.

Andy whooped and hugged Wyn and Zita. "I can wear pants again!"

Zita hugged her friends back and escaped their grips. She shifted to her own body for the first time in days and stripped off her mask. "Next time mythological creatures tell us we have to finish quests before we can go home, can we at least try to go home on our own first? Good job, Wyn."

Wyn tapped her throat, and her Muse illusion dissipated. She bit her lip. "Definitely, even if it defies the mythic cycle."

The angry cat voices ceased.

Andy voiced Zita's worry. "Let's find out how much we missed."

As he took a step toward the stairs, Wyn stopped him with a hand on his chest. "What if someone's here? They can't see you in your costume, and they might've heard us."

"I don't hear anyone, but I'll check. Don't worry. No one will notice me." Zita shifted to a lavender-point Siamese and darted up the stairs. She pawed open the door.

A claw shot toward her face.

Her instincts took over, and Zita hopped up and backward, landing half on two different steps, with her hind legs scrabbling for purchase. She slashed her tail, lifting her nose in the air, and settled her fur back in place.

From below, she heard her friends snicker.

This time, when she opened the door, Zita was ready for an attack.

But none came.

Instead, Wyn's two cats flowed past her and down the stairs, ignoring her presence as they surrounded Wyn, meowing.

Shaking her head, Zita slipped into the kitchen, avoiding a fresh hairball, and checked the house. "It's clear."

Her friends came upstairs. Wyn withdrew a phone from her bag and turned it on. "It's three fourteen, Monday afternoon, June second. I've got days before my aunt is due for another spell, though I'll have to apologize for missing work today." Her shoulders slumped in relief.

Zita and Andy both swore. Hers was annoyed. His was fretful.

"We've lost four days? I've missed work, Quentin's art thing, and coffee with Miguel." Zita swore again for good measure.

Andy moaned. "My interview! I really wanted that job, but I've only got forty-five minutes to get there and rush hour starts soon. Plus, I'll need to change clothes, so I don't look like I just woke up after a frat party."

"No worries, mano, I'll take you to your place, and that'll get you halfway there. If you hurry and cheat with your powers, you can make it."

He rubbed the back of his neck and sighed. "It could be a sign. The job is too good to be true. I mean, I'd be in the same department as Farnswaggle himself. How can I possibly be good enough to make the cut? I mean, the whole physics department must be filled with awesome scientists, and I'm just me..."

Wyn touched his elbow, sympathy on her face. "You can do this. They wouldn't have called you back for an in-person interview if you were a poor candidate."

With less sympathy, Zita gave his arm a light punch. "Knock it off. We all know you know Fartswallow—"

He couldn't help correcting her. "Farnswaggle"

"Whatever. You're a total fanboy and know his physics better than anyone else. You rock. If you start feeling intimidated, remind yourself that you've got a lot of experience that they can't hope to duplicate."

"What's that?" His tone was glum.

She grinned at him. "You will undoubtedly be the only person in the interview who has ever punched a dinosaur or thrown a hydra head into a volcano. What's a bunch of old farts around a table got on that?"

A half-laugh escaped Andy. He opened his mouth, but then paused, pursing his lips. "You're definitely right. However, I'm not certain how well that translates to an assistant professorship position in theoretical physics."

Zita snorted. "What's that you always say to me? Who better to study the laws of physics than someone used to breaking them? Now, enough pity party. If we go now, you can shower and get there in time. Mamá's already in town. I'm supposed to be having an early dinner with her, my brothers, and Miguel's girl in about fifteen minutes."

Glancing up from where she had been absorbed in petting her cats, Wyn said, "And take a shower. You're a bit, ah, ripe from that dip in the water to rinse off the hydra spit."

Zita plucked at her outfit. "Yeah, I'll need to do that. It'll make me late. They'll just assume I'm being irresponsible again." She sighed inwardly.

Wyn touched Zita's shoulder. "Speaking of that, should you choose to date the mercenary, you have my support, if not my agreement that the decision is at all wise. Be careful."

Her voice gruff, Zita grunted. "Thanks for that and all."

"Here's to irresponsibility and punching extinct predators! Later, Wyn." Andy touched Zita's shoulder.

Wyn tried to wave, but a cat insistently batted at her hand.

Zita teleported with Andy.

***

After dropping off her friend, Zita teleported to her bedroom, skipping her usual ritual of traveling in feline form to the roof and checking her apartment for witnesses before breaking in. An outfit was laid out on her bed, and the scent of both of her brothers lingered in the air.

"Quentin can't be too mad at me if he's picked out something I should wear. Gracias a Dios," she murmured, eyeing the clothing. After swapping out the beige shirt for a hot pink one, she gathered the outfit and stepped out of her bedroom.

"DMS! Get your hands in the air!" a masculine voice barked.

Instincts screaming, she dropped the clean clothing and flattened herself with her back against the wall. Her arms shot up, every muscle tense. "Don't shoot!"

Belatedly, she recognized the voice. "Miguel, hermano, if you shoot me, Mamá is going to kill you." She turned to face her eldest brother.

Miguel stood in the entrance to her living room, gun drawn. He tucked the weapon away in a tidy shoulder holster under the plain black suit he wore. "Zita?"

Lowering her arms, she raised her eyebrows. "Who else were you expecting in my apartment?"

Quentin breezed by him and swept her into a hug. Cologne overlaid the odors of metal and his favorite steak torta in his scent. "Zita! Gracias a Dios! Nobody's been able to reach you for days! You missed work and my pottery class, and when we found your phone on the kitchen table... well, Miguel worries."

"That was this weekend? Oops. Yeah, I must've left that here. Sorry," she said, returning the hug.

Miguel hugged her as well, as soon as her Quentin released her. His dry cleaner's detergent and favorite pine soap didn't completely hide the women's perfume that clung lovingly to him. "How did you get in? I didn't see you."

"Funny, I didn't see you guys either. You must've been in the other room when I came in." Backing up, Zita stared at her brothers, willing them to believe her.

Innocently, Quentin helped. "It was probably when you were in the bathroom, and I was picking out something for her to wear to dinner. That is not the shirt I picked, by the way."

She collected the clothing she'd dropped. "I liked this one better."

Miguel barked questions at her, his eyes narrowed. "What happened to you? Where have you been? What is that outfit you're wearing? Why didn't you tell anyone where you were going? At your age, you should know better than to take off without telling people where you're going."

"And why do you smell like dead fish?" Quentin added.

Zita opened her mouth, and a huge lie dropped out. "Sorry to worry you. I was backpacking over the weekend and fell in a river. Lost all my stuff. When I got out of the water, I was pretty far downstream. I hitched a ride with these tourists. Since my clothes were soaked, the wife loaned me the outfit. This was all she had that would fit me."

Her brother frowned at her. "Where were they from that this would be an option?"

She said the first thing that came to mind. "Canada?"

"What does that have to do with a toga?" Miguel frowned at her.

"Canadian actors! Always ready to jump on stage. I was just going to shower and change and meet you guys." Zita clutched her clean clothes to her chest.

Quentin leaned in, mischief dancing on his face. "She didn't have any socks?"

"Hippies. Canadian artist hippies who only wear sandals. Folks be loco. What are you going to do? I got to shower and dress, or we'll be super late for dinner," Zita said desperately.

Miguel's expression remained skeptical.

When he opened his mouth, undoubtedly to pepper her with more questions, Zita beat him to it. "So is your girlfriend pregnant or what, Miguel?"

He made a choking sound, his face turning red.

Quentin howled with laughter. "Like you'd be that lucky."

"Got to shower!" She escaped to the bathroom.

****

For the first time, the silence felt uncomfortable. Physically, squirm-inducing uncomfortable.

Five days after returning from Chiron's Greece, Zita sat at the top of a cliff in her Arca guise. A few feet away, Freelance perched on a nearby rock. She watched the acres of green forest below, letting the heat of their climb dissipate in the pine-scented breeze. The rock under her was rough and lumpy, but most of her attention was internal.

She ran a hand over her hair, back and forth, and broke the silence. "Sorry I didn't text sooner? Magic stuff exploded, and we got stranded in this weird place. It took a few days to get back. We don't know yet what happened to Zeus and his people, but Jen Stone was definitely with them. Since they were standing somewhere else, they may have been vaporized, but Muse says that's unlikely. I'll let you know if we find anything. Will you do the same for us?"

He inclined his head.

While she normally preferred his stillness to someone asking a million questions she couldn't answer, this once she might not have minded an irrelevant tangent that would let her avoid either of the awkward subjects she needed handled. *Am I turning into a wuss or what? I need to get off my culo and just talk to the man.*

To her surprise, he spoke first. "Good you're back. People must have missed you."

She waved a hand and shrugged. "Sí, but anyone would have been missed. You would've."

A soft exhale escaped his voice changer, so quiet she almost didn't make out the word it contained. "Unlikely."

"No, I know you would've." Heat rose in her face, and she looked away, flexing her shoulders.

He said nothing.

She scrabbled through her pockets desperately. "I brought snacks. It's pasteli. It's like a Greek power bar made with sesame, honey, and nuts. I know that climb was a tie, but I don't mind sharing." Zita stopped herself from babbling that it was made by surprisingly domestic centaurs using honey from man-killing bees. *That would make things weird. Weirder.*

After a pause, he shook his head. Deft and sure, his hands almost caressed the rope he'd brought, checking it for faults.

"You don't mind if I do though, right?" Zita stuffed part of a bar in her mouth and chewed.

Rope coiled in a neat pile beside him as he worked.

Around a mouthful of the treat, she blurted, "We need to talk. Carajo, I sound like Muse. Or a girl." She frowned.

Freelance paused, his head tilting.

Zita inhaled. *Start with the easy one.* "First, let's get business out of the way. Apparently, if a real powerful super is killed, they blow up. Or their power does? I don't really understand the reasoning, but apparently, the type of explosion is based on their abilities, and it's like a mile radius or something."

"No."

She blinked. "What?"

His capable hands slowed, and he took a moment before answering. If she hadn't been so attuned to him, she might've missed the tautness that came over his body. "Killed supers."

"Oh. It's not all supers. Just the most powerful? Like Dragon or Wingspan or Muse. Possibly Jen Stone," she said. *How sad is it that he's had to kill multiple people since last year this time?*

He sat motionless for a moment. "You."

She puffed out her cheeks and blew out air. "That's what I'm told. Muse suggested that's what happened with all the weirdness and conflicting reports at Chernobyl and Tiananmen Square since Shining Woman and Fu Dog were pretty powerful."

"Way to tell?" Nimbly, he resumed his painstaking examination of the rope.

Zita lifted her hands in the air. "The people we met claimed it was obvious to them, but couldn't explain it to us. Anyway, I thought you should know. Not just because your team's been trying to bring in Jen Stone for her dad, but also because you're the person I know who's most likely to kill a super."

His fingers stilled.

Too late, she realized how her comment could sound. "Just keeping it real with the mercenary gig given that you're way competent and all."

He inclined his head, his body relaxing slightly. "Fair. Thank you."

She flexed her shoulders, releasing tension she hadn't realized she'd been holding. Of course, her muscles knotted up as she realized the next topic.

I have to ask. Even if he bails, at least I'll know, and I need to, one way or the other. I won't be stuck in my own little world never knowing. I'll give it a few minutes and lay out our options and the rules in a nice, logical way.

All of two seconds later, Zita blurted out her question. "So, not that this has anything to do with exploding corpses or whatever, but are we dating or what? We didn't finish talking before, and I suck at people things, so let's just put it all out there, right? No more assuming things about each other because that gets into creepy stalker territory, and I'm so not into that."

She gulped a big breath of pine-scented air and barreled on. "I'm willing to give it a try if you are, but you have to actually tell me that it's what you want. While I normally enjoy pretending you agree with me when you don't correct me, not saying anything will just muck things up." *Worse than I'm doing now. He's just joined the legions of people who think I'm an idiot. Life would be so much easier if we could just show our attraction through kick-ass stunts or something and snacks. Carajo. Now not only do I sound like an idiot, but I'm hungry again.*

"Interested."

Zita laughed, trying to ignore the silly warmth that single word ignited in her. "How about a deal? We lay it all out. If one of us wants to change things, go all exclusive or not do it anymore or whatever, we tell the other person outright. No assumptions, because clearly, we don't do too good with those."

Rope again slid through his hands. When he spoke, his answer wasn't anything she had expected. "Equitable. I am... new to such things."

Her jaw dropped. More words poured out. "What? What was your longest relationship?"

"Eight."

She blinked. "Eight years? That's pretty impressive." *Better than my track record. My longest was two years, minus the summers I was off doing cool stuff without my boyfriend.* His answer yanked her out of musing over the catastrophe of her prior relationship.

"Nights. Vacation."

We're doomed. I'm the relationship expert? My friends would die laughing, assuming Wyn didn't have a heart attack first. She tilted her head. "You're a one-night stand type of guy? Yeah, that's not me.

Not one for strangers manhandling me. I'm more of an eventual long-term maybe commitment girl. My parents had the happy marriage thing, and I want that someday, but not for years and years and maybe decades. What do you want from me?"

Freelance's goggles whirred as he studied her. "Your time?"

Clearing her throat, she said, "That's doable. I can do one step at a time." *I think. He's obviously not into me for all the sex we're not having.*

His voice changer made a humming sound she chose to take for understanding.

After a pause, he nodded.

Cards on the table. She cleared her throat and watched him. "I can't go total monogamy because of my family and our masks."

His head tilted, and a question escaped his mask. "Your... family?"

Zita rubbed her forehead. "They get to line up one guy a month for a blind date until I start dating someone on the regular. So far, their choices have sucked. Since I can't tell them anything about you, I've got to keep going on these disasters. I told you about one, the drunk bull and the ice rink?" *Not that I did that well on my own before, admittedly, but my brothers haven't helped.*

He nodded.

"How about we call it casual for now, not exclusive, but if either one of us wants to get serious with someone else, we're done. Being a side piece is insulting and unhygienic for both of us."

Another nod.

"Do you want to talk about anything?" she asked. "Fair's fair and all."

"Sex?"

Zita almost said please, but caught herself in time, mentally shoving her hormones into a trunk and sinking it in an abyss. One with a handsy giant squid. "You're hot and all, but I'm not ready to take off my mask, let alone my pants. It's on the table for the future, though, if we want. Got to warn you though—if we get down to it, we're monogamous until we call it quits."

His head inclined. "Fair. Secret. Your reputation matters."

Zita nodded, or her head wobbled, close enough. Though her balance was fine, she felt a swirl of dizziness run through her. When it had passed, she said, "Right, secret, excluding Wingspan and Muse and your crew if that's how you want to play it."

When he said no more, she filled the silence with the babbling she couldn't seem to stop. "Chido. Dating's cool. We're cool. You ready for the descent? We can go back to doing stuff now. I don't mind."

He offered her a rope.

"Works for me." Her cheeks hurt from her stupid grin, and she let her fingers linger on his as she accepted the rope.

Languages Glossary

These are definitions of the words as used in the book and may not include all possible variations. The Spanish is primarily Mexican in usage and slang. Needless to say, anything marked with "Vulgar" should not be used in polite company.

abuela: Spanish. Grandma.

ándale: Spanish. Let's go.

arca: Spanish. A chest or ark. Zita originally used it referring to Noah's ark in *Super*.

ay: Spanish. An interjection, similar to "Oh."

ay papi: Spanish. Ooh, baby, used in sexual situations. Literally, Oh daddy.

buey: Spanish. Dude.

buena suerte: Spanish. Good luck.

capoeira: Portuguese. A fast, fluid Brazilian martial art known for its acrobatic and dance-like kicks, spins, and other techniques.

carajo: Spanish. Shit. Vulgar.

caramba: Spanish. A mild interjection of surprise or dismay.

chido: Spanish. Cool.

chingado: Spanish. Fucked or fucking. This has other meanings as well, but this is how Zita generally uses it. Vulgar.

culo: Spanish. Ass. Vulgar.

Diné: Navajo. The People (i.e., the Navajo People)

Dios: Spanish. God.

eso es la vida: Spanish. That's life.

frío: Spanish. Cold.

ginga: Portuguese. The most basic capoeira footwork, a moving fight stance.

gracias a Dios: Spanish. Thank God or Thanks be to God.

hermano: Spanish. Brother.

hombre: Spanish. Man.

Hypatus: Greek. Title for Zeus meaning Supreme or Most High.

kykeon: Greek. An ancient Greek beverage. In this novel, it refers to a mixture of water and barley, flavored with herbs, ground goat cheese, and a touch of honey. Other recipes also existed, including alcoholic ones.

loco/loca: Spanish. Crazy man or woman.

mano: Spanish. Bro. Abbreviated form of "hermano" as Zita uses it.

momentito: Spanish. Just a moment.

neta: Spanish. Really, for real, you know.

Nihalgai: Navajo. This world. The Fourth World or Glittering World of myth.

no hay bronca: Spanish. No problem.

no sé: Spanish. I don't know.

órale: Spanish. An interjection. Can be used like heck yeah, right on, listen, hey, or hurry up.

oye: Spanish. An interjection that can be used as hey, listen, or yo.

pan comido: Spanish. Piece of cake, literally "eaten cake."

pendejo: Spanish. A jerk or asshole. Vulgar.

Pheletes: Greek. Title meaning Thief or Robber. Used for Hermes, not Zeus, in actual Greek legends.

por supuesto: Spanish. Of course.

pues: Spanish. An interjection, equivalent of well, then, or since.

qué: Spanish. What.

qué onda: Spanish. What's up? Literally, "what wave?"

sí: Spanish. Yes.

Sublime Gracia: Spanish. The "Amazing Grace" hymn.

tiganites: Greek. Greek-style pancakes, frequently topped with honey and nuts or sesame seeds.

tía: Spanish. Aunt.

torta: Spanish. A big Mexican-style sandwich, almost always on a roll, usually including veggies, a protein, cheese, and a soft spread (like refried beans).

verdad: Spanish. True or truth.

xenia: Greek. The ancient Greek version of hospitality, the mutual courtesy and care shown between those who are far from home (the guest) and the host. It assumes both host and guest will treat the other like a treasured friend. Guests are expected to offer xenia to their host if the host ever comes to their home.

From the Author

Thank you for reading!

First, a note for any history buffs. The lack of historical accuracy in the book's mythological Greece is a plot point and acknowledged a few times in the novel. One of the major issues is that Zita and friends are not really wearing togas, which are Roman garments, not Greek. However, there are a lot more toga jokes than chiton ones.

Additionally, the specific cave with the poisonous air that features in the early chapters is an imaginary amalgam of existing caves, placed in the very real Cape Matapan. All other locations are real, even if they lack the creatures and buildings I may have placed upon them.

Please consider leaving reviews for any books you've enjoyed, positive or negative. Reviews assist other readers in finding books and let authors know what they've done right (or wrong).

For the latest on past and future releases, monthly chatter, free short stories, and the occasional other freebie, subscribe to the newsletter on my website, https://www.karendiem.com/. You can also use the website to contact me, browse free content (cut scenes, sample chapters, my abbreviated autobiography, and more), or find me on social media sites (Twitter, Facebook, etc.). Since I'd hate to read the same stuff everywhere, I do try to put different content in each place. New release notices are the exception and go everywhere.

Arca Chronology

This list only includes novels. For the complete, up-to-date chronology, including short stories, see https://www.karendiem.com.

Super
Human
Power
Monster
Toga